Praise for *Code Name: Dove* by Judith Leon

"*Code Name: Dove* launches the new Bombshell line with guns blazing. Judith Leon's hard-edged thriller is not your traditional series romance. She delivers an exciting, action-packed read with expertly drawn main characters, complex relationships, a lightning-fast pace and a truly creepy villain."

—*Romantic Times BOOKclub*

* * *

"He said that if I injected one, it would make me immune."

Ya Lin hurriedly opened the cosmetic bag and stripped back white paper, revealing three vials topped with stubby needles. "The minute he left I used one."

"So you are immune?" Nova asked.

"If the man is right. But I'm not staying in Italy to find out. Here." She pressed the vials into Nova's hand. "Maybe they'll make you immune. That might help you if you try to stop him. And I can feel less guilty."

Ya Lin was right. If the drug conferred immunity, chances of stopping these madmen would be tremendously increased. Otherwise, approaching them without bulky and confining Hazmat gear would be a death sentence.

Nova stared, undecided, at the vials, her heart racing. The stuff might infect rather than create immunity. Was it worth the risk?

Dear Reader,

I'm often asked what inspires a particular story. With Bombshell books, the inspiration is virtually always based on four things, the same four that influence me in the creation of any story.

First, I love being in the head and heart of a brave, strong woman who can take charge and make a difference, so I am right at home in the Bombshell world. I'm not Nova Blair, but for a time I can dream as though I am.

Second, I want to explore places of beauty and interest that I've not seen before. I pick a setting where I think I'll enjoy spending time, in the case of *Iron Dove,* the absolutely beautiful Amalfi coast of Italy, and a bit of Rome itself. I traveled to both places as research for the book. If I write well, my readers—you—get to experience those same things.

Third, I consider what kind of villain or antihero is a worthy opponent of my heroine: Who should she take down? What kind of mess in the world needs fixing? I spend a lot of time thinking about the nature of the evil she will confront, and I find inspiration in taking him or her out in fiction. We can't always make things right in the real world, but why not in our imaginations, right?

And finally, and perhaps most satisfying of all, my heroines find love—if not right away, eventually. Love is the greatest force I've experienced in my life, and I thoroughly enjoy finding it anew in one fabulous hero after another.

I'd be delighted to have you visit my Web site to learn more about my other books: www.jhand.com.

Judith

JUDITH LEON

IRON DOVE

Silhouette®

BOMBSHELL™

Published by Silhouette Books

America's Publisher of Contemporary Romance

SILHOUETTE BOOKS

ISBN 0-373-51379-8

IRON DOVE

www.SilhouetteBombshell.com

Printed in U.S.A.

Books by Judith Leon

Silhouette Bombshell

Code Name: Dove #4
Iron Dove #65

JUDITH LEON

made the transition from left-brained scientist to right-brained novelist. Before she began writing fiction some twelve years ago, she was teaching animal behavior and ornithology in the UCLA biology department.

She is the author of several novels and two screenplays. Her epic of the Minoan civilization, *Voice of the Goddess,* published under her married name, Judith Hand, has won numerous awards. Her second epic historical, *The Amazon and the Warrior,* is based on the life of Penthesilea, an Amazon who fought the warrior Achilles in the Trojan War. In all of her stories she writes of strong, bold women—women who are doers and leaders.

A classical music fan, world traveler and bird-watcher, she currently lives in Rancho Bernardo, California. For more information about the author and her books, see her Web site at www.jhand.com.

To my steadfast friend, staunchest moral
supporter and talented writing partner—
a true visionary and a gifted editor,
Peggy Lang.

Chapter 1

"I don't want to die!" Robin Scott's quavering voice shot through the green canopy of Costa Rican cloud forest. A pair of Emerald Toucanets, in a flash of yellow and green, exploded from a treetop, taking flight into pearl-gray mist.

Every muscle in Nova Blair's body tensed. Her youngest adventurer on this isolated birding tour, sixteen-year-old Robin, was dangling a hundred and fifty perilous feet above the ground.

This wasn't your usual tame, gray-haired birder tour, where senior citizens poked around with their binoculars into low-lying bushes and safe pathways. This was an entirely different tour where adventurers traversed distances of more than a hundred feet from one wooden observation deck to another, suspended on leather harnesses, fifteen stories above ground. Safe, yes. But scary as hell if you weren't familiar with what you were doing. And Robin wasn't.

With the mist the way it was, you couldn't even see the ground. Nova had told Robin to focus, instead, on reaching the next deck. Now the young girl was flailing at the air and at the sling harness in which she sat supported on a small leather seat.

"I'm going to fall!"

Nova called back, "Robin, you're okay. Just stop moving, love. Your security line is tangled. I'll free it from the traverse line and you'll be fine."

Four other members of the tour, who had not yet crossed the traverse line to the next deck, stood beside Nova, holding their breaths. Through the misty green came the raucous who-who-who-whos of howler monkeys, an eerie sound that matched the girl's own wails.

Two traverse lines were anchored to the sky bridge platform situated a short fifty paces from the Treetops Hotel's canopy-level patio. Nova's group would use seated slings to pull themselves across five such rope passages to reach today's observation deck, a wooden perch overlooking the nesting site of a showy pair of resplendent quetzals, birds famous for their reclusive habits and long, fancy tails.

The quetzal observation deck—nestled among branches at the tops of figs trees, tree ferns and lianas— had been lowered into place two years ago by a blimp. Researchers needed a secure platform but couldn't afford the cost of attempting from-the-ground-up construction in the heart of a jungle. By selling this tour to enough wealthy adventurers, Cosmos Adventure Travel was making the scientists' quetzal research possible.

For Nova, this was a win-win-win situation; she loved sharing a life of adventure and travel with fellow daredevils, she admired field scientists who searched for truth in dangerous places and she loved the beauty of birds.

Yesterday, Jeeps had dropped her group here after a torturous four-hour drive from Costa Rica's capital, San Juan. Aged sixteen to an athletic fifty-six, they pluckily climbed a 150-foot wooden ladder to the surprisingly elegant hotel, Treetops, named for its famous Kenyan predecessor. Nova's adventurers would not touch Mother Earth again for ten days. Rooms were small for two people but fitted with comfortable beds and elegant native furnishings.

"Bruce!" Nova called out. Her assistant waited for Robin on a platform out of Nova's sight at the other end of the traverse line. "I'll untangle her security line. You pull her the rest of the way yourself."

"Roger," he called back.

If Robin would just hold still, she should be in no danger, but Nova's heart went out to her. After a day of travel and another day of orientation with father and daughter, along with this tour's eight other clients, Nova had concluded that Robin had, more or less, been coerced into coming on this trip by her father.

Charles Scott, a hard-charging CEO in the import/export business, wanted to share an adventurous vacation with his daughter in one of Costa Rica's most beautiful rain forests. But not Monteverde, a secure tourist preserve with several miles of sky bridges. No.

He'd chosen an isolated region of rain forest, used mostly for a Smithsonian-sponsored research project and, by special contract, also by Nova's tour company, CAT. A trip here was expensive, exclusive, and not for the faint of heart.

As Nova snatched up an extra sling harness and stepped into it, she again called to Robin. "I'm coming across on the other line."

"I'm dizzy."

In a calm, this-happens-all-the-time-voice, Nova said, "Stop moving, hon, and just sit tight." *And please, PLEASE for love of your life, sit still.* "I'll be over to you in just a few minutes."

The senior Scott, a veteran of seven CAT tours, had been acting as though he believed this experience would turn his aspiring artist and poet into a thrill-seeker like Nova. Robin was an only child. Dad had probably counted heavily on having a son.

Nova pulled the sling's harness over her shoulders as James Padgett, a pudgy, nervous conservationist from Panama, finished his thought out loud. "I'm going to quit working for the conservancy after this trip."

James, now is not the time to talk about quitting your work. Nova bit back the thought before it could escape her lips.

James had been talking about the encroachment of cattle ranchers onto a strip of pristine forest preserve he'd worked years to save. His failure was obviously eating him up. When a man got that burned out, it was hard to care about anything.

Nova snapped her sling's metal ring, located over her diaphragm, to the carabiner of her harness line. "I bet you know, James, that if the good guys quit, it means the bad guys win. I hope you don't quit. You're good at what you do."

"Easy to say," he muttered.

And also true. Quitters are always the losers.

"PLEEZE!" Robin yelled.

Another carabiner, those cleverly designed metal loops that were staples for rappelling and mountain climbing, attached her harness line to a pulley on her traverse line. She checked it. It was secure. In moves she'd made hundreds of times, Nova climbed over the guardrail and onto the three-foot-square launch platform.

Charles Scott elbowed his way past Padgett. "Robin," he yelled, "Stop that screaming."

You jerk! A hateful memory of her stepfather, Candido Branco, flared into Nova's mind. "Mr. Scott, she's understandably afraid."

"If she'd pulled herself the way you said, the rope wouldn't have gotten tangled and she'd be okay. She needs to learn to pay attention to details."

Her stepfather's voice had always been soft, his words encouraging. Candido Branco had never spoken to her harshly. *But then, there's all kinds of abuse. I probably would have been less screwed up and my life would've been less screwed up if he'd just yelled at me.*

A magnificent butterfly—electric blue and iridescent green, with bright yellow spots on each wing—landed on her hand as she double-checked the carabiner linking her to the pulley. *I'm thirty-three and Candido is finally losing his control over me. I hope Robin gets over her father a whole lot sooner.*

"Let me have your unipod a sec," she said to Padgett, urgency and some disgust with both men putting a sharp edge to her tone. Padgett turned his back, and from his day pack she fetched a collapsible aluminum pole that he used to steady his camera while taking photographs. The camera platform at the tip end of the pole would make a serviceable hook.

She hurriedly extended the unipod to full length, let the sling harness and traverse line take her weight, then let herself off the sky bridge. The movement disturbed a flock of violet sabrewings. They burst in a shower of green and purple, flapping from the crown of a towering strangler fig ten feet away.

Nova started pulling toward the girl, Robin's "I don't wanna die" still ringing in her ears. There were lots of places to die. Lots of places and times already in her life where she had come close to dying. For her this beautiful place would actually be a good one.

A shriek cut the air. Nova's head snapped in the girl's direction. Robin now hung, rotating slowly, ten feet below the traverse line. *Merciful God!*

She had been saved only by her safety line from a fall that would surely have killed her. The harness line was still attached to the traverse line—but not to Robin. *How could that have happened?*

"Robin, Robin," Charles Scott yelled.

Nova's pulse beating loudly in her ears, she yelled, "Robin! Do. Not. Move. Do you understand?"

"I…I do."

Pulling fast, her heartbeat pounding against her breastbone, Nova raced back toward the skywalk. *Be calm! Be cool!*

Training and discipline took over, her thoughts sped

up and her senses sharpened. Now, in addition to the unipod, she would need a length of nylon rope, a rescue pulley and possibly a replacement carabiner.

That's what safety lines are for. It will hold. It has to hold. Please, make it hold.

"Novaaa!"

Chapter 2

"So, Mr. Cardone, who's so important you have to fetch him out of the middle of the jungle?"

The Huey's flight engineer had left her place up front. She perched on the jump seat beside Joe. She'd removed her headset, looping it around the back of her neck, and was yelling over the beating of the chopper blades.

With Costa Rican permission, Joe, the flight engineer, and the Huey's two pilots had come inland from the USS *Reagan*, stationed off Costa Rica's Pacific coast.

"How long until we get there?" he yelled back.

"Ten minutes. You didn't answer my question. Big secret?"

"Not really. At least *who* isn't a secret. *Why* we want her is."

"A her? Who is *she?*"

Joe pictured Nova. Dark black ponytail and bangs, delicate fair skin. Nondescript makeup and a nondescript "look." That's how she had struck him the first time he'd seen her. But there was nothing nondescript about those startling emerald-green eyes. He recalled the first time he'd seen her dressed for a seduction for the Company. Man, had he ever been one bowled-over Texas boy. She'd let her straight hair down to her shoulder blades and tucked it back behind one ear. A crimson red gown clung to every mouthwatering body curve. Dangling crystal earrings had glimmered in the ballroom light.

Jesus, she was the most incredible chameleon. Nova could disappear into the woodwork when she needed to, but dressed up she could morph into a movie star or Paris model. Code name: Dove. It fit her perfectly because she seemed so gentle and sweet, someone you could trust. But she was also as tough and professional a spy as he'd ever known.

Well, Nova wasn't really full-time CIA as he was. A contract agent, Nova served only when she chose to and when called in because one of her special talents or gifts was needed. Sometimes she was called upon because of her beauty, but mostly it was when the Company needed someone with an unsurpassed ability to win trust. Within the inner circles of the agency, she was famous for "spinning silken threads of either trust or desire." She'd rescued the daughter of an Argentinean diplomat by winning over the hostage taker's mistress. She'd convinced a Saudi prince that she was a doctoral student studying falconry, and by doing so, obtained information that enabled the Company to prevent the bombing of a disco in Malaysia.

"Nova Blair," he yelled back to the chopper engineer. "She's a world-class photographer. Also a tour guide for an action/adventure travel company." CAT was a legitimate travel company and also a CIA cover, the one Nova used most often.

The flight engineer grinned. "My name's Katie Donovan. And I'm a damn good dancer. You guys staying on the ship tonight? We've got a party planned."

He gave Katie Donovan one of his better smiles. Quite a few women had complimented him on that smile. "Sorry," he yelled. "After I get Nova, it's back to the *Reagan* to jet off ASAP."

"I'm sorry, too." She paused a moment, then, "Does she know you're coming?"

Now there was a good question. She didn't. In fact, he'd been told by Langley that since his last job with her, Nova had twice turned down assignments. In Germany, she'd fallen hard for Jean Paul König, a charismatic German politician with the looks of a movie star, but when the mission was over, she'd decided König wasn't right for her.

In Joe's opinion, she'd been seriously let down. Hell. He'd caught her with tears in her eyes after making her parting speech to König, and Nova definitely wasn't the crying type.

He hadn't pressed her for details. Nova just might be the most private person he'd ever known. And she owned some very deep and dark secrets, some he knew having to do with the stepfather she refused to discuss. Those secrets must be the explanation for why such a beautiful, intelligent, talented woman undertook the dangerous and sometimes murderous things she did for the Company.

He thought it unlikely that Langley knew about her genuine affection for König. He wasn't about to break her confidence and tell them; Nova's private business was her private business. But the Company was clearly aware that the assignment had put her off working for them. "Look, we need her for this assignment," he'd been told when his controller had awakened him in his D.C. condo at three-twenty this morning, "and we need her now. You'll be going to Italy. To the Amalfi Coast."

"If she's burnt out, maybe you should get someone else," he'd replied, pleased that she'd quit Company work, a dangerous business mixed up with the scum of the earth.

"You'll get your briefing in Italy. Time is of the essence here. The bottom line is that fast and accurate translation is the key, and it may have to be done on-site. For that we have to have someone who can translate and speak fluently in Russian, Italian, Chinese and, of course, English, and who is intimately familiar with the lingo involved in virus research. The Italians don't have any one person like that. We have Nova, and we've told them we'd get her for them."

He'd been surprised. "Nova knows about viruses?"

Now irritated, the Company man had muttered, "You'll get your briefing in Italy, Cardone. All you need to know now is that Nova is uniquely qualified, that's she's needed urgently for this assignment, and a fucking lot of lives are at stake. I'd say, conservatively, millions of lives. Your job is to get her to do it. Get her

involved again for the Company or expect to feel big
heat from higher up. All the way higher up."

Joe yelled to Katie over the helicopter's racket. "No.
She doesn't know I'm coming. And if she's like most
women, she'll probably be pissed when I show up."

Grinning, Katie Donovan tilted her head, eager for
his explanation.

"The last time I saw her we were about to spend a
nice weekend together when I got called away. The
usual thing, right?"

"Uh-huh."

"And about the last thing I said to her was that I'd
call. I didn't."

"Oh yes. You *are* in big trouble." Katie used his
shoulder for support as she pushed to her feet. He liked
it. The feel of a woman's hand. "We should be about
there." She made her way forward.

He gazed out the starboard door over the rolling sea
of green, the earthy-smelling warm wind hitting his
face, thinking, *Why didn't I call?* He had intended to.
But his next assignment kept him fully occupied for the
first ten days, and when he finally caught his breath, he
remembered how Nova, who was five years older, always treated him like a kid brother.

And König was an urbane sophisticate, quite the opposite of a Texas-ranch-raised, ex-Naval aviator jock.
Calling Nova had suddenly struck him as stupid. Besides, they led crazy lives. When could they ever real-
istically get together? So at first he'd put off calling her,
and then finally he'd quit even planning to.

Now he was going to have to pay the price.

But then, maybe not. Nova wouldn't really have expected a call. *What a monumental ego you have, Cardone.* She would have assumed that his saying he would call was like a Hollywood producer saying, "We'll do lunch soon."

Nova Blair was one woman who wouldn't be sitting around waiting for some man to call her.

Chapter 3

Nova halted on her traverse line immediately above Robin. The terror-stricken girl was still rotating, but more slowly now. Pale, she was gazing up at Nova.

"You hanging in there?" Nova said, wishing with an aching heart that she could be the scared one, not Robin. "Pun intended," she said, forcing a reassuring smile.

Robin actually smiled back, but with thin, white lips. "Yep, ha-hanging in there."

"I'll attach a rescue pulley to your traverse line. Then I'll let down a rope. Put the rope under your arms, and together we'll haul you back up. Okay?"

"Okay."

Using the unipod, Nova pulled the girl's carabiner, dangling at the end of Robin's harness line, across the short space between the two traverse lines. The carabiner was fine, but somehow Robin's thrashing had been enough to yank the metal ring off her harness.

Nova clamped the rescue pulley onto Robin's traverse line. She fed one end of the thirty feet of half-inch nylon rope through the rescue pulley and tied a figure-eight knot. Feeding out rope, she said, "Put the loop under both arms and make sure the fit is good and tight."

In less than a minute, Robin was ready. Nova ran the rope under both of her arms and across her back. "Here's how we do this. I'll count to three. When I say three, you pull yourself up on the security line as much as you can. That takes weight off the rope. We're both dangling. I don't have any real leverage. But if you pull yourself up on the security line while I'm pulling on the rope, we will hoist you back here. Okay?"

Robin nodded.

Please let this work right! "Okay. One, two, THREE!"

Nova pulled, and took in at least a foot and a half. "Good," she yelled. "Perfect! Okay. Again. One, two, THREE!"

Nova took in another foot and a half.

"It's working," Robin called out.

Charles Scott yelled, "You're doing it!"

It took maybe ten minutes, but finally Nova had Robin face-to-face. She immediately refastened a thick nylon strap on Robin's sling harness to the carabiner of the harness line.

"You okay, hon?" Nova asked, squeezing Robin's hand, elated and relieved.

"I have never been so scared in all my life."

"You're going to have a great story to tell your friends."

Robin grinned. "Yeah." The smile faded quickly. "I am so sorry to be such a wimp. My dad's furious. I can never please him. I try, but I just can't do this stuff."

"Here's a guarantee. Trust Bruce and me and yourself, and when you leave here ten days from now, you'll be amazed. I know you want to please your dad, but the person you most want to please is you. I promise, you will have learned that you can always do more than you first believe. Just don't give up."

"If you'd said that an hour ago, I'd have laughed out loud."

"Right!"

Robin's brow wrinkled in a frown. "What's that sound?"

Nova hesitated, listening, as she, too, heard a thrumming. "Helicopter," she said.

They searched the sky, and within seconds a gray-green military-type helicopter—a Huey, Nova noted—appeared, moving directly toward them.

"Oh, it's coming our way," Robin said, her voice again in a quiver.

"It's not going to shake us out of these slings. We're fine."

The blissful stillness of the jungle, already assaulted by the chopper's blades, suddenly crackled with the sound of bullhorn being turned on.

Just wonderful, Nova thought. *This cannot be good news. Why in the world would anyone come out here in a helicopter?*

"I'm from Cosmos Adventure Travel," rumbled a voice over the loudspeaker. "My name is Joseph Cardone. I need to speak to Nova Blair."

Joe! My God! If Joe was here for her, whatever was brewing must be serious.

Her tour folks were pointing her way. The helicopter edged overhead. She and Robin swayed.

For a second, Nova was transported to a street in Germany and Joe was kneeling beside her, his face ashen. He'd just saved her from being run over, maybe even killed. She remembered the strength of his hands, the rich chocolate of his brown eyes, that football quarterback body.

She briskly hand-signaled the helicopter to back off, afraid the downdraft might break branches or topple nests. The pilot responded, lifting the craft higher but still keeping it above them. Joe, holding the bullhorn, stood inside the starboard door.

"Hey, Nova!"

She recognized his voice and her heart—which was already pumping from the adrenalin rush of the rescue so hard she could feel it in her throat—sped up still more. *The goddamn idiot never called.*

She gave him a thumbs-up of recognition.

"CAT needs you to do something. Urgent. No time to get a Jeep out here. You should turn over the tour to Bruce, collect your stuff, and then we'll pick you up from the hotel's deck. Say, ten minutes?"

How about, say, never! How dare they assume she'd jump when they called! She couldn't have made it clearer that she no longer intended to work Company jobs. She gave a thumbs-down.

"Bruce," she called out. "You can pull Robin across now."

Robin started moving away toward the far side of the canopy.

From the sky, "We'll pick you up. Ten minutes. Okay?"

She looked up at him, happy to see him and furious at the same time. She wanted to climb up there and ask him what he'd been doing lately. Again, she gave him the thumbs-down.

"Are you saying you aren't going to come?"

She nodded and simultaneously gave a thumbs-up.

She began to pull back to where Padgett, Charles and the others waited. The helicopter followed, hovering high over her at first, and then slid swiftly to hover over the hotel. She wondered what havoc the blades were stirring up with anything loose on the deck. A rope ladder dropped down from the starboard door.

No is no, she thought.

By the time she reached her group, Joe was halfway down the ladder. She unhooked her carabiner and stepped out of the sling.

"Sorry, folks. This shouldn't take long, but I've got to deal with it before we can go out today. Clearly CAT has some special problem they think I can solve. Everyone wait here, until I get back. Or you can come back with me to the hotel."

"I'll wait here since Robin is already across," Charles said.

"I'll wait here, too," Padgett added.

"Don't leave us in the lurch," said a teacher from Ohio.

"I'll be back in no time," she assured everyone. *No is no!*

Chapter 4

Her feet felt light, as though her tennis shoes had the power of levitation. Nova closed the space between herself and Joe, who had just dropped a couple of feet from the helicopter's ladder onto the broad Treetops deck.

The khaki, lightweight military jumpsuit showed off his dark brown wavy hair and deeply tanned skin in a way that triggered a too damn familiar sexual fantasy she had of being swept off her feet by Joe, and more. Lots more. Across the narrowing distance between them, he sent her one of those goddamn fantastic smiles.

Her pulse beat a tattoo at her throat. She didn't even try to suppress the smile she sent in return. How wonderful to see him again. How amazingly good it felt.

He grabbed her hand for a handshake. She embraced him in a bear hug. He smelled wonderfully like fresh air and Texas sage—soap or shampoo, she thought. She'd never known him to wear cologne. Then she pushed him away. "You are a typical male jerk."

"You're pissed."

"You betcha."

He tilted his head, gave her a sheepish half grin.

"As I recall you uttered something about keeping in contact, and I haven't heard word one from you. How many months now? Since I know you're a man of your word, I decided you must surely be dead."

They were yelling over the sound of the chopper. Joe waved the pilot to back off farther, noting as he did that Nova had a bit of tan on that extraordinarily fair skin, something she'd not had the last time he'd seen her.

He also wondered whether her greeting was the kind she'd use with a kid brother—or a friend—or one she used with a man she was attracted to. So far, he couldn't tell.

She'd braided her glossy, long black hair into a twist at the back of her head. He checked her earlobes and found a plain pair of silver studs—not the dangly silver doves that he'd given her as a parting gift. He suddenly realized he'd been hoping she'd be wearing those. She always wore earrings, acted as though she was somehow naked without them, but it certainly made more sense out in the middle of the jungle to be wearing simple studs.

She might not be wearing his earrings, but she clearly had remembered his promise. And she was right that promises should be kept. "My humble apology." He added a little bow at the waist.

Judith Leon

She laughed, and the deep, throaty sound made the small hairs at the back of his neck stand up. He enjoyed looking at the curve of her breasts beneath the tight, gray tank top, and then at the long legs exposed below her gray shorts. He forced his eyes to her lips. He sure wasn't thinking about business and why he'd been sent here. He was thinking of sex.

Gazing at those moist, luscious lips didn't solve his thought problem, so he turned sideways and, staring out at the expanse of green foliage, said, "Look, I know you've turned down a couple of Company assignments. But this one, I promise you, is critical."

A man and woman approached from the other end of the deck. Nova said, "Joe Cardone, this is Hans Licht and his wife, Jennie. They pretty much make Treetops happen. Joe works with me at CAT."

He shook hands with them, and Hans Licht said, "Is there anything wrong? What is happening?"

"It's okay, Hans," Nova said. "CAT has hit a snag and they think they need me. I'm quite sure they don't, but..."

Joe and I... hosts that they obviously had to be, given their exclusive clientele, the Lichts made a swift departure. Joe was again alone with a reluctant Dove.

"I'm stunned they would send you all the way out here," she said at once. "I'm finished with CIA business."

The irony of this scene struck him, momentarily interrupting the argument he'd prepared for her. Here he was, tasked to get Nova to work for the Company again on pain of professional discomfort, or worse, if he didn't succeed. Yet during the last conversation he'd had with her, he'd asked why in the world she ever worked for the Company. He'd even said something to the effect that he didn't understand why someone with her many gifts would spend any time dealing with the lowlifes of the world, even for her country.

He shook his head. A smile must have accompanied the headshake because Nova said, "What's funny?"

"Sorry." He leaned back against the sturdy deck rail—one guaranteed to keep distracted or tipsy guests from tumbling a hundred or more feet to the ground. He crossed his arms. "Not funny. Just ironic. I should be glad you want to quit, but here I am, and I've got to convince you to take just one more job. Just one more."

"No."

He waited. He'd let her wonder a bit just what they might need her for.

"Look," she said.

She leaned against the rail beside him, close enough so that he felt the skin of her arm brush his forearm. Would she stand so close to a man she thought of as a kid brother?

"I'm burnt out. I lost a man I loved. I had to kill people again. I hate it. I'm out of the game."

"Okay. You don't need to convince me. I'm not someone who wants you…well, I'd just as soon you quit. But we've got a megaproblem, and we need you."

"That's ridiculous. They can always find someone else."

"Someone else who speaks and reads, fluently, English, Italian, Chinese and Russian?"

She snorted in disbelief. "Why in the world would they need…?" She studied his face. "You're not authorized to explain unless I agree to take the job, are you?"

"Correct."

"Does it really have to be one person with all of those languages?"

"That's what they tell me."

"I don't want to do it, Joe."

She frowned in a way he'd never seen before. A look of true hurt. She wanted to be free, to take her beautiful photos and spend her days in magnificent and exciting places with interesting and nice people. And why not?

"When we were in Virginia training for the German mission," he said, "someone told me that you never took jobs for the Company unless people had been killed. Not agents, and not bad guys, but ordinary people. I can tell you one thing. No one has died yet, but if we don't succeed in this mission, thousands, maybe hundreds of thousands of people will die."

"You're exaggerating."

He said nothing. He waited a moment more to let that sink in, and then, "You're unique, Nova. You are fluent in all the languages we need." Another pause. "Just one more job."

"Why do they need me? Us? Why not use local talent? Use several of their own break-in specialists and translators?"

"I wasn't told that, but you can be sure they have their reasons. If I had to guess, I'd say maybe they need someone on-site to translate, for whatever reason, and to avoid leaks or generating suspicion by the target, they don't want to have more people on location than is absolutely necessary. They require one person with heavy-duty language skills. And who knows about viruses. He definitely mentioned viruses. You know about viruses?"

"I did a job several years ago in Pakistan that involved bioweapons."

"Well, a translator fluent in a bunch of languages who knows about bioweapons is an exceedingly rare bird. That's you. Or maybe they think they need an on-site translator with a good cover who won't obviously smell like security. We're foreigners. We, as a team, would fit. Maybe they want all of those things."

"I cannot tell you how much I don't want to do this."

"Look, it's not going to be like last time. No wet work involved. This is a break-in and translation job, and I do the break-ins. I'll even tell you where. It's in Italy. The Amalfi Coast. What could be more beautiful? It'll be more like a vacation. How's that? A great, paid vacation for a little translation work and the potential to save thousands."

She remained silent. "You'd be lead agent," he added with an encouraging smile. "In charge, just like in Germany."

Nova sighed and shifted her weight. She put her hand over Joe's. She could tell from his tone that he was honestly reluctant to drag her back into this, but reluctance wasn't stopping him. He believed she was, in fact, essential.

Her stepfather's sexual and verbal abuse had hardened her. Killing Candido to save her younger sister Star from that same abuse and the years she'd served in prison for the killing had toughened her still more. Being recruited for the CIA by a man she thought had loved her but who'd dumped her when she no longer served his purposes, had been the finishing touch. She was capable of taking out the bad guys, and if Joe was being honest—and she believed he was—then how could she turn down this job and live with herself afterward? All they asked from her was translations. Was she going to call Claiton Pryce at Langley and say, "I absolutely refuse to translate one word for you or the Italians no matter how many people might die if I don't?"

"Okay," she said. A heavy weight descended onto her shoulders. "One more time."

Chapter 5

The young man's feet felt like great stones, every step requiring a huge effort. His palms were clammy and even though he had rubbed on massive amounts of deodorant to prevent perspiration in his armpits lest he be detected too soon, he felt some wetness there.

Scarcely one block away, he saw his target, Madrid's famous and busy Gaudi Galleria, a shopping and entertainment center that at this afternoon hour would be crowded with hundreds—no, thousands—of infidels. Although people were dashing across the boulevard, he crossed the street at the light. He must do nothing that might call attention.

Half a block from the entrance, his vision of the glassy Galleria structure ahead momentarily blurred. He stopped, his legs shaking, and sucked in a breath.

"Don't stop," Ahmad al Hassan had coached him repeatedly. "It will seem strange."

To cover the moment, he glanced in the window of the shop beside him. Nothing he saw registered in his mind. He turned again to his target and walked at the same practiced pace. Not too fast.

But his heart raced with his eagerness to get there, to have it done. He prayed he would not lose courage at the last minute, that he would be the one to press the button. If for any reason he froze, two others were with him on this mission, and one of them would do it for him. There was no way out now, no way back, only forward to honor and paradise.

No one seemed to notice a clean-shaven, nicely dressed youth with dark, intense eyes and well-combed hair.

Fifteen paces inside, he put his shaking finger on the detonator button. "God is great," he shouted in Arabic. He pressed, the circuit completed connection.

The roar, which he did not hear, was deafening.

In his small, tidy office on the second floor of a building in Amalfi that housed a bakery on the first floor, Ahmad al Hassan fought the urge to squirm in his desk chair. The aroma of fresh bread seeped into the room from below and his mouth watered despite his anxiety. His two assistants, Mohsin and Brahim, appeared to be busy laboring at their desks.

He stroked his beard, kept short so that he would not draw excessive attention to that fact that he was Muslim in this heathen land. So much was happening all at once. In his pocket he carried the e-tickets that would take Nissia and the children out of Italy, and he was anxious, now, to tell her she must leave. But he could not possibly leave work until he knew if today's attack had succeeded. Ahmad had spent enormous emotional energy and substantial Al Qaeda financial resources to get the bomber in place.

To Mohsin he said, "If the boy is caught—"

He spoke in Arabic, which he allowed his assistants to speak only in the office. Outside it, they were never to speak anything but Italian, the better to blend in.

Success meant he could concentrate his efforts immediately on the still greater spectacle, one that would bring Italy and the continent to its knees. Failure in Madrid meant he would have to deal with criticism from Syria.

Again he checked the television screen. The station put out continuous news but Ahmad had ordered Mohsin to silence the sound. He simply had too much to do to have the monstrous machine blaring at him in Italian.

He checked the clock. If the boy had succeeded, the Galleria would be in chaos at this moment and the boy in the presence of Allah. The news should appear on the screen soon.

Mohsin sneezed. His head, a small round ball atop a long skinny neck, nodded over the fake documents he was preparing for Al Qaeda recruits due to arrive soon from Palestine, Egypt and Syria, on their way to Germany.

By habit, the *dua* associated with sneezing spilled from Ahmad's lips, "May Allah have mercy on you."

"May Allah be praised," Mohsin responded.

Mohsin was a graybeard of fifty-five, much older than Ahmad's thirty-six years. They had met in Palestine. Then ten years ago, Ahmad had become a sworn member of Al Qaeda and the two of them had been sent here to Amalfi. Now fronted by Ahmad's profitable and legitimate fishing business, both of them were deep undercover. And although Mohsin felt the creeping affliction of Parkinson's disease, the fire of jihad still burned hot in his soul. He would sacrifice his life, if he had to, to get all Westerners out of the Holy Lands.

"I am sure that all will go as we have planned," Brahim said from across the room. His voice, high with anxiety, betrayed his confident words. Brahim, twenty-five years old, short and plump, was a financial whiz, skilled at laundering money through the fishing business.

Ahmad studied Brahim for a moment, fascinated as always by his remarkably fat yet agile fingers, then he snapped, "Concentrate on your work. The list of weapons needs to be sent to Greco by tomorrow at the latest."

The weapons, to be secured from the weapons dealer Fabiano Greco, who lived in Positano, would be smuggled via Lebanon into Syria. The heart of Al Qaeda now resided in Syria under the leadership of the Saudi imam, Ramsi Muhammad.

Ahmad forced his eyes once again to his own work. Because of his language skills, one of his tasks was to translate all-important, sensitive messages from Kenya, Libya and France, brought by courier to this office, into Arabic. Another courier carried them on to Syria. The secret to remaining undetected by the electronics of the infidels was to avoid electronic devices for all really critical communications. At the moment, he labored over a report from the Al Qaeda cell in Kenya.

"That's it," Brahim shouted.

With his two assistants, Ahmad turned to the TV, his gaze transfixed by the scene of twisted metal, broken glass, scattered paper, here and there, something recognizable as a body.

"Allah be praised," Ahmad said, almost a whisper, his head bowed.

Mohsin leapt to his feet and turned on the sound.

The news anchor spouted the basics: how many known dead so far, twenty-three but the death toll swiftly rising; that it was the work of a suicide bomber, but as yet no clues and no one claiming responsibility; that the wounded were being taken to nearby hospitals.

Ahmad turned to Brahim. "I am going to be busy with preparations for the fourteenth. You are in charge of getting the information out to the usual outlets that this is our accomplishment. Make sure Aljazeera receives it first, by at least an hour. They are fanatical about having priority. And the video, too."

Brahim nodded.

Mohsin said, "I have the article for the Web site ready. Do you still wish it to be posted tomorrow, not today?"

"Yes."

From the beautifully carved cedar PrayerKeeper on the wall came the call to prayer, interrupting Ahmad's growing sense of joy, swelling sense of pride and relief that the boy had not been caught and they were all still safe. As the head of the Al Qaeda cell in Italy, keeping

this Amalfi operation safe—their home base in Italy—
was his most solemn duty.

Like the good Muslim that he was, he prayed five
times daily at the appointed hours, and the Prayer-
Keeper let him know the correct moment. It could indicate the time for prayer at any place in the world. In
addition to playing the call to worship, it indicated the
direction of Qiblah. The time was 16:09, the time for
mid-afternoon prayers.

The timekeeper had been a gift last year from his
son, Saddoun. A good son. Smart. Devoted to Allah.
Ahmad could never have hoped for a better seed. He
had tried to have at least one other boy, but Allah, the
one true God, had blessed him with three daughters instead. Allah's will be done.

He made ablution, as did Brahim and Mohsin. Afterward, he unrolled his carpet as they did theirs. They
all took the position of reverence. *"Allahu Akbar"* they
intoned.

Praying on clean ground would be better, but even
the Prophet, peace and blessings be upon him, had used
a carpet. Although Islam was growing in fertile soil in
Italy and the country now had more than four hundred
mosques or cultural centers, there were none yet in
Amalfi, so they prayed together at the office.

He prayed thrice, at the end said Aameen, and used
both hands to rub his face. He stood and rolled up the
carpet.

"I have to leave now," he said. "I cannot return, so
you should close up."

Ahmad rushed out the door, down the outside
stairway and to his ancient Audi. As he seated himself

inside and turned the ignition, he said the appropriate *dua*.

He pulled into the Amalfi traffic, heading for home. Nissia was not going to want to leave, but before the fourteenth, his entire family must be out of Italy.

Chapter 6

Joe hung above her, climbing quickly, halfway up to the hovering Huey. Someone had hauled up her minimal gear. She'd taken only four minutes to change from walking shorts into a pair of light gray cotton slacks and matching short-sleeved top.

"It's such a shame they can't get someone else," Charles Scott said, his hair and clothes rippling in the downdraft. "Robin is going to be horribly disappointed. She admires you enormously."

James Padgett grabbed Nova's hand. "Take care," he bellowed. "I'll try to remember what you said. 'Don't give up.'"

Joe disappeared into the Huey. James Padgett gave her a leg up onto the first rung. She grabbed the ladder with both hands and climbed swiftly.

Joe and a blond, blue-eyed, and quite young military woman pulled her into the Huey. With Joe beside her, Nova buckled herself into a jump seat, and the blonde went forward to join the pilot and copilot.

"Where are we headed?" Nova yelled.

"The USS *Ronald Reagan*. About thirty minutes off the coast."

The blonde then reappeared carrying two cups. She handed one to Nova. "Coffee?" she yelled over the noise of the helicopter blades.

"Yes, thanks." Nova loved Costa Rican coffee. Better still, a cappuccino made with Costa Rican coffee. She was pretty much hooked on cappuccinos.

The blonde extended the second cup to Joe. "How about you?" She gave him an unabashedly come-hither smile.

Nova snapped her gaze to Joe's face. He captured the blonde's gaze with those dark chocolate eyes of his, returned her smile and, when he took the cup, managed to let their fingers touch.

Or had the blonde arranged that?

This guy is absolutely incorrigible.

He's a jock. Women are crazy about him—beautiful women younger than me. He's younger than me. And if I let him get under my skin again, I'll richly deserve the disappointment I'll eventually have. I've got to stow it.

The blonde went forward. Nova gave Joe a cocky smile. "Still got that winning way with women, I see."

He just grinned and shrugged.

Twenty minutes later, they touched down onto the carrier's deck. They had barely dashed out from under the still rotating blades when a young, sun-blistered lieutenant colonel met them. "We have an EA-6B Prowler waiting for you," he said. The lieutenant colonel's aide carried a couple of bags Nova assumed must belong to Joe.

The blonde deposited Nova's two bags at Nova's feet. She gave Joe a parting smile and strode off, back straight, hips in a swagger. Nova felt a flash of admiration for the confidence in her stride.

Looking at Joe's gear and the large duffel bag and aluminum camera case at her feet, the lieutenant colonel added, "I don't think the Prowler will handle that much."

"Sure it will," Joe countered.

"I'll leave the clothes if I have to," Nova said. "I won't leave the camera equipment."

"While we take a quick anticipatory trip to the head," Joe said to their contact, "you check with the pilot and find a way to bring all her gear."

"Yes, sir," came the man's crisp answer. "You'll find the heads one deck down that ladder," he gestured with his thumb, "and to your right."

Joe took Nova's arm. Her body remembered at once the feel of his hand on her arm—firm, warm and a bit possessive. And she didn't mind any of that. Not at all.

He steered her toward the ladder. "Here's the deal," he said. At last she was going to get a better feel for what was afoot. "We need to be in Rome as soon as possible. We're going to be picked up by SISMI, the Italian version of the Company."

"SISMI. Right. Servizio per le Informazioni e la Securezza Militaire. And Rome. I haven't been to Rome for about eight years."

"It will be easier for them to pick us up from Rome's Leonardo Da Vinci International Airport than from the American military base, so we're going to make the last leg of the trip on Alitalia, out of Atlanta. And we have to be there by 17:30 this afternoon, Atlanta time, to make the connection. It's sure a better deal for us. We'll be a lot more comfortable in Alitalia's business class than on a military transport."

"If I'm not mistaken, my niece, Maggie, is in Italy right now. Or should be soon. You remember I told you my sister Star has three kids. Maggie, the girl, is their ten-year-old."

They reached the lower deck and turned right. She spotted the sign for the women's head.

She met him back on deck where he was waiting with the lieutenant colonel. In short order, she slipped into flight gear and a helmet; as she climbed into the Prowler, she felt her pulse picking up. Joe had been a naval aviator before an accident had ruined his vision and he'd traded flying for spying. This would all be old hat for him, but she'd never flown in a jet with this much power before.

The takeoff from the carrier's deck was a thrill ride times a thousand, the jet's thrust slamming her hard into the seat. "That was way too quick. I want to do it again," she said into the intercom.

"You'd have made a great pilot," Joe's voice came back.

"Glad you enjoyed it, Ms. Blair," she heard from the pilot. "Always my pleasure to give a hot woman a thrill."

Yes, she thought with a grin. *Flyboys do love their thrills—of all kinds.*

The flight to Pensacola left her too much time to wonder about what job could be so complicated as to require uncommon linguistic skills.

Time to think, also, of how much she did not want to deal anymore with the brutality and destruction some people seemed compelled to commit. She was quite certain why they'd sent Joe to rope her in. They knew she would trust him. And she did. If Joe believed it was important for her to do this, then they figured she'd go along.

At the Pensacola air station, she and Joe ran to a waiting private executive jet, were whisked inside and were quickly once again airborne. Free of the uncomfortable flight suit, she stretched her legs and arms and sighed. Except for the pilot and a copilot, they were alone at last, Joe sitting facing her in one of the comfortable leather seats. "So what can you tell me?"

Joe removed one shoe and then the other. "It's bad, Nova. Potentially a disaster."

He started massaging the ball of one foot. With a grin, he said, "Sorry, but the sneakers are new. My feet ache like hell."

She pinched her nose in fake revulsion. "As I recall, you're the guy with a great perfume connoisseur's nose. How can you think of subjecting me to male foot smell?"

"Gonna pass out?"

She let go of her nose. "No. I'll just cut down on breathing. So, what kind of disaster?"

He talked with his eyes closed. "On the plane coming down here, after I got the call instructing me to fetch you, I received some further information. Not much, but here's what I know." He opened his eyes, propped one leg across his knee. "SISMI has obtained reliable information that someone in the Amalfi area has their hands on the formula for a new strain of the Ebola virus."

Icy fingers brushed a chill across her throat.

"It's a modified form of something called the Reston strain, which apparently means you don't need physical contact to get it. It can be spread in the air."

From her op in Pakistan, Nova was all too familiar with the early symptoms of the Ebola Zaire strain: fever, headache, muscle ache, rash, diarrhea, vomiting and stomach pain. The Zaire strain was the first one recorded, named after the African country of Zaire, where the first outbreak was recorded. To date, it was the most lethal strain, with a fatality rate of eighty to ninety percent. During her pre-op briefing for Pakistan, she'd been shown a photo that had been taken during an outbreak in Gabon. A woman held her child, both of them in the final stages of the disease. A bloody rash covered their bodies and they were bleeding from the eyes, ears and nose. They would likely die from shock before they bled out.

Nova shuddered. She thought about the Reston strain and what she knew about it. As bad as Ebola Zaire was, becoming infected required physical contact with body fluids. The Reston strain was not as fatal, but had the potential to be much worse because it could be transmitted through the air.

"So you're saying that someone is selling the information needed to take the rather tame but airborne Reston strain and turn it into a deadly, airborne strain. Right?"

Joe shook his head. "What does it mean if it has a 'carrier phase'?"

Bad to horribly bad! "What that means is that they have modified it so that a person can have the disease but not show symptoms for quite a while. Days or even weeks. And all the time they're walking around, they're spreading it."

"Holy shit!"

"Is it the virus that's being sold, or just the know-how to make it, if someone gets their hands on some Reston?"

Joe shrugged. "Don't know. The message only said that SISMI had evidence that someone has their hands on the formula for creating a new strain of Reston Ebola virus with a carrier phase and is going to sell it. I presume *it* refers to the formula."

"Let us pray that *it* doesn't refer to the actual virus, either the original Reston or, even worse, the modified form."

They were quiet a moment. The world was rapidly becoming a bloody scary place. So many seriously misguided men and women were willing to kill thousands, and technology made it ridiculously simple and possible. A wave of sadness pulled at her.

Joe was absolutely right. She couldn't walk away.

"So, how's your love life?"

She laughed. The question was such a complete switch, but she welcomed anything to take her mind off the mission for the moment. "We never talked much about our love lives in Germany, did we?"

"No. I'd say we pretty much had other things on our minds. How *have* you been doing? I mean, about cutting König loose?"

"It was tough for a while, but I've met someone new. His name is, um, James Padgett." James Padgett! Why would she make up such a dumb thing? "He's crazy about photography, like me."

Well that proved it. When she was with Joe, she lost her grip on reality. A mild case of disconnect, to be sure, but enough to make her fabricate a romance!

She countered. "So what about you?"

Now he grinned. "Been really busy for the Company. Until two days ago, I hadn't even been to my D.C. condo in over a month."

"I didn't know you lived in D.C."

"There's a lot of stuff, isn't there, that we don't know about each other."

She let it go at that. They settled back to their own thoughts. That was something she remembered liking about Joe. He didn't need to talk all the time. And he knew when to stop asking questions. At one point he went to the rear and returned in civvies.

Their Alitalia flight, direct to Rome, would take off at 5:30 p.m. They made the Atlanta airport in good time, close to 4:45, and were ushered through security by the local Company man who met them. Using her computer, she checked her e-mail. Nothing important. Everyone was expecting her to be in Costa Rica for another two weeks.

She felt a caffeine twitch. "How about we hit Starbucks for a cappuccino?" she asked Joe as he closed his own laptop.

He nodded, and they made their way to the food court. "I pay," she said.

He laughed out loud. "Yep. You sure do. Every cup of cappuccino we ever have together, you pay for."

So Joe remembered their bet. In Germany, she had

made a bet with him on who was the bad guy. He had won. She paid for all future cappuccinos.

They checked into the boarding area and, as they sipped, she called her sister Star in La Jolla. First, she asked about their mother's condition; their mother had had another small stroke.

"It's not too bad," Star assured her.

Nova also asked about Maggie and learned that the girl was indeed going to Italy in two days.

Star explained, "It's another hiking trip like the one the Robertsons took her on last year."

"After Costa Rica, I might be going to Italy. If I get some time, I might try to hook up with Maggie and the Robertsons. I'll call if it looks like I might be able to work it out."

Maggie was the closest thing Nova had to a daughter. She'd been at the hospital, in the birthing room, when Maggie was born. In Nova's life, Maggie was a bright, lovely light.

She didn't tell Star about the abrupt change of plans from Costa Rica. Not one person in her life, not even Star, knew about her work for the company.

She called her close friend, Penny. She and Penny, the gay owner of La Jolla's most prestigious beauty salon, had side-by-side apartments. He, bless his heart, took care of her plants and her cat, Divinity, when she was away.

"The Costa Rica trip might be longer than two weeks. And I may take a side trip to Italy."

"No problem," Penny said.

When she and Joe had settled into their seats in Alitalia's business class, she watched as the flight attendants, both of them, fawned over Joe. Yes, the two women were gracious to her as well, but they absolutely glowed when they talked with Joe.

When she and Joe had privacy again she said, "It's actually fun to watch you at work."

"Nova, I swear I usually don't do a thing. Yes, I know I can turn on the smile and charm if I need to. But it's always been like this since I was, maybe, fourteen. It's a blessing, sure. But it's also a curse. Look at how you're dressed. Hair hidden by that braid, that gray outfit, no makeup. It must be a relief to, sort of, be able to disappear. A guy can't change his hair or leave off the makeup."

"Ah, the burden," she said, her amusement showing in a wry smile.

One of the flight attendants offered them magazines. Nova took *O* and *InStyle,* but for a while she and Joe talked about Italy. Both had been there twice before. Both of them loved the astounding history of Rome, the republic and then the empire.

Dinner was served, including wine. Joe raved about his *boeuf bourguignon.* Her stuffed manicotti melted in her mouth. They talked long into the darkness. She was tired and she knew he had to be as well, but somehow the flow of conversation about sports and movies seemed too exciting to break off.

But eventually it did. He beat her to sleep. As she started to drift off, she opened her eyes again, just to catch a glance of him sleeping. She couldn't remember ever having seen him sleeping before.

The urge to reach out and touch the brown hair that curled onto his forehead was so strong that she nearly had to sit on her hand to keep from doing it.

Chapter 7

The home Ahmad had made for his family lay a short five-minute uphill drive from Amalfi's distinctive Moorish-Norman cathedral. When he arrived, the smell of lamb cooking greeted him. Nissia had promised shish kebab for dinner. He would also have her make atayef. The pancake—filled with walnuts, cinnamon and sugar, and drenched in syrup—was his favorite dessert, and tonight was a night to celebrate.

Leila, his fifteen-year-old daughter, and fourteen-year-old Hanan sat at the dining room table dressed in jeans and T-shirts. Leila was fixing her sister's hair. Saddoun, his eyes riveted to television news about the Madrid bomb blast, seemed not to even register that his father had arrived.

Leila glanced at Ahmad and smiled. "The peace of Allah be upon you, Father."

"And upon you, Daughter. Where is your mother?"

"She's in the bedroom with Fatima."

Leila's greeting smile had entirely faded when he asked about her mother. Clearly, something was wrong. Yesterday had been Fatima's twelfth birthday. She had reached puberty and today was the first day she had gone to school wearing a hajib. Had something gone wrong? Had someone insulted her? Some in the Italian government proposed to ban the head scarf in public schools.

Finally Saddoun noticed his presence. "Look, Father," Saddoun said. "One of our soldiers has struck a heavy blow in Madrid. I can almost feel the fear of the infidels coming through the television."

"Have they said yet who is taking credit?"

"No. But I'm sure it's one of ours." Saddoun looked at Ahmad, his mouth open, perhaps to ask Ahmad to verify if this was true.

Ahmad shook his head and indicated with a nod toward the girls that Saddoun should not speak of men's matters in front of them. Saddoun grinned. "I earned highest rank today for my marksmanship in gun class." He turned back to the television.

At only sixteen, Saddoun had yet to fill out. He was slender and wiry like his mother, and like his youngest sister, Fatima, he had high spirits. But while Fatima already at twelve was proving a difficult handful, drawn like so many of the young to sinful Western ways, Saddoun was filled with the righteous spirit of Allah. On his fifteenth birthday, Saddoun had begged Ahmad to let him take a gun class and a class in karate. He was, in fact, becoming quite good at both. Ahmad felt a warm glow of pride just looking at his son's fine hands and strong shoulders.

Nissia joined them, but without Fatima. Usually everyone came to greet him.

"Where is Fatima?"

"We have to talk about her," Nissia replied. "And you will have to talk to her."

"First I want you all to listen to me." He looked at Saddoun. "Turn down the TV."

He immediately had their attention. "I have not been able to tell you something sooner, and I regret that. I know what I'm going to say will not please you. But it is necessary."

"What can be so serious?" Nissia frowned. She shook her head and softly muttered, "Allah deliver me from this horrible day."

"I have purchased airline tickets for all of you to leave Amalfi on the fourteenth of this month. The tickets will take all of you to your mother in Jordan, Nissia."

For a moment, the only sound was the low background chattering of the television.

Then their protests burst forth all at once. "I can't leave school," Leila cried. "I have a party on the sixteenth," declared Hanan.

"That's impossible," Nissia said, lips set in a hard line.

"I won't go," Saddoun said.

Ahmad held up his hand and stared each of them down. "This is not debatable. This is essential. It is necessary that you submit to my will."

Only Saddoun and Nissia knew that he was far more

than a very successful dealer in fresh fish. He saw both of them struggle to resign themselves to what they could not question.

Hanan said, "Father, why do we have to leave? Just us? Aren't you coming?"

"This is something I can't explain. It's something you must accept."

He turned to Nissia. "Now, what is this problem with Fatima? Where is she?"

Saddoun continued to stare at him, his young jaw set firm, but Leila returned her attention to Hanan's hair with only a protesting pout on her lips.

"Come with me," Nissia said. She turned and headed for Fatima's bedroom. He followed, his good mood having entirely evaporated. He could tell from Nissia's straight back and stiff neck that she was in foul humor.

Fatima lay on her bed. The room held the scent of jasmine. Quite inappropriate for a twelve-year-old.

Like his other daughters, Fatima wore jeans and a T-shirt. He accepted this in the home, provided that in public the garments covered their arms and legs and that they wore a hajib to cover their hair and necks. Nissia had sided with Leila and Hanan about being casual at home, so he found it the only way to keep even half the peace. Hearing them enter, Fatima sat up but did not greet him. She stared straight ahead.

Nissia walked to the chest of drawers and picked up a photo. She handed it to Ahmad and said flatly, "I found this in her bottom drawer."

The photo had a signature identifying the subject— Christina Aguilera. The young woman in the publicity photo wore a shape- and skin-revealing red outfit characteristic of a woman of the streets. Arms, shoulders, neck and practically all of her legs were exposed.

He felt the warmth of anger at his neck. "Why would you keep a picture of such a woman?"

Finally Fatima looked at him. "She's beautiful."

"She's shameless!"

Nissia sat the picture back onto the dresser. "The picture is only a symptom of the problem, Ahmad. I am sorry to say that your daughter tried to deceive us."

At the word deceive, he felt his pulse begin to thrum against his temples. "Explain."

"She left the house wearing her head scarf, and she was wearing it when she came home. But Hanan told me she took it off at school."

Ahmad stepped to Fatima, grabbed her wrist, pulled her to her feet and slapped her face. "Repent at once!" he commanded.

She pulled away and sat on the bed; tears welled in her eyes and spilled over.

"I said, repent."

"I—I don't want to stick out. I don't want them to stare at me and make fun. I will lose all my friends."

"You will wear the hajib. You will wear it both to protect yourself from the unwanted stares of men and to honor Allah, who alone is worthy of our worship. If you do not, if you disobey me, the next time I will beat you."

She seemed to shrink a bit.

"Do you understand me?"

For a moment, she simply sat in sullen silence. Finally, she nodded.

"Repent!"

She took a shaky breath. "O Allah, I repent before You for all my sins and I promise never to return to the same."

"I am shamed," he said. "I pray to Allah that this is the end of it."

He paused, glaring at her a moment to be certain the message had sunk in, and then spun on his heels and strode back toward the living room, at the same time both heartsick and furious. The infidels, if they could, would rob him of his children, but very soon he would strike a blow for Allah that would bring the cursed Westerners to their knees.

Chapter 8

With Joe leading, Nova stepped from the offloading ramp into the Alitalia boarding gate at Rome's Leonardo Da Vinci International Airport at roughly 8:15 a.m., local time. She had checked her duffel bag through, as he had, but she carried her aluminum photo equipment case and a briefcase with personal items and her laptop. Joe, too, had briefcase in hand.

"What's our contact's name?" she asked.

"Cesare Giordano."

A tall, thin, clean-shaven and extravagantly dressed man of about thirty-five with bright blue eyes and a neatly trimmed van Dyke held a small sign that said CAT—Blair/Cardone. They walked up to him. Still leading, Joe stuck out his hand.

"I'm Cardone. This is Blair," he said, nodding toward Nova.

Nova took in the man who should be Cesare Giordano and hid her surprise, although she did share a
quick glance with Joe. Joe's slightly lifted eyebrows
suggested that he was having a similarly amazed reaction.

The man's perfectly cut slacks were black; his long-
sleeved silk shirt purple with a red crown pattern over
one pocket. It was either an expensive Armani or a fine
knockoff. Open at the throat, the shirt framed a heavy
gold necklace, the chain holding a massive, two-inch
bull's head with sapphire eyes and polished black horns,
probably onyx. Very expensive—with cuff links to
match. The shoes were Bruno Magli, of O.J. Simpson
fame. He whipped off a pair of sunglasses with metallic, hide-your-eyes lenses. If this was a disguise for a
SISMI agent, it was certainly a good one. Her thought
was, Beverly Hills pimp but with lots of class.

"Delighted, delighted. I'm Cesare Giordano," he
said smiling effusively. "So pleased to welcome you to
Rome, once the capital of the known world. While you
are in Italy, you will be my responsibility."

Before either she or Joe could respond, sleek Cesare
Giordano was at her side with the speed of a sprinter.
She smelled just a delicate hint of a fruity cologne. He
reached for her photocase. But she was also quick. She
pulled it back before he could relieve her of it.

"No, no. Really. You must let me carry your case.
A beautiful woman should not be toting luggage
through Rome."

"How about some ID?" she said.

He held up a hand dramatically, smiled, nodded. He
pulled out a wallet from his slacks pocket and flipped

it open. A SISMI badge bore his picture and the name Cesare Giordano.

She handed over the camera equipment. "Very thoughtful of you."

"My honor, I assure you. Shall we proceed to baggage claim area. I presume you do have luggage?"

"Right," Joe said.

"And how was your flight?" Cesare asked. Without waiting for an answer he commented on what he felt was the excellent quality of Alitalia service, comparing it one after the other with Lufthansa, British Airways and Aeroflot.

Side by side, she and Joe followed the SISMI agent through the airport to the baggage carousels. With pleasing speed, their bags arrived.

They followed Giordano outside into a warm bright June morning, marred by the stink of petrol and the noise of heavy traffic and landing airplanes. A car—a black, four-door Alfa Romeo—waited nearby, presumably granted this parking privilege because of the importance of the arrivals being picked up. Or, perhaps, because of Giordano's pull.

Giordano clicked open the trunk. He had been making more or less one-sided conversation from the moment he had led them toward the baggage claim. As he put Nova's aluminum case inside, he said, "It is my task to make you both comfortable." He relieved Joe of his duffel bag, stowed it in the trunk, and then Nova's. "I shall take you to a hotel at once. You may wish to relax a bit. I suggest you also sleep if you can today so as to readjust to time lag as quickly as possible. Right?"

Nova heard a sound from his car, looked up, and

there in the back window she saw a small, white dog. A Lhasa apso.

"That's my dear Principessa," Giordano said.

Maybe it was the *dear,* but Giordano suddenly reminded her strongly of Penny. *Giordano's gay too. He has to be gay.* Either that or he'd created a brilliant cover.

He held the door for Nova to sit in the front seat. Joe settled himself in the back. Principessa settled herself into Nova's lap, at first wiggling and licking, but quickly curling up to be petted.

"Are we to stay in Rome, Mr. Giordano?" Nova asked.

"Oh please, please. Not Mr. Giordano. I am Cesare."

The car, with Cesare in enthusiastic control, pulled into the traffic. They were out of the airport area in good time.

"Yes," he finally said as they moved onto the freeway leading into Rome. "Tomorrow you will meet at a SISMI office here, in Rome, with Aldo Provenza, the case officer in charge of operation Global Dread."

Cesare suddenly stuck his long arm across Nova's chest to point out her window. "Now you see that splendid mansion! I am the creator of its absolutely glorious interior. I certainly wish we were not so pressed for time. I would love to show you some of my work. But we will save that for another day."

Joe said, "Don't you work for SISMI?"

"Would I be guessing correctly if both of you are thinking, 'It's just not possible this charming man is a SISMI agent.' But I am. I'm accustomed to that reaction. But I assure you, I am their most important asset

in all of Italy. Yes, I am. I am—with all due humility—
Italy's premier *artiste* of interior design. I have access
to the homes of not only the rich and famous, but also
the would-be rich and famous. And if I show up at
someone's door, anyone's door, I am welcomed with
open arms. And now, seeing you both, I am certain we
shall make a perfect team. You are foreigners and, like
me, you look nothing like agents. Amalfi, for her na-
tives, is a small world, and outsiders are always noticed
if they are not obvious tourists. You two are perfect."

Again, Nova flashed on a comparison of Cesare with
Penny. Her neighbor owned La Jolla's most prestigious
beauty salon and was every bit as proud of his work as
Cesare. But while Cesare was showing every indication
of being garrulous, Penny was a man of few, but carefully chosen, words. He shared with Cesare, though, a
belief in his importance and artistry. Before long, it
should become obvious whether Cesare was a blowhard
or the real thing.

He continued to describe every notable point of interest along the freeway leading into the capital. Nova
continued to stroke Principessa, who seemed to be a
perfect lady.

All at once, Joe chimed in with, "You know, Cesare,
Nova and I have both been here before. Several times."

Nova turned to look back at Joe. He let his eyes roll
skyward, clearly not thrilled by Cesare's steady verbal
stream.

"Oh, of course. I would imagine that both of you are
experienced travelers."

The car lurched left, Cesare changing lanes abruptly,
ostensibly to avoid crashing into the bakery truck in

front of them. She saw Joe grip his briefcase tightly just as she swiveled forward again to watch the road—and Cesare's driving.

"I myself travel relatively little out of the country as my work consumes any spare time I might have. But it is such a pleasure to point out those features of Rome that only a native is likely to know."

Nova glanced back at Joe. His arms were crossed, his eyes staring out the window. He was too good an agent to let his feelings show on his face unless he chose to, but she knew him thoroughly and imagined that in his mind he was gritting his teeth.

Poor Joe, she thought, but with a secret smile. She was actually enjoying Cesare—although he did seem a bit too excited by his own conversation to be driving.

"Have you heard about the bombing in Madrid yesterday?" Cesare asked.

"I haven't heard or read any news since day before yesterday," Joe answered.

"I predict it will be the handiwork of Al Qaeda," Cesare continued.

"Determined bastards," Joe replied.

Soon they were within the city's embrace. Narrow streets ran beside the arches of a thousand-year-old aqueduct. She simply could not imagine how anything made of bricks and concrete could last that long. What fabulous stories those bricks could tell! Flowers gaily graced second floor windows and balconies of buildings that seemed to sag with age. A constant flow of people in cars and on bikes passed going in all directions.

Their car swept through the Piazza Venezia past the

Vittorio Emanuele monument, and then down the crowded Via dei Fori Imperiali. On her right she recognized the grounds of ancient Rome's heart, the Forum, and farther ahead she could see the northwest side of the Coliseum. She felt an elated buzz. No one could be blasé in this place. From this spot on the globe, the Romans had conquered and ruled the world for a thousand years.

Before they reached the Coliseum, Cesare lurched the car left into the rushing traffic of Via Cavour. From previous trips, Nova knew that not far ahead lay Rome's central train station. Cesare, however, braked to a teeth-clicking stop in front of the Hotel Imperial Cavour. She gave it a quick assessing appraisal and ranked the seven-story hotel tentatively as three-star.

Again with sprinter-like speed, Cesare leapt out of the car and rushed around to open Nova's door. Setting Principessa on the passenger seat, she let Cesare play gentleman, which, judging from his happy smile as she stepped from the car, pleased him. Joe, she noted, was glowering.

"Registration is in your own names. Tomorrow morning I will pick you up promptly at nine. You will spend the day in briefings. We are somewhat short on time, so I myself will be making final arrangements for our lodgings in Positano and for our transportation the day after tomorrow to Sorrento by helicopter and from Sorrento to Positano by auto."

He opened the trunk and took out Nova's gear. Joe, with quick-time speed to match Cesare's, grabbed up his own gear. As the doorman piled everything onto a luggage cart, Cesare said, "Tomorrow I will pick you up after your briefings. By the way, don't let Provenza frighten you."

Joe blew his breath out.

Cesare looked first at Joe and then at her and shook his head. "But, of course, neither of you will be. What *am* I thinking? I myself am from Milan and the man is Sicilian, and I never really trust Sicilians."

He turned, sank into his Alfa and, with a wave and a *ciao,* took off.

"At last," Joe said as they strode toward the hotel entrance.

"I think he's funny. And informative."

"He's going to drive me nuts."

She patted Joe's arm.

The stones of the street and the pavement already throbbed with heat. By noon, Rome would be as hot as Costa Rica had been.

Once inside the hotel and registered, she said, "I'd like to walk down to the Coliseum and maybe through the Forum. Want to come?"

He hesitated, clearly undecided. "Aren't you tired?"

"Not really." In truth, the thought of what they might be facing had her wound up tight. Maybe a walk could calm her. "But you're right. Tomorrow we need to be bright-eyed and clear-brained."

"Funny. I'm surprised that I actually forgot your insomniac thing about only needing three or four hours of sleep. I would want to come with you. Anywhere with you. But let me crash now. Tomorrow, after the briefing, we'll do something."

They stepped into the elevator and the bellman followed them in with the luggage, crowding the modest space. Her shoulder pressed against Joe's strong, hard, and utterly male one. She suffered the outrageously out-of-place wish that they weren't headed for separate rooms, followed immediately by an urge to ruffle his cocky feathers. "I know how kids need their sleep."

He shrugged. "Just a *normal* guy who needs the *normal* amount of sleep. Unlike some *weird* folks I know."

He followed her down the hall. Her thoughts switched again to tomorrow. What would they learn? Were they only concerned with the sale of deadly information, or was it the virus itself that was to be sold? Tonight, even four hours of sleep might be hard to come by.

Chapter 9

Ali Yassin stared at his brother's bier, but his thoughts were on his mission in Rome.

"Now, Ali," his uncle said softly, bringing Ali back to the squalor of the tent he and his mother, brother and two sisters called home.

His brother was dead, killed because he had been throwing stones. As dead as his father and two uncles before him. Ali became once again aware of the noise of the crowd outside, the sounds of the wailing of women and the chanting of prayers by men.

His mother touched Ali's hand. "Carry him proudly." Tears welled in her eyes above the veil that would cover her as she followed yet another of her loved ones to his funeral.

"Pride," he said as he stepped over to the crude bier and, with his uncle and four other men, lifted it off the wooden table. "You can't eat pride. Pride won't put clothes on a man's back. Pride won't get a man an education. Pride is good, but it's not enough."

With the other men, he moved toward the door, and then out into the street.

Shouts of "Revenge! Revenge!" rose. The women's wailing grew louder.

Waving palm branches and Hamas flags, the mourners moved slowly down the narrow and filthy street toward the camp's humble mosque.

Soon his mother, sisters and uncle would have reason to be proud of what he would do, something that would make his name famous far beyond Palestine—and his mother would have the money given to the families of all martyrs who went to Allah.

Chapter 10

Cesare and Principessa dropped off Nova and Joe in front of a business with a sign that said Condolezzi, Importo e Exporto. The office occupied the middle of a block in a modest, tree-lined neighborhood halfway between their downtown hotel and the airport.

A small fountain in a pocket park in the center of the street gurgled pleasantly. Shops on either side and across the way proclaimed that they were a bakery, tobacco shop, shoe repair, Internet café and a copying and business supply establishment. The smell of cinnamon and coffee from the bakery lent the whole neighborhood a spirit of hominess.

"When you are ready to be picked up, call me on my cell," Cesare announced, as full of energy and enthusiasm as he had been yesterday.

With Joe at her side, Nova entered Condolezzi. She would have preferred to be wearing something more professional than casual slacks, but so far she'd had no good chance to shop.

The balding middle-aged man reading a newspaper behind the counter removed his glasses. The smell of his pipe smoke suddenly evoked her father's presence. Kind, strong, world diplomat, excellent father, loyal husband. His death in a plane crash into the water at Capri when he was much, much too young had changed everything in Nova's life—for the worse. Her throat tightened.

How very different it all would have been, Papa, if you'd lived. I still miss you.

How ironic that beautiful Capri was such a short distance away and would be even closer tomorrow, when she and Joe reached Positano.

Her father had been, like Nova, tall and dark and with the same emerald-green eyes. Her straight hair and the slightly oriental almond shape to her eyes, though, came from her mother, who now lived in a full-care facility in La Jolla, an hour's drive from Nova but quite near Star.

Nova's mother was half Chinese and half Scottish and had been, in her day, an extraordinary beauty. Her father said that the moment he'd set eyes on her mother, at a diplomatic function in Hong Kong, he'd been her slave—or so he'd always claimed, laughing. The very language gifts that brought Nova into this smoke-filled room in Rome began with her life as a diplomat's daughter.

She traveled, learning about so many places in the

world right up until her father's death and her mother's tragic marriage to Candido. Rape, killing Candido and prison—that had been the beginning of learning about evil.

The balding man gestured with his pipe stem toward the door at the far end of the sparsely furnished room, then returned to his newspaper. There would be no ID check here in this public section.

Nova shook herself. To focus, she made note of the room's number of desks (five), number of personnel (two young women, in addition to the senior man), the miscellaneous phones, faxes, posters and a wall clock with times around the world that suggested Condolezzi might actually do some importing and exporting.

The two women smiled at Joe, and Nova felt them watching her as well as she followed Joe to the rear door stamped with a sign saying, in Italian, Private, Store Personnel Only.

Joe opened the door for her. A large room full of shelved items held one man, dressed casually in slacks and sport shirt but armed with a Beretta 92F semiautomatic. He stood up. She and Joe showed the IDs that Cesare had supplied. These indicated that they were Jane and James Blake, Private Investigators. A small mark in one corner gave them immediate access to SISMI channels of communication or operations involved with Global Dread.

In Italian, he said, "Take the elevator and press the Loading Dock button."

They went down. When the elevator door opened, they entered an entirely different world—ultramodern, with computers on every desk. Condolezzi was actually a SISMI operations center and safe house.

A nattily dressed bull of a man—her immediate thought was Olympic wrestler—stood at once and strode toward them with firm steps. She guessed his age at fifty. Clean-shaven and a bit jowly to match his bulk, he still had a full head of wavy, dark brown hair. He'd been perched on the edge of one of the ten desks in the room, talking to a man whose turban and coloring indicated he was probably a Sikh.

Fourteen SISMI personnel toiled at various tasks. She noted big blow-up maps of Italy and Europe on two of the walls and six huge, wall-mounted TV monitors.

"Glad to welcome you both," said the Olympic wrestler in flawless English with a British accent. "I'm Aldo Provenza."

So, she thought, letting a small smile curve her lips. *The Sicilian whom Cesare claims not to trust.*

Provenza introduced them, using English, and then steered them into a side conference room. Only the Sikh, Sandeep Dev, joined them.

"Would either of you care for something to drink?" Provenza asked, continuing in English. It looked as if Provenza felt the meeting would go most smoothly in English. "Water? Coffee? Tea?"

"Two coffees, black, would be nice," Joe said. He glanced at her to make sure she, in fact, wanted coffee. She nodded.

Dev sent out a request for three black coffees and one Earl Gray tea. Provenza indicated that she and Joe should take seats at the starkly functional but expensive chrome conference table that occupied the room's center. The chairs were matching chrome with extremely comfy blue upholstery.

"We're profoundly glad to have you help us out here, Ms. Blair," Provenza continued. He took the seat at the head of the table.

Nova sat across from Joe. She noted three thick manila file folders neatly lined up in the table's center. Two other folders, also labeled in Italian, lay in front of Provenza. "May I call you Nova? I understand you speak quite a few languages."

"Eight," Joe chimed in.

"Nova is fine," she answered.

"Eight. Quite impressive indeed. Although," Provenza patted one of the files in front of him, "as an ex-field agent, I'm even more impressed with your ability to shoot, bomb, steal and just plain out-wit a lot of other people through your years of work for the Company."

This sort of talk always made her squirm. "Perhaps we'll have time for me to show you some of my more positive skills."

"And these are?"

"I'm a photographer."

"Oh, yes. Of course."

The coffees and tea arrived. Dev took the tea.

"Let's get right down to Operation Global Dread, as we are calling it," Provenza said. "Neither of you have yet had time to be briefed. Actually, I assure you that we are all acting under the pressure of time. Here is what we have so far.

"On the twenty-second of June, that's only twenty days from today, an individual or more likely, a criminal group living somewhere along the Amalfi coast is going to sell the instructions for creating a deadly strain of Ebola virus to someone else, apparently terrorists."

When Provenza said *Ebola,* the hair rose on the back of Nova's neck. The name alone again conjured that unforgettable vision of dying mother and child.

"We know this because of an informant," Provenza continued, cool and calm. But of course, he'd had more time to grow accustomed to the horror they were tasked to prevent. "Our informant is an electrical repairman. He was working outside the window of an apartment in Amalfi when the apartment's male renter came home very angry. The disgruntled renter told his sister, who also lived there, that he and 'Lynchpin' just had a big fight.

"It was obvious to our informant that this angry guy worked for someone he called Lynchpin and that he had been making big bucks doing so. But he told his sister, 'I'm finished with the whole thing,' explaining that Lynchpin bragged about having this information about a major modification to the Ebola virus that would make it extremely deadly, something that would be spread in the air, and had arranged to sell it to some terrorist group. The informant thought he heard the name Rexton. Ebola has four strains. Clearly the word he must have heard was Reston, for the Reston strain."

Nova said, "I've seen pictures of what this stuff does to people. Is there any chance it's the virus itself, not just information? Either the original Reston or, God forbid, the modified strain?"

Provenza shrugged. "The informant claims the angry guy told his sister, 'The stuff is right there in the safe.' We have no more specific information than that. 'Stuff.' The sister then said he should go to the police and he became furious, saying he feared Lynchpin more than he feared the police. Also, when the sister asked who Lynchpin was, all he said was, 'It's better you don't know.'

"So the repairman reported what he'd heard to the local police. They contacted us. We've put a task force on this, of which I am the head. I contacted the Company looking for information about Lynchpin. Although the informant was working in Amalfi at the time, there are a number of coastal towns where the seller could live. From the informant's story we've deduced the most likely suspects.

"But regarding your specific question, Nova, the Center for Disease Control is fairly confident that they know every lab in the world that has the Reston strain, and they say there are no known records of any losses. In which case, it's only the information that's for sale. But they admit they can't be certain that scientists, rogue or otherwise, from unfriendly countries don't have the virus. Say, the Russians or Chinese. Because of our informant's accidental but very fortunate eavesdropping, the CDC is in the middle of intense investigations of all of their known sources of the virus. They are double-checking for any possible 'accidental' transfers within the last several years to other labs or scientists. Such accidents have been known to occur, you know, even with these very dangerous bugs. Even if they got a sample of the virus, it would take quite some time, though, for whoever had it to successfully create the airborne strain."

Nova nodded, recalling the scare not long ago about a mistaken transfer of deadly smallpox samples to several unauthorized labs.

"We can't take anything for granted," Provenza went on, his arms crossed over his wide chest. "So we're working on the assumption that, at some point, terrorists may have gotten their hands on some Reston and now what they need are directions for modifying it. That makes it imperative that we stop this sale, even if what is being sold is only information."

"Who are your suspects?" Joe asked.

"Before we move on to the matter of suspects, you need to know that our informant is certain that what is being sold—whether it's on paper or stored on some electronic medium or is the virus itself—whatever it is, it's in the home safe—not a business safe or some other place, but in the home safe—of this person with criminal connections. We have no idea yet, none at all, of who the buyer is, but as I've said, the seller's code name is, in English, Lynchpin. Unfortunately, we do not know who Lynchpin is and neither does the CIA or Interpol."

Nova repeated Joe's question. "So who are your suspects?"

"We have three. The first is an Italian. He is the one we think most likely to be selling information about weapons of mass destruction. Fabiano Greco. He is a member of La Cosa Nostra. While your branch of the Mafia has been rather thoroughly taken down in the States, they continue to thrive here in their homeland. Greco originally made a fortune as a middleman for any kind of deal—art, coins, antiques. From the beginning of his career, Naples authorities suspected him of dealing in stolen items. He lives in Positano. We suspect he's selling weapons, major sales, from RPG launch-

ers to land mines to out-of-date jet fighters from the
Russians and Brits, some legally, some not."

Nova interrupted. "Would he sell terrorists a deadly
virus? Something that could be used right here and kill
him?"

"First, we don't know it's the virus. If it's simply information being sold, this guy Greco would have no
problem. He'd sell practically anything for a sufficiently big payoff. But more importantly, it's very possible that when dealing with a sale of this sort of
material, the original source might not let the middleman—in this case, let's say Greco—know what he's
selling."

Joe said, "Why is Greco first on the list?"

"Because he is a legitimate arms dealer with the le-
gal permits to sell weapons that can be legally sold. We
know he's dirty, but unfortunately he's also clever. We
have no proof of any of his illegal dealings. Although
dealing in WMDs is quite a specialty, he does deal in
weapons, so that makes him our strongest suspect. He
knows all the major international players—buyers and
suppliers. He'd be a likely middleman for a source to
contact, whoever the source might be. As you know,
Nova's first job will be to distract him while you, Joe,
break into his safe."

Nova jerked upright, sloshing coffee out of her cup.
"What do you mean, distract him?"

Provenza didn't seem to understand the question.

"My job, as I understand it, is to do translation."

Provenza continued to stare back, blinking.

"Translation," she said again. "That's all. No personal contact of any kind."

"Well, then, it seems there has been a miscommunication." Provenza looked at Joe. "Was that your understanding as well? It will be very inconvenient, actually impossible, to find someone else with Ms. Blair's qualifications in terms of seduction and languages."

Nova leaned forward, both hands on the table. "Seduction!"

Joe seemed to finally have found his voice. "No one said anything to me about personal contact, let alone seduction."

The room fell silent.

Dev finally said in a matter-of-fact tone, "Ms. Blair, you need only to distract Greco and the others. Signore Provenza's use of the word *seduction* was infelicitous. And I, too, have read your file. Simply distracting this man—apparently, simply distracting any man for a few hours—is well and easily within your capabilities. This is an unfortunate miscommunication, but combined with your facility with languages, it is a critical part of the reason you, specifically, are so important to the success of the mission. And surely seducing a man is not all that important, given the gravity of what we face."

Well, there. Just fine. The three of them were staring at her, all of them knowing that simply distracting one man a few hours while Joe obtained the goods should be, as they implied, a cakewalk for her.

She sat back in her seat, took a sip of the coffee, set the cup down and laced her fingers together, grasping them tightly. She thought for an eyeblink to insist on replacing Joe, she was so pissed at him for luring her into this. But taking time to set up a new partnership was a waste of time, which was surely why they had picked Joe since they both worked well together, and he was the only operative who could have gotten her to agree to the mission in the first place.

"Okay. Go on, Mr. Provenza. Who are your other suspects? And what—" she sent Joe a look she hoped would skewer him to the back of his chair "—what exactly am I expected to do with respect to each of them?"

"The second suspect is a Russian émigré, Pavel Sorokin. He belongs to the Russian mafia. Along with his brother back in Russia, Sorokin traffics in opium from Afghanistan, among other things. The thought is that the brothers could very well have come into possession of such information about a bioweapon via some rogue Russian scientist. Or they might simply be the middleman, Lynchpin."

Provenza pointed to the three folders in the table's center. "You will find photos, backgrounds, in Italian and English, a good introduction to what we have on all three suspects in those files."

Joe shoved his cup over to Dev. "How about another?" His request sounded more like an angry command. He turned back to Provenza. "And the third suspect?"

Dev looked to her. She shook her head. She was so enraged, so pissed at being sucked in, that the coffee roiled inside her stomach.

"The third is the Chinese actress Ya Lin," Provenza said as Dev left the room.

"No kidding?" Joe said. "She's hot."

"You know about Ya Lin?" Nova was truly surprised. A lot of things about Joe surprised her.

"I like foreign movies."

Provenza ignored their side chat. "It turns out that Italy's famous Ya Lin is also believed to be a Chinese spy. And we know that, contrary to her image of great wealth, she's nearly flat broke. If by chance the seller is someone, a scientist from China, she might have been able to set herself up as the broker for the deal."

"Why these three?" Nova asked.

Dev returned and gave Joe his fresh coffee.

"Because they live in the Amalfi area and we have been watching them. We have to start somewhere," Provenza explained.

Joe said, "Obviously neither SISMI or the CIA knows who Lynchpin is. But why haven't they gotten his identity from the man who worked for Lynchpin?"

"Gone. Along with his sister. When we went to pick them up for questioning, they had disappeared. A number of agencies, including Interpol, are searching for them as we speak."

"So the idea," Nova said, "is for me to distract the suspects while Joe breaks in and gets access to what's in their safe. And then what?"

"He makes a copy of everything in the safe—papers, disks, anything on a laptop—and brings the copies out. As I say, you translate at once to see if there is any information about the virus. Reston or any other kind. Cesare also sends copies to us and we'll have translators here also to work on whatever you get. You are on site, however, and the first call goes to you. If you get anything at all about viruses, Cesare is positioned to get a search warrant immediately.

"But let me emphasize—and I can't overstate this— we have to be very careful here. All three suspects are well-known, influential people. To accuse them wrongly without proof is not an option. We have to know with absolute certainty what is in the safe before we even say the word warrant, let alone arrest them. Understood?"

She nodded.

Provenza turned his attention to Joe. "And there's something else. We don't want any of them to know they're under suspicion, that we've been watching them. They must remain ignorant of our attention to them. So you are to be especially careful to leave no evidence of the break-in behind."

"Understood," Joe said.

Dev said, "You'll need a cover. We've been working on that."

Nova shook her head. "We have a cover. It's perfect. We've used it before and practiced it before. I'm a photographer. We'll be doing a series on beautiful beaches of the world. Or better yet, astonishingly beautiful beach drives. Or maybe Mediterranean architecture. Whatever we settle on, Joe is my assistant."

She grinned wickedly at Joe. A little payback for his misleading her. When they had worked in Germany, it had been obvious that he had chafed at being a woman's assistant. Now he would be her assistant, to be bossed around publicly, again.

Provenza grinned. "Yes. Your experience together. Another reason the Company thought it good for us to bring Mr. Cardone on board."

Her stomach had settled enough that what she really needed now was a double espresso. "What if none of these suspects are your seller? And what if we find other incriminating materials in the safe?"

"If you find other evidence linking them to other crimes, we'll pursue it through ordinary channels. And if none of them is the Ebola seller—" Provenza paused and downed the last of his coffee "—I am developing other leads. But if that is the case, well then, unless some other lead turns up, we are in deep shit."

Chapter 11

Striding down the dim passenger ramp from his Egypt-Air plane, Ali eagerly scanned the well-lit exit door only steps ahead of him, buoyed by spirits as high as they had been when he'd taken off yesterday from Jordan. The flight to Cairo, and now the flight to Rome, had treated him to one exciting moment after another. He felt not the least bit weary.

How could he be weary? He was special. His brothers had not only given him the first two plane rides of his life, he'd been given business-class tickets. Never had he tasted more delicious foods, not even for holidays. The serving woman had, of course, offered him alcohol, which he had declined, although he'd been tempted to sip just once since he would never again have the chance to experience this famous evil of the West.

And the view from both planes so captured his attention that, really, it was only the food that tempted him to look away from the bedazzling white clouds, the unfolding brown earth, and the royal blue Mediterranean Sea. He had strained to drink in those beautiful, astonishing sights as they were, for him, more precious now than even water and food. They were last memories.

Ali stepped into the full light of day of the reception room. He shifted his single boxy old suitcase into his left hand. An older man, perhaps his uncle's age of thirty-eight, stepped toward him, stopped, and stuck out his hand Western-style, something he probably did to make him blend into this foreign place. Ali responded in kind.

"I am Ahmad al Hasan," the older man said in Arabic. His suit and shoes were also Western but he still wore a beard, although closely cut. And who knew if this was his real name. Ali could tell from his accent that he was Syrian, and Ali had been told that al Hasan was also the head of Al Qaeda in Italy. That such an important and heroic figure would pick him up at the airport reflected yet another measure of Ali's importance.

Ali's face warmed with pride as the man let go of his hand.

"I trust your flight was enjoyable," Ahmad al Hasan said. "Come. I have a car waiting."

They walked side by side through the terminal, past stores selling perfumes and books, then a coffee vendor, then down the extraordinary moving metal stairs, past still more crowds and finally outside. They walked on sidewalks heated by the midday sun to a big parking lot and eventually stopped at a plain white Audi, at least ten years old.

Ahmad al Hasan opened the door to the backseat and sat Ali's suitcase onto faded brown cloth. He indicated that Ali should take the passenger side.

When they had navigated out of the airport and were on the highway, the Al Qaeda man said, "I live in Amalfi. An apartment there will be our base. Tomorrow, a brother will pick up another when he arrives from Lebanon. The remaining three will arrive soon. We will be all together and prepared by the appointed day."

He scanned Ali, head to toe. "We must change your appearance as soon as possible. You must not stick out in any way. Tomorrow morning, in Amalfi, we will buy good quality Italian slacks, and shirts. A pair of good walking shoes. But most important, we will go right now to a barber and have that sprouting young beard of yours removed."

"I'm ready to do whatever Allah asks."

Al Hasan looked at him again and smiled. "I know. I admire and envy you."

After their briefing with Provenza, Cesare dropped them off at the hotel. Joe asked Nova to join him for dinner. She was inclined to say no and sulk in her room or defiantly go off on her own, but they had to work together. Refusing to eat with him simply wasn't reasonable.

Nor could she face a dinner with Joe wearing the same clothing she'd worn for what seemed like days, and the only other pants she had with her were shorts for a jungle trek. They agreed to meet in the lobby at eight, and she went in search of the hotel's dress boutique.

When she met Joe in the lobby at eight, he looked her over carefully. She'd purchased an emerald green pair of linen slacks and a matching sleeveless top, cut off short at the waist and trimmed on the low-cut neckline and hem with black silk cord.

"Nice earrings," he said. She'd purposely set aside the silver-and-emerald earrings he'd given her, wearing instead glazed emerald green wooden hoops. He didn't say anything else. Neither did she, but she was certain that he was wondering whether she still had his earrings and if she ever wore them.

Few cities matched Rome, in Nova's view, for having so many fabulous restaurants per square block. They walked six doors down from the hotel to La Frescata, a restaurant she knew from her last trip here eight years earlier. Judging from the fact that all the tables were filled and that she and Joe had to wait for twenty-five minutes at the small bar, she decided La Frescata must be doing a good business.

While they nibbled on antipasto, prosciutto and marinated mushrooms, she listened to him talk about flying jets. She watched his lips and then studied his eyes, considered the strength in his hands. When she imagined what it might be like to have Joe touch her skin or hair or lips with a lover's touch, she shivered and felt foolish.

The spell was broken when their entrées came; their talk switched to climbing gear and what they might expect on their flight tomorrow to Sorrento. The food presented a different pleasure, but it didn't match the delight she'd had feasting on Joe—the rat who had played his part in tricking her into this mission.

When they stepped out onto the street, reality hit full

blast. People strolled by her on this pleasant Roman evening unaware that it was very possible that unless she and Joe were successful, within a few weeks the how-to recipe for a deadly virus would reach the hands of terrorists willing to kill everyone breathing in this beautiful balmy air.

Chapter 12

The four-seater helicopter dipped abruptly right, toward Naples. Nova's stomach lurched.

In her headphones, she heard Cesare blurt excitedly to the pilot, "I do not like flying. Please, please make your turns more slowly." Cesare sat up front in their bubble-like cockpit with Principessa in his lap. She and Joe occupied the two rear seats.

An extraordinarily clear, stunning vista surrounded them, especially now on their approach to the green-and-blue Bay of Naples. Were she not still in a foul mood, she would probably be brimming with delight. Contact with deadly lowlifes was exactly what she no longer wanted.

Joe touched her hand to get her attention. He grinned. "Look at this view! Terrific. Didn't I say this would be like a vacation?"

She gave him an icy stare.

He tilted his head and shrugged. "Nova, I swear I didn't know."

"Uh-huh," she said, and returned her attention to the view.

The enormous bay made an almost perfect gentle concave sweeping arc. Dead ahead, Vesuvius poked its smooth crown into a turquoise sky full of scattered, puffy white clouds. Vesuvius's last significant eruption had been in 1944 when ashfall displaced thousands. Much of the village of Ottaviano had disappeared under lava. Earthquakes plagued the whole region around Naples. But of course what gave the volcano its fame far and wide was its eruption in 79 A.D. which had destroyed Pompeii and Herculaneum.

The ashfall had so perfectly preserved artifacts and bodies of the people of that long-gone world that few archeological sites could match it. Nova recalled the dark, gray-black cast of a woman still protectively clutching her child that she'd seen in the Naples Museum. Frozen in time, bent to save her child, if not herself, the small brave woman had drawn Nova into a deep sadness. She'd stared at the dark remains for many minutes, pondering how fate overtakes everyone.

Naples covered the hills that formed the westernmost stretch of the bay. Hills rose up again in the east at their destination, Sorrento.

"Have either of you been to Naples?" Cesare asked through the headphones.

Joe looked at her and mouthed the words, *Can he never be quiet?*

Nova remembered the great surprise of her one trip

to the sprawling, hilly city famous for *amore* and pizza. "Do you know the Capodimonte Museum?"

"Of course," Cesare chirped back. "World-class. The art. The architecture. The furnishings. All superb."

"Well, I have a friend who lives in San Diego, my town. Susan Vreeland. She wrote a book called *The Passion of Artemisia* about a woman painter who did a Caravaggesque painting called *Judith's Beheading of Holofernes.*" Nova looked at Joe and gave him a wicked smile. "I can well imagine that Holofernes must have lied to Judith."

"I didn't lie. I was misinformed," he muttered.

Nova continued, "I loved the book, and then when I wandered through the Capodimante, there, hanging on a wall in front of me, was the painting. Just as my friend had described it."

"My last surprising memory of Naples," Joe said with edge in his voice, "was having my pocket picked in the central train station."

"So sorry," Cesare lamented, his voice bursting with good spirits. Her fondness for Cesare seemed to increase as quickly as Joe's irritation with him. "La Cosa Nostra is still powerful and widespread in all the region around Naples. They have a hand in everything, big and small, including picking pockets. The train station is particularly notorious."

The pilot swung them left, and the crest of Vesuvius slid by on Joe's side. She surveyed the ground. They were sufficiently high up that at first she couldn't spot what she was looking for; then she did. "There." She pointed out his window to a patch along the coast that, in the midst of the sprawling mass of modern development, stuck out as a big brown area on the volcano's southern skirt. "That's what's left of Pompeii."

In less than twenty minutes, their pilot put them down in Sorrento. A black Laforza 351 SUV awaited them, as Cesare had arranged. Joe moved toward the driver's side.

"It does make more sense, doesn't it, if I do the driving?" Cesare said, heading Joe off at the pass. "I do know this area, having driven this coast many times."

Nova took the front passenger seat again, noting that Cesare had once again managed to set Joe's teeth on edge. This continuing clash did nothing to lift her gloomy mood. Principessa took her place, demurely curling up and resting her head on her paws in Nova's lap. Nova enjoyed the pleasure of scratching the small white bit of fluff under the chin, something Cesare said Principessa particularly favored.

"We have a choice," Cesare said, pulling out of the local airport. "I am dying to discuss what emerged from your briefings with Provenza yesterday, and it is nearly time for lunch. We could have lunch here in Sorrento. I know a hotel, the Victoria. Five stars. It has the most astounding view of the bay. We could dine on their patio and have sufficient privacy to chat."

"Or?" Joe said from the seat behind Cesare.

"Or we could proceed at once to the coast and on to Positano."

"That would get us to our lodgings sooner, wouldn't it?"

"Perhaps a little."

"Then I vote we head right to Positano. What do you think, Nova?"

Joe wanted to rush ahead to their rooms to escape from Cesare ASAP. "A five-star hotel with a smashing view," she said sweetly. "Oh, my. That does sound like a vacation, doesn't it?"

She looked back and caught an ever-so-small narrowing of Joe's eyes. He figured she was going to go for the lunch in Sorrento with Cesare in order to torment him further. She'd scored.

But then, Positano would also have lovely views, and she knew what it was like to be cooped up with someone who irritates you. Even if Joe was being unreasonable, and as much as she might like to pretend otherwise, this was no vacation so she and Joe needed to be in sync, not at odds. "On the other hand, I'd like to get settled in myself, Cesare. Let's go on. As Joe says, we can talk while we drive," she added.

She looked back to Joe again. *Thanks,* he mouthed silently.

From Sorrento, the road at first climbed inland away from the water past small towns and the orchards that produced lemons for Sorrento's famous lemon liqueur.

"Jesus, Cesare!" Joe exclaimed. "That BMW!"

Rather than brake the SUV, Cesare revved into the lane for oncoming traffic, accelerated and passed the BMW. Her heart skipped more than a few beats. Had he even checked to see if it was safe to go around? His reaction had been so fast Nova wasn't sure.

After an uncomfortably long pause during which he seemed to be considering whether or not to throttle Cesare, Joe started talking about how to execute the break-ins. Their first target was Fabiano Greco.

"Ah. I know him personally," Cesare said. "Handsome devil. Single. A thoroughgoing womanizer. And as crooked as they come. I decorated the home of his close neighbor in Rome and have chatted with Greco on occasion about doing his place here on the coast. He has a condo in Positano that is famously talked about as being utterly elegant, with a perfect gem of a view. I was there once and I agree with that assessment."

"Tomorrow or the next day, I'll 'accidentally' meet him at the beach," Nova said. "He habitually has cocktails at the same beach restaurant in the late afternoon."

"Well, then, we are going to have to take you shopping. Please don't misunderstand. You are certainly a lovely, lovely woman. Any man can see that. But, well, I think you're not going to catch the eye and certainly not capture the attention of a man like Fabiano Greco in the wardrobe and, well, let's say, the 'look' that you display so far."

She grinned. "Yes, shopping is already on my schedule."

Joe laughed. "Cesare, your eyes will pop. Nova is a master of the duckling-into-swan routine. What you see now is, in my view, the duckling. Plain Jane, as we say in America. For Greco, she will come armed as a swan—a divine sex goddess."

"My, my. That should indeed be a most amusing change to observe."

Cesare glanced at Joe in the rearview mirror. "But I'm sorry, Joe, for interrupting. You were saying?"

"Do you *also* know suspect number two, Pavel Sorokin?" Joe spoke with a touch of sarcasm, apparently irritated now by Cesare's seeming knowledge of everyone in Italy.

"Certainly. Two years ago, I actually did some re-decoration of their magnificent villa in Ravello. He has a lovely family. His wife is Italian and quite social. One child, a daughter. His wife loves music. She explained to me that's why they bought in Ravello. She attends all the festivals and drags Pavel with her whenever she can. I doubt seriously that his wife has any suspicion of any nefarious doings. No, no. Not possible."

Cesare honked the SUV's horn, pulled out into the oncoming traffic lane, and passed a slow-moving but absolutely darling little black car with elegant silver trim.

"What is that?" Nova exclaimed. "It's adorable."

Cesare smiled. "It's a minicar, the most *in* car imaginable. The Smart cars are perfect for narrow streets and miniscule parking spaces."

Joe snorted. "Can you imagine the effect of a collision of a Hummer and one of those? Elephant sits on hummingbird."

They crested a hill and suddenly a wedge of the blue Adriatic lay exposed before her. Just a hint of blue. Traffic flowed bumper to bumper going north and south on the narrow two-lane highway. "I really hate being behind these tour buses," Cesare announced as he hit the gas and zoomed around a big one, skipping back into their own southbound lane just barely in time to avoid taking out a ponytailed honcho on a motor scooter with a young girl clinging behind him. Neither wore helmets. Nova's heart once more clogged her throat.

Joe said, "I suppose you know suspect number three, Ya Lin, too. And by the way, would you like me to drive? I know we're in a hurry, but we do need to arrive intact."

Acting as if he'd not heard Joe's snide remark, Cesare said, "I don't know her. She's quite the big star in Italian films. But she is extremely private. Although I do know where she lives in Amalfi. Guards are always posted at her gates."

Nova zoned out. She stopped listening to Cesare and Joe and just let herself go into what was now magnificent coastline. Rocky points, breaking waves on a rugged shoreline, and now and then a white, sandy beach. How would the water feel on her body? Slick with salt. Warm with Mediterranean June heat. Glorious. Tomorrow she would buy a swimsuit.

Soon she caught a glimpse, well in the distance, of white and sandy-colored buildings perched in descending row upon row on a steep slope, like birds nesting on a sea cliff. The houses of Positano seemed to defy gravity. The road wound through the town, pressed by businesses on either side. Shops on her left climbed up the hills, and those on her right plummeted toward the sea.

Before they reached anything she would consider as the center of a town, Cesare made a left up a narrow street and they climbed. And climbed. The road weaved upward until they reached a high, wrought iron gate.

"The Contessa Rimaldi is one of my best clients. She is also, without question, Positano's biggest gossip. By this time tomorrow, day after tomorrow at the latest, all the locals will know about the two American photographers who are here to ferret out and document the most beautiful vistas and imposing homes along the Amalfi drive," Cesare said as he rolled down the window and pressed the button on the gate security box. "Time to start setting up your cover."

Chapter 13

Ahmad counted each hour that passed. Only five days remained before Operation Awesome Vengeance would shock the world. He felt tense, like a man before battle, and also excited.

He had great faith in the man he had chosen to be in charge of the six bodyguards for this operation. The soldier was Khangi, a seasoned Jihad fighter who looked, acted, and dressed Western, right down to his jeans, T-shirt, clean-shaven face, and short, military haircut. Like Ahmad, Khangi had been raised in Syria, but unlike Ahmad, who had an education, Khangi cut his teeth in the brutal back streets of Damascus.

Ten minutes earlier, when Ahmad dropped by the safe house with groceries for the four men who had already arrived—the boy Ali, Khangi, and two other volunteers—Khangi had been explaining to Ali how to clean and reassemble a Kalashnikov AK-74. Along with a Markarov pistol, which each bodyguard would carry, two of them would hide an AK-74 under their long dust cloaks. Dust cloaks were not uncommon in fashionable cities or towns in Italy these days, and the long overcoats would actually be common dress at the Doomsday rock concert where Awesome Vengeance would be inflicting the most immediate damage.

"Only Ali and Khangi will go through the security check points and into the concert venue," Ahmad instructed the four of them. "The rest of you can hold their weapons for them until they come back out."

The call to serve Allah had saved Khangi from a life dedicated to thievery and petty brutalities and sent him to learn the ways of armed resistance in a camp in Lebanon's Bekaa Valley. He was accepted for this mission, as were all the others, because Al Qaeda headquarters knew that he had no record as yet with international security agencies.

"Your main task as bodyguards," Ahmad continued, "is to protect Ali as he moves through open public spaces. We can't risk him being harmed by an accident. Or, a mugging. Or for that matter, arrest. Although arrest isn't likely, it's the reason for having six of you instead of the usual two that accompany a suicide bomber. He must not be arrested. Letting him go inside the concert space alone with only you, Khangi, to guard him, is risky. But worth the risk. Thousands will be attending. You and the boy go in. Circulate widely for an hour. Then leave. Your next target is the subway."

Khangi nodded.

A knock at the door stopped their talk. A soldier from Egypt looked out the peephole. He turned to look at Ahmad. "It's Saddoun. It's your son."

Baffled and angry, Ahmad said, "Let him in." How did Saddoun know this place?

Saddoun eagerly took in the men and the weapons. "Mohsin sent me," he said to Ahmad. "There's another arrival at the airport and he is very early. Mohsin thought you'd want to know so you can go pick him up now."

"Mohsin should have come himself," Ahmad said, his tone sharpened by displeasure. He did not want Saddoun near weapons or men like these. The boy already had an unhealthy attraction to guns. He would have preferred it if Saddoun didn't know the location of the safe house. Mohsin should have known better.

"I'll go now," Ahmad said to Khangi. "I'll return tomorrow and we will make further plans. Our final three men will be here by the fourteenth. We can fill them in as they arrive." He strode to the door. "Since you're here," he said to Saddoun, "you may as well ride with me to the airport."

Once in the car, Saddoun immediately exploded with excitement. "Something big is happening, isn't it?"

"This isn't your concern. Mohsin should not have involved you."

"But it is big, isn't it?"

"You may as well put it out of your mind."

"I don't want to leave with the family. I want to stay. I want to take part. I saw that boy. He's no older than I am. And I'm good with guns, you know that."

"I have humored your desire to learn about weapons and to be able to shoot a gun. A man must be able to protect himself and his family. But it is out of the question for you to be involved with my work here."

"Why? I want to serve."

"And you will."

"I've asked to go train in Bekaa over and over. I'm a warrior."

Ahmad swerved sharply across two lanes of traffic and into the right lane for the airport. "Boy, be quiet! I nearly missed the turnoff!"

"Please, Father."

"You are going to college in England. I have not given you English lessons for nothing. You have a fine mind. You must train to be the finest thinker and planner for Allah and for our cause. Anyone, Saddoun, can be a soldier. But we need men who have lived among the infidels and know their weaknesses and how to use those weaknesses against them. You have great promise."

"I don't want to be like you. I want to fight them. Kill them."

Ahmad sighed. "You are my only son. I love you. And I forbid it."

"You let that boy go. Why not me? Am I better than him? Or am I not as good? Why is it all right for him to risk death, but not me?"

Ahmad felt his neck grow warm from a strange anger, as if Saddoun had stuck a knife of accusation in his back. How dare his son question him, question his motives, question the rightness of his choices? Did the sharpness of the accusation sting because the boy, Ali, was not just going to risk death, but also be marked for death, and a gruesome one at that? That was something Ahmad had not made altogether clear to Ali.

Chapter 14

Joe stood on a Positano beach beside Cesare, who was holding Principessa, as they watched Nova slowly descend toward the sand. Above her billowed a parasail flaunting vivid stripes of yellow, red and purple against the azure sky. The motorboat towing her was slowing just enough to bring her down to a safe landing with impressive precision.

Like Nova, Joe and Cesare wore bathing suits; in Joe's case, his had been purchased this morning when Nova bought hers. Ten minutes earlier, he had made the same flight and landing. Nova was clearly having fun, reveling in the view and feeling the wind on her skin. He caught himself grinning with empathetic pleasure. He loved to see her smiling like now, as her feet hit the ground running.

Cesare shook his head. "You were quite right, Joe. Nova is a stunning beauty and she hides it well. All that was required, really, was to take her clothes off. You will note that there is not one man on this beach—or one woman, for that matter—who doesn't stop to look at her."

Nova had picked a crimson bikini trimmed with a pattern of small diamonds as coal-black as her hair. Against her fair skin, the red stood out like a cherry on top of vanilla ice cream. Her hair was still French braided at the back, like it had been when he'd picked her up in Costa Rica, but no one was looking at her hair, or even her face. "She works out more religiously than I do," he said to Cesare.

"How much is real and how much is surgery?"

Joe snorted, amused. "Do you really expect me to know?"

"I do. Clearly you've spent a great deal of time with her. You seem to read each other's minds."

"Okay. I do know. It's all real."

"Umm. I like your Nova. I would be deeply grieved should she be hurt. Of course, you are both professionals. Naturally. But Greco's ruthless. He is La Cosa Nostra. And if he is our guilty man, and he gets any hint that Nova is not the photographer she will claim to be, he will not hesitate to…. Well, I don't like to think what he might do to try to find out exactly who she really is."

For the first time, Joe felt kinship with the endlessly chatty Cesare. "First, let me assure you that Nova actually *is* a world-class photographer. She's not going to make any slipups there. Also she has this amazing effect on people. She seems so vulnerable—to say nothing of beautiful. You can trust me, Cesare. She'll have the same effect on Greco. Greco should pray she doesn't find reason to damage *him*."

Did he believe that? Yes, of course. Oddly enough, he'd never yet seen Nova in a fight. He'd always been somewhere else when the fighting started. But he knew that in Germany, she had single-handedly incapacitated two terrorists, killed six others and blown a small mountain sky high. He also knew that the higher-ups at Langley considered her to be almost spookily competent.

"Well, I shall take some comfort in that. But I do not forget that while you two are in Italy, you are my responsibility."

Joe suppressed a chuckle. Cesare, the garrulous interior decorator, may have read her file, but that wouldn't tell the half of what Nova was really capable.

Today Nova and Cesare were going shopping for the clothes Nova would need to dazzle Greco and make an appropriate impression on Sorokin and Ya Lin, as well. Joe had thought she would go boutique foraging first thing, but instead she'd said, "Let's hit the beach for an hour or two. I'll have time to shop this afternoon." The parasailing had been Joe's idea.

When Nova reached them, she grabbed his arm, grinning. "Fantastic," she said. "But I need some real exercise. How about a swim?"

He and Nova headed for the water. Cesare stayed put. Perfect, from Joe's perspective. But Nova said, "Aren't you coming, Cesare?"

"I don't want to leave Principessa. Do go on without me."

Joe grabbed her hand and pulled her into a run. They splashed onto water-soaked sand. He let go of her hand. They ran to the edge of the gently breaking surf, strode side by side until they were waist-deep. Then she put her hands over her head, dove in and started stroking out to sea; he followed.

They passed two rows of anchored sailboats and yachts and still Nova swam outbound. He kept up. He would let the Amazon decide how far she wanted to go.

When eventually she stopped, he turned to look back toward Positano. They were out about half a mile. "As always, you're in top condition," he said.

She brushed water from her face, shook her head and leaned back to float. "It's beautifully quiet, isn't it?"

They rested that way for long moments.

A sudden splash of water hit him on the chest. Another splash, and water hit his face.

He righted himself, treading. "So you want to fight?"

"Are you too tired?" She grinned and a glint of fun put green fire in her eyes. "I should drown you."

He balled his fist and used his forearm to blast water at her. She swam toward him, then dived. The next thing, Nova had her arms around his waist and was pulling him under.

He grabbed her shoulders and, kicking like crazy, drove them to the top. Their heads breached the water's surface and he grabbed a lungful of air. He heard her do the same. She wrapped her arms around his chest, he wrapped his arms around her arms, and down they went again. This was going to be a test of who could stay down the longest.

She lost. She released her grip on his chest, he let

her loose, and she kicked to the surface. He followed her up and, when he surfaced, wrapped his arms around her again. He felt her breasts, her kicking legs, her belly touching his. He was amazed that, under the guise of punishing him, she'd started a game that smacked of intimacy. He wanted to kiss her. *What the heck am I supposed to do?*

"You win," Nova said, letting her hands sweep slowly across Joe's back, testing just exactly how firm his muscles were. They were rock-hard.

He grinned that electric, cowboy-from-Texas grin. "Didn't I tell you this would be a vacation?"

She felt their legs as they kept brushing together, a decidedly exciting sensation. "Yes, you told me a vacation." Now she felt his hands exploring her back. Of course he would do that. She'd started this whole thing, and it was dangerous to think she could play at being intimate with a man like Joe and expect that he'd take it any other way than that it was real. "But I'd be having a real vacation if you would make peace with Cesare."

"You want me to make peace?" His grip did not lessen one tiny bit.

"Yes. Peace."

"With Cesare?"

"He's bursting with enthusiasm, Joe. And well-intentioned."

"He's going to drive me crazy with all his talk. Or we'll all be killed in the car." He grinned. "I'd much rather be cooped up on a mission with Principessa."

She couldn't stop the laugh that popped out. Then it suddenly grew very quiet as they held each other, slowly treading water.

"Maybe we should start back," she offered.

"Should we?"

The look in his eyes suggested he wasn't thinking about swimming. "I'll make a deal with you," she said. "If you promise to let Cesare do his babbling routine and let it slip off your back like this water is slipping down your skin, I will insist that, when we're all together, you will be the one to drive. Deal?"

His arms loosened their hug; his hands grabbed her shoulders. Their bodies, which had been moving almost as one, moved apart again.

"It's a deal. Partner."

Partner. Yes, they were just partners.

She started back, a brisk breaststroke. "Tomorrow's the big day," she called over her shoulder.

"Greco arrives at the restaurant pretty promptly at six." He talked between kicks as he caught up. "I should be into his condo by six-thirty or six-forty-five at the latest. The safecracking program is good, but he may have a safe that's a real time-consumer, in which case getting into it and copying the hard drive of his laptop, any papers, and whatever disks are stored along with it could take me up to two hours. You need to keep him away until eight, just to be conservative."

"Eight o'clock it shall be."

"You know, Cesare is worried for you. I told him not to be. That you can handle yourself. But guys tied into La Cosa Nostra are by nature superparanoid. You know. You do need to be extra cautious not to spook Greco."

She looked to him, but he was looking forward, toward the beach. She couldn't read his expression. He was worried for her. Maybe with a bit of special worry?

Chapter 15

Nova rose early the next day. Now armed with various outfits from Versace, Armani, and Gucci chosen to sexually distract Greco, intrigue the drug-smuggling Sorokin and impress the famous but nearly broke Chinese movie star, Ya Lin, she felt the thrill of adventure when all systems were go—the thrill of risk. Nature's natural high.

True, Joe and the Company had deceived her by their omission of information, and she experienced a moment of angry brain sizzle every time she thought about that. But she couldn't deny the charge that the suspense of a good hunt always gave her. More than once, she'd been accused by one of her high adventure tourists of being an adrenaline junkie. It was, for better or worse, true.

She worked out in her bedroom. The apartment

building looked like a thousand others from the outside, but their unit had three spacious bedrooms. While Cesare concocted a breakfast feast of cheese omelets with bacon crisps, five different fresh fruits, café au lait and croissants, she and Joe had another go at the SISMI-provided photos—from the ground and the air—and the layouts of Greco's condo and the Sorokin and Lin mansions.

Finally it was time to climb into their Laforza SUV and do their own on-site recon of all three target properties. Summoning consummate tact, she said, "Cesare, I love Principessa and I love you, but to keep peace, I want you to please let Joe do the driving."

Cesare stopped, stroked Principessa, who was perched on his arm, and shook his head. "They don't like my driving, sweetheart."

"Oh, I love it," she countered, smiling and casting a glance at Joe from the corner of her eye. "I love excitement. But humor me. Joe is the insecure sort who will be easiest for us to get along with if we let him feel he's in control."

"Get off it, Nova!" Joe said, although he smiled at her latest attempt to rile him.

Cesare grinned at Joe. "You know, I do so understand. I don't have that sort of problem myself. Principessa and I will happily sit in the rear." He tossed the keys to Joe, opened the rear door on the passenger side and slid in.

Joe took the driver's seat.

Positano was the location of their rented home base. The cities on this famous coastline formed a necklace of colorful seashells, all about a twenty-minute drive from each other. Going north to south down the coast, first came Positano and then Amalfi, both clinging as if by the tips of their fingers to hillsides overlooking the glittering blue water of the Gulf of Salerno. And then Ravello, reached by a winding, steep uphill road into equally steep hills where it nestled surrounded by the exquisite green of Mediterranean shrub and oaks.

Fabiano Greco's bachelor pad was in Positano, their first destination. They arrived at ten o'clock and parked two blocks away. Cesare agreed to remain with the SUV. "We do not want to be a crowd. I am simply your guide, if anyone asks," he said.

Nova carried two cameras. Joe lugged a camera case and tripod.

Last night, Cesare, who had once visited Greco's condo, described in detail the interior. Very little recon was required here. The plan was for Nova to connect with Greco at the beach. Then the live-in maid, who also cooked for Greco, would receive a call from her priest, arranged by SISMI, saying she must come at once to the church because a gift had arrived for her from her daughter in America. Then Joe would break in. The cook would return two hours later, five hundred dollars wealthier. And Nova would disengage as soon as possible after two hours with Greco had passed.

They strolled past the condo, Joe taking a particularly long look down the side alley. Then it was back to the SUV and off to see Ya Lin's place in Amalfi. The drive was so beautiful—azure sea, sheer drops to sandy beaches, sails against the water, white-washed homes and businesses with their red-tile roofs dazzling in the strong sun. She let down the window and savored salty air and seaweed.

They arrived at eleven-thirty, and once again they left Cesare parked a block away on the narrow, steep street. Were there any flat streets on the entire coast, she wondered wryly as she and Joe trudged uphill past the entries to two mansions situated below Lin's.

To make their cover as photographers interested in architecture plausible, she snapped photos of both mansions, the fronts of which could be glimpsed through their gates if she aimed at just the right angle. At Ya Lin's gate she did the same.

Joe muttered, "This place will be a bitch to get into if the housekeeper doesn't accept my cover as a city fire inspector and let me onto the grounds. It's evident from here that all the windows are easily accessible with the rope and hook, but there isn't any place along this damn wall with a good blind spot. If I can't get in during the day... Well, thank God, she doesn't have dogs."

"The housekeeper will let you in. Your Italian is perfect—great northern accent. And then, there is always the trusty smile."

Nova hoped her optimism was justified because they had already agreed that their backup plan, for them to come in together at night, would be much more difficult and risky since at night Lin put the guards outside the house, and they walked the open grounds.

A car braked to a stop nearly on top of them. Nova's skin crawled with goose bumps as she and Joe spun around. The front doors of a black sedan flew open, and two very large and grumpy-looking men with Mediterranean complexions and beautifully tailored suits stepped out.

"What are you doing here?" one with a bald head demanded in Italian, his tone reminding her of Star's Doberman pinscher when you tried to take a bone from him.

"I'm a photographer," she said in a rush and in English, praying as her pulse accelerated that they wouldn't understand her and so be confused. "I photograph architecture."

Apparently he didn't understand. He came back again in Italian. "I said, what are you doing taking pictures here? No paparazzi allowed!"

"Paparazzi," Joe echoed. "No. No paparazzi."

Bald Head stepped up to Joe, close, inside any man's zone of acceptance. "Get away from here," he growled one last time in Italian.

Nova grabbed Joe's arm, gave both men one of her best, most innocent and quite apologetic smiles. "Sorry," she said. "It's a beautiful home on beautiful grounds. Sorry."

She and Joe sauntered back down the hill, all innocence. She turned once to check, and they were still watching. She waved, then turned and relaxed.

Joe said, smiling broadly, "Well, I never thought I'd be glad to be taken for paparazzi."

When they explained to Cesare what had happened, he frowned. "You know, if they are up to no good and thus inclined to be suspicious, we could have a problem, because paparazzi are virtually always men—not attractive women. We don't want them getting overly defensive. They may have said paparazzi, but they may have second thoughts and try to check you out. Hopefully the contessa will have done our job for us."

He stroked Principessa, thinking, then grinned. "In

fact, this little encounter may work out fine since, if they do check you out, the grapevine gossip will have primed Ya Lin to accept Nova as a photographer."

Since it was past noon, they agreed to have lunch in Amalfi. Cesare took them straight down the road past the Cathedral of Sant'Andrea to a restaurant on the beach. They shared a huge pizza, washing it down with red wine.

The drive to Ravello took them inland, past orange groves of divine scent and vineyards clinging to steep slopes. Cesare, who had been unusually quiet all morning said, "You said you once stayed at the Astoria when you attended the music festival, Nova. The view of the bay from its dining terrace is really quite stupendous, don't you agree?"

"I do indeed. I was ten. I was with my father and my mother. He loved great music. He loved Italy. He died flying in a seaplane to Capri for holiday."

"I am so very sorry," Cesare said.

"The drive here is bringing back bits of memory."

The heart of Ravello, where the Cathedral San Pantaleone dominated an intimate piazza, was blocked off from car traffic. Nova remembered sitting with her father, licking her first gelato and watching tourists mingle with locals: dark-robed priests linked arm in arm strolling toward the cathedral, women with straw hats to fight the sun, couples having someone take their picture. The hotel had been only steps away; at least, that was how she remembered it. And the concerts had been performed in an outdoor place where she could watch birds flying and see the sea at the same time.

Her throat tightened and she blinked hard against

threatening tears as she remembered her father smiling and leaning close to whisper to her, as a middle-aged man passed by them. "That's the famous writer, Gore Vidal," her father had said. She had no idea who Gore Vidal was then. She'd later learned that he was indeed famous, and that he owned a villa in Ravello, as many famous musicians and writers did.

But that day her father was sharing something that had pleased him with her. They had spent the entire day together, a rare event. But though his responsibilities as a diplomat kept him busy and often away, she never once in her life doubted his love. Her father had set a very high bar for any man to reach. That was probably one reason why she was unmarried and unlikely ever to be so. That, as well as the fact that of the two men in her life after her father, the first had abused her and the second had betrayed her.

They passed the point where cars had to park if people wanted to go into the town center. Not much farther on they turned left onto a narrow road that led past expensive homes.

Joe said, "I'm going to drive past the entry so we can get a first look. We'll walk back downhill."

The Sorokin property appeared to be as formidable to get inside as Nova had feared, based on the recon photos of the long and narrow house. The architect had essentially built the house's backside flush with the mountain behind it. Most of the main rooms fronted onto the lawn. The front entry gate opened onto a sweeping drive through a huge lawn decorated with metal and marble sculptures.

Walking back to the SUV, she said, "There's no way

to get in from the sides or front without being detected. The entry will have to be at the rear."

"I agree," Joe said.

"That means a long rappel down the side of the cliff and then entry through that chimney."

"Agreed."

"Much as it pisses me off to say it, Joe, we need to change plans. We need to set it up so that you distract Sorokin and I go in."

"Like hell!"

They reached the car and Joe yanked his door open. She slid into the passenger seat.

"Welcome back," Cesare offered cheerily. The usually silent Principessa barked once.

"I mean it, Joe. Clearly I'm the one best suited."

"Clearly you're not."

"Tell me you haven't been worried that the chimney might be just a bit too tight a fit." She added, even as she sensed the irony of the fact that she was going to be doing exactly what she'd said she didn't want to do, "I'm also a more experienced climber. Did you figure from the photos how sheer that seventy-five foot drop down to the roof is?"

Clenching his jaw, Joe turned the key and the SUV roared. He put it in gear and they took off, heading back downhill. "I can make the climb just fine," he said, "and I can get down that damn chimney just fine."

"What seems to be the problem?" Cesare asked, his tone for once stern.

"I am a better climber than Joe, and I'm smaller in size, especially my shoulders. He also knows, although it hasn't come up before, that I've gone through the training at The Farm and although I'm slower, I can get into the safe as well as he can. If we're going to do this right, and we are, I am the one who should go in. I was going to distract Sorokin by claiming to sell a fancy Ferrari. Joe can just as well be the seller. It doesn't have to be me."

Again, Joe exploded. "There's no need to change anything, goddamn it."

Cesare now sat perched on the edge of his seat. "I must say that I myself found the nature of the cliff much more daunting than it appeared to be from photos. Is it true she is the better climber?"

After a long pause and some more jaw clenching, Joe grumbled, "Technically."

"Well, then," Cesare said, sliding back into the seat and resuming his easy manner, "I am formally in charge here. And I say, let's do it her way."

He sounded amused. And all the way back to Positano, he kept up a friendly commentary on homes he'd decorated and the infamous exploits of their owners.

She and Joe said little. Joe's one comment was that if there was any bright side to the switch, it was that he would be the one to take a long drive with the Ferrari, whose owner had allowed SISMI to use it only after SISMI's front for the deal—an agency claiming they were going to use the car in an advertisement—ponied up money for insurance against theft or damage.

She didn't really understand why Joe was so angry. The switch made sense. She had thought that by the end of the German mission, he'd accepted her as equal to any task, certainly any task like climbing. She wondered for a moment if maybe he was concerned for her, maybe worried for her, even if irrationally. Because if she cared for someone and they wanted to do something dangerous and she couldn't forbid them, that might come out as anger. More likely, though, he just felt his macho Texas-flyboy pride had been dented.

But the next evening, she got a clear message that it had been concern. In the late afternoon, she went to the beach restaurant that Greco frequented dressed to melt all male resistance—in her new red bikini. Greco religiously came for cocktails at six o'clock and stayed for dinner; he never showed up.

In the ladies' room, after calling Cesare and telling him that they would have to cancel the op and try again tomorrow, she changed into her gray slacks and blouse. She drank alone and then ate alone, disappointment her dinner companion. She always felt let down when an attempt to contact a mark fell through. They still had plenty of time; the sale wasn't due to take place until the twenty-second, twelve days away. Still, the sooner this business was finished, the better.

Just as her waiter brought an after-dinner cappuccino, Joe arrived. He ordered one, too, and afterward he asked if she wanted to walk on the beach.

They left their shoes at the restaurant. At first, they talked about reasons why Greco might have changed his plans. She loved the feeling of wet sand slipping through her toes. Then she persuaded Joe to talk a while about his father and their small ranch in Texas. Then she said, "Why were you so opposed to having me go into the Sorokin home?"

He stopped walking and took her hand. The rush and then sigh of the water against the sand seemed to echo the rush of her blood to her heart and the catch of her breath at his touch. He said, "I should have called you. I said I would."

"For a long time, every call I got I thought might be from you."

He turned her hand over and traced the outline of her fingers. "Is that true?"

"Have I ever lied to you?"

"No. You don't lie. But you don't share much, either."

"It's a habit, I suppose."

"Maybe because of your stepfather?"

He tugged her hand toward him, and she took a step closer, her blood pounding in her ears. "I hated my stepfather, that's for certain."

"What he did, did it make you...distrust all men?" There was an unmistakable glow of passion in his eyes, gentle yet determined.

"I don't distrust all men."

"Do you distrust me? Or do you still think I'm just a kid?"

She now stood so close to him, she imagined she could feel the heat from his body. She resisted an urge to throw herself into his arms. "Dumb questions. You know I'd trust you with my life. I already have, more than once. And I haven't thought you were a kid for a long time."

He put both hands on her shoulders, and alarms screamed in her head. He was going to kiss her. "Don't," she said.

As if she'd zapped him with a Taser, he froze, and she thought she saw the glow in his eyes turn to wariness.

She cared. She'd known she cared a great deal when his failure to call hurt so much. She might hold his interest for a while, but not for long. Someone younger, someone pretty and new, would eventually steal his heart. He was only twenty-eight years old. And she wasn't up to any more heartbreaks. She hurried to explain, "I don't want to mix the personal with business. Things get very sticky. You said you'd call. You didn't. I figure that's pretty self-explanatory."

"I said I was wrong not to call."

"And you were right."

He let go of her shoulders. "Okay. No mixing of personal and business. Let's just forget it."

Nevertheless he took her hand and they walked that way for a bit, until she pretended that she'd stepped on something that needed to be brushed off and took her hand away.

Chapter 16

Mohsin handed the phone toward Ahmad, halting Ahmad's plan to leave the office. Irritated by the interruption, Ahmad snatched the phone from Mohsin.

"This is Alberto," said the deep male voice on the other end of the line.

Ahmad felt the uncomfortable tightening of the chest he experienced whenever the Don's consigliere or any one of his lieutenant's called. The Camorra family had been in control of La Cosa Nostra in the region surrounding Naples for many years. And from his third month of arrival in Amalfi, almost ten years ago now, Ahmad had paid the family's demands for protection money. Not just for the legitimate fish business—nearly eleven percent of everything—but even more expansively, for keeping his Al Qaeda operations secure.

"How can I help you?" Ahmad replied, keeping his voice calm and reminding himself to make sure he used none of the words that would trigger the interest of those all-prying ears of Italian, British, American or Soviet agencies.

"We have noted a lot of activity from your business lately. My employer wants to know what it's all about?"

"Please assure him that nothing special is happening. Nothing." Ahmad felt a moment of panic. Would they buy it? No one, not even La Cosa Nostra, was to know that Operation Awesome Vengeance was organized by the Italian cell of Al Qaeda. Information would be leaked to Aljazeera that implicated Al Qaeda operatives in Lebanon. If any hint of his connection to the operation leaked out, he might have to leave Italy permanently. He sat down, his heart racing.

Alberto continued, "I'm calling to remind you that you are not to touch anything under our protection. If anything serious happens without our permission, you will not be welcome here. And if any financial transactions occur to your benefit, we expect to have compensation."

"I am, as always, grateful for the consideration and assistance I receive and I would do nothing to injure our relationship."

"So. You have been reminded."

Ahmad's palms were sweaty. He wiped one hand and switched the phone receiver to it. "I appreciate that."

"Then you will also appreciate knowing that we have information that a certain agency is hot on the trail of something coming down in the Amalfi area. Your area. While you don't appear to be one of their subjects of interest, we're putting everyone in the Amalfi area who we feel might be involved on alert."

Ahmad immediately thought of the seller. "I can absolutely assure you that no party of the kind to which you refer is aware of my actions or existence."

"Yes, of yours. But perhaps you are dealing with others who are under suspicion."

"Who are these suspects?"

"Unfortunately, our informant does not know. Just consider yourself warned. You would be well advised to take extra precautions."

"Yes. Of course. My gratitude once again. And please extend my respect to your employer."

Alberto, if that was his real name, hung up. Ahmad did so, as well, and wiped both sweaty palms on his pants.

"What is it?" Mohsin asked.

"SISMI seems to be snooping around Amalfi. You contact our broker right away. Urge extra caution."

"This is not good."

"The Don has somehow sensed that we are up to something. These pigs must have a paid informant for every ten people in the country. They know, or sense, everything."

"You did not get permission from the Camorra? Syria thinks we have their permission."

"We do not need the permission of infidels. This operation is the will of Allah. I will find a way to deal with the Camorra. They listen to money."

"Not if their people die."

"We will deny having anything to do with it. They

will have to accept that because they will have no proof to the contrary."

Mohsin shrugged. "God is great. And I hope you are right."

Chapter 17

Nova's swimsuit had dried out enough to be comfortable for walking but was still damp enough to cling to every curve. Now would be the perfect time to contact Greco.

She lay on a beach towel on her stomach, gazing at the parking lot where Cesare was on lookout in the SUV. This late in the afternoon—quarter to six was really more like early evening—the sun held little heat. She actually felt a bit chilled.

After yesterday's failed attempt to make contact, she'd felt positively twitchy all day, antsy to get on with it. In theory, they still had plenty of time to stop the sale, but her instinct was never, ever to assume anything.

Her cell buzzed. He's in place, the text message said.

She scrambled to her feet, rolled up the towel, picked up her sandals and big woven beach bag, and trudged through the sand toward the Hotel Dolphin's bar/patio. As she neared it, she saw that Greco was seated at his favorite table next to the sand. With him sat a pretty brunette that Nova figured must be no more than twenty-three.

She washed sand off her feet in the big conch shell the restaurant placed at the patio's beach entrance for that purpose. With her pulse elevated, just enough so she felt incredibly alive, she sauntered up to Greco's table.

In Italian, she said, "Excuse me, but I sat here earlier and I can't find my sunglasses. I think I may have left them on your table."

With the predictability of a Pavlovian dog, Greco ran his eyes over every curve of her body.

"We didn't find any glasses," the girl offered in Italian, smiling.

Nova returned Greco's frank gaze, bending her head and looking up at him from seductively lowered eyelids. With her tongue, she moistened her lower lip as Greco maintained unbroken eye contact. She said, "Perhaps they slipped to the floor."

She bent down at the knees in a way calculated to give him a male-pleasing view of cleavage. Whether the glasses Cesare had planted were still there wasn't relevant. The ploy worked either way. In this case, the glasses were right next to the pedestal. She plucked them up and stood. "Lucky me," she said. "Here they are."

"Right. Lucky you," Greco countered. "I haven't seen you here before."

"I'm only here for a week. Doing some photography. I ate here last night. Wonderful food."

He checked out the cleavage again as he said, "The

best in Amalfi." His gaze connected again with hers. "Here for a week. Photographing what?"

"Mediterranean architecture."

He laughed. She liked the laugh—deep, very male, and sincerely amused. No doubt about it, Fabiano Greco was a singularly handsome hunk of Italian male. Dark, permanently tanned, flawless skin, clear intelligent eyes below a high forehead, and a Roman nose that gave the face strength where it might otherwise have been just pretty "Such a stunning woman cannot possibly be a serious photographer of architecture."

She let herself laugh, went with the flow. "I assure you, I'm quite serious. It was nice chatting with you."

"So you are you leaving now?"

"No. I'm going to change and then have dinner."

"Alone?"

"Quite alone."

"I don't believe it. It's not possible. It's not natural." She laughed again.

"Look," he said, "why don't you change and then join me, join us, for dinner?"

The brunette's eyes had been shooting darts at Nova since the moment Greco asked Nova if she was leaving. The woman's eyes were now shooting daggers, each one carrying the message, "Leave now, or I will slit your throat!"

"Are you sure," Nova said with all the sincerity she could muster, "that you wouldn't mind my intruding?"

"Change. Come back. I live here and I know a bit about the architecture. I'll find out if you are telling the truth, and if you are, you can find out what I know about Amalfi's buildings. Perhaps I can be of help."

She leaned down, touched his arm—very quickly, but the message was clear. "Your offer is delightful and accepted. I'd love to have your…help. I'll only be a short time in the ladies'."

She left the table, and her naked skin experienced that sixth sense that said he was watching her walk away toward the restrooms. His driver/bodyguard sat at the bar drinking, and as she walked past him, she felt his gaze as well.

In the bathroom, she went at once to a stall, entered, and sent a text message to Cesare. The op was on, the priest should make his call. In a short time, Joe should be free to enter Greco's condo. Getting into the safe would take at least an hour and a half, they hoped, not more. She noted the time.

Greco's housekeeper practically flew out the condominium's front door. She must need money badly, Joe thought. He estimated it couldn't have taken her more than a minute to get her purse and get in gear.

With his safecracking kit, which included a digital camera and blank CDs, and a laptop in hand, he picked the lock and let himself into a cool, serene haven for what Cesare had said were priceless antiques. The spacious entry led first to a powder room to the left and the secondary entry into the modern kitchen on the right. He walked forward into the living room, the walls of which were covered with tapestries and old paintings. He knew from Cesare that the den was the first door down the hall to the left, the maid's room at the end of the hall, and the master bedroom off to the right of the living room.

He went straight to the den, the most likely place for a safe. Fifteen frustrating minutes later, he said, "Shit," and began to worry. Maybe SISMI's information was wrong, and Greco had the stuff for sale stored in a safe at one of his two places of business.

He lost another ten minutes searching another small bedroom down the hall from the den. Twenty-five minutes gone.

Statistically, the kitchen and dining rooms were the least likely places to install a safe. The next most likely was the master bedroom. He crossed through the living room, entered the hallway and then stopped. Something—his gut, intuition, whatever—said the living room. He backtracked and began to search again, starting with the most likely places.

Sure enough, behind the third painting he checked, he found the safe encased in a two-foot thick layer of concrete and steel. Modern and electronic. Very expensive. No ordinary thief would be able to break in. But then, the Company was no ordinary thief. He set the safecracking kit aside and opened up the laptop.

The software, an upgraded version of the program developed by J.D. Hamilton, would be able to interface wirelessly with the lock at its programming port. He started punching keys. The program simply ran number sequences at an astonishing rate of speed. The safe, a Manlichman, used a six-number combination. It would be impossible to know exactly how long the program would take to hit the right combination. Maybe five minutes, maybe two hours. He'd already used up thirty minutes.

For a moment, he watched the flickering of the LED. Then, satisfied, he pulled out his latest Ken Follett thriller and started reading. God forbid it took more than an hour and a half, because then he'd have to alert Cesare, who would signal Nova. She would then have to put into play some ruse to keep Greco away.

Chapter 18

After letting Cesare know that the op was on, Nova stayed in the bathroom stall to change out of the bathing suit. By what struck her as an interesting coincidence, Greco had come dressed in white cotton slacks and a lime-green, silk, short-sleeved shirt and she had brought white jeans and an emerald-green spaghetti strap silk top with plunging neckline. She smiled, zipping up the jeans and thinking what a lovely color-coordinated couple they would make.

She sat the large woven beach bag on the sink counter, returning the smile of a Muslim woman wearing a hajib who then dried her hands and walked out.

One secret Nova had found effective with men over the years was to surprise them in ways that played to their senses. Surprising them did marvelous things to rev up their libidos. She had purposely done up her hair in a single French braid twisted up in back. She'd made sure it didn't get too wet when she had been in the ocean, but the hair was nevertheless damp.

She removed the hairpins and undid the braid, letting her hair fall to her shoulder blades. From the basket, she took out a blow-dryer and brush, found an outlet, plugged the dryer in and heated the straight, silky black strands of her hair and bangs to total dryness. The change should fascinate him. She tilted her head a couple of times and noted with satisfaction that her glossy hair swished freely, as if lubricated with silicone.

While she'd worn lipstick and subtle eye colorations to meet him, she now enhanced the lipstick with a glistener and also darkened the eyeliner. The overall effect was to bring out strongly the emerald color of her slightly almond-shaped, large eyes.

She completed the transformation with earrings, dangling silver doves in flight, their eyes made from tiny emeralds. She always felt undressed or incomplete without a pair of earrings, even if only studs. They seemed to somehow ground her. Noting her fetish, Joe had given her these doves as a parting gift in Germany.

She touched the dove on her right ear, thinking of Joe, thinking what a babe magnet he was, thinking that he should be in the condo by now and, with luck, have found the safe. She checked the time. Six twenty-eight.

Passing through the bar on the way to the patio, she noted the absence of Greco's driver/bodyguard. Had Greco invited him to join them for dinner? Did Greco intend to foist her off on the bodyguard, a dinner foursome? Controlling Greco would be much more difficult if that were the case.

The music playing throughout the restaurant was something suitably romantic and Italian with mandolins. Seeing Greco alone at his table, she inhaled a deep satisfied breath of relief. The girl was also missing.

"Where is your friend?" she asked, sticking to Italian.

"She suddenly discovered she needed to go home." He smiled and, while remaining seated, pulled out the chair for her.

"Well now, I am sorry about that."

He cocked his head, and his lips curled into an even more satisfied grin. "Yes, so am I."

She undid the fresh napkin and laid it across her lap.

He switched to English. "Would I be right if I guessed you are an American."

"Is my Italian all that bad?" she replied, in English.

"Of course not. Your Italian is delightful. And you are American? Or perhaps Canadian?"

"No. Your first guess is right. American."

"Do you mind if we speak English? I like to practice."

She leaned forward, placing her hand on the table as if sharing a secret and said in English, "But I like to practice my Italian."

"Perhaps I should speak English," he said, "and you can reply in Italian." He covered her hand with his.

She laughed, and as the waiter stepped to the table, she withdrew her hand to her lap.

"Do you like fish? Specifically sea bass?" He had switched to English. "It is one of the Dolphin's specialties."

"You're the local expert. I bow to your choice."

"Two of the Black Sea bass with spinach ricotta ravioli," he said. "But I think we'd like drinks and to talk first." He looked at her.

"Yes. Drinks and talk. I'd like a Cinzano on ice, please."

He ordered another single malt Scotch, a brand she didn't recognize.

The waiter hustled off. Greco leaned toward her and put his hand, palm up, on the table. Things were certainly moving along swiftly. The guy was clearly of the don't-let-any-grass-grow-under-your-feet persuasion. She put her hand into his. "What does this signify in Italy?"

He laughed as he closed his fingers around her hand. "I don't know. I just felt like doing it to see what you'd do. Maybe it means I find you a very beautiful woman."

"Well, there is certainly no doubt you are an extraordinarily handsome man. And I say that as a professional."

"A professional?" His raised eyebrows indicated a bit of shock.

"A photographer, remember."

He let go of her hand as the waiter returned with their drinks. "Ah yes. Architecture. So tell me, what do you think of our Cathedral of Sant'Andrea?"

"Shall I be honest?"

"By all means. Let's have a very honest evening."

She must not seem too eager to be with him, or to be too easy. "We are having dinner, not an evening."

"I'm hoping to change that."

The conversation stuck on architecture, although he twice mentioned some item of her outfit that he thought brought out a particularly fine physical feature. The truth was that Fabiano Greco was proving to be a first-rate conversationalist with an extraordinarily wry sense of humor. Wealthy women paid a lot of money to gigolos to be entertained so skillfully by glorious men whose claims that they were beautiful came off with utter conviction.

Near the end of the dinner, she checked her cell phone for the time, telling him she needed to see if she had messages from her partner. It was only seven thirty-five and she must keep him away from the condo until, at the very minimum, eight. Circumstances clearly required that she indulge in a slow, leisurely dessert. She would enjoy every minute of it.

"Partner?" he said, a slight frown creasing the beautiful brow.

"My cameraman and all-around assistant. He also writes copy with me for my books."

"You do books as well?"

"That I do. I can give you my Web site."

His cell phone apparently vibrated because he stiffened and reached for his pants pocket. He withdrew his phone and checked the display. "Please excuse me," he said. "I have to take this call."

"Not a problem."

He rose and disappeared toward the restaurant's entry lobby. She appreciated his courtesy in not subjecting her, or anyone else, to his private chatter. On the other hand, since his private chatter might very well be something requiring secrecy, his thoughtfulness might be more a case of being discreet than being polite.

He returned with a sincerely disappointed look on his face. "This call is somewhat urgent. I need to send information to someone. I don't have it here with me. I need to return home."

She felt a little thud in her chest as her heart did a double beat. Super…potential disaster on the horizon. Not surprising, really. Everything so far had seemed disconcertingly easy. Joe needed at the very minimum another twenty-five minutes. "Could we not finish dessert, at least?"

"I truly apologize. Look, come with me. I find your company a pleasure. I'm certain to find us something sweet for the palette at the condo."

"Absolutely. Good idea," she said as she rose, her mind already wondering how to stall or distract him to the maximum. And wondering also how she was going to get out of Fabio's condo gracefully after she had distracted him there. Going to his condo had not been in their plans.

The waiter appeared as if conjured. "Put it on my marker," Fabiano said as he took her elbow and guided her toward the entrance. When they stepped outside into a balmy Mediterranean June evening, his driver had already brought up the car, a midnight-blue Jaguar sedan. The man must have returned from dropping off Fabiano's lady friend while she and Fabiano were eating.

Fabiano wasn't giving her any opportunity to call Cesare to warn Joe. In the car, she tried to think of some plausible excuse to make a call but he began earnestly describing various architectural wonders they passed. To a mind inclined to be suspicious, interrupting his conversation to make a call for any reason she could think of would trigger major alarms.

In what she estimated was less than seven minutes, the driver dropped them off. At the ornately carved oak door, as he put his key in the lock, she said in a voice she was praying would reach Joe's ears if he were still there, "Fabiano, this place is extraordinary! What a view you must have. I am so glad you brought me."

"Fabiano!"

That was all Joe had to hear from Nova to jet him into overdrive. The laptop, which still had not come up with the safe's combination, had to be hidden immediately.

He snatched it off the antique glass-topped table and slid it on the floor under a sofa, then tossed some kind of fancy dark cloth over it. Fortunately, the computer would continue its work wirelessly.

He launched himself behind the nearest couch, a poor hiding place at best since it had claw-footed legs and if anyone looked at the right angle, he'd be seen. But he'd already checked out other possible quick hiding spots, and the sofa was the best bet.

He held his breath.

Nova entered, doubtless with Greco.

A floor lamp in the room turned on. "Maria," Greco called out.

Of course there was no reply. Hair at the back of Joe's neck prickled up. *No one bends down to look under furniture.*

"Please," Nova said, loud enough so that were he in any of the rooms, he would be able to hear it. "Show me to the balcony before you rush off to do whatever it is you have to do."

"This way, then," Greco said.

Footsteps crossed toward Joe, passed by and then stopped at the French doors leading onto the balcony.

But the door didn't open. Nor did Nova or Greco say anything. The silence was strange. What the heck were they doing?

Then Greco said, "I've been wanting to do that since the moment I saw you in that red bathing suit."

Damn it! Greco had kissed Nova.

"Do it again," she said.

DO IT AGAIN! Joe felt the heat of blood rush into his face as he clenched his fists.

The silence dragged on even longer this time.

"So, show me the view," she said in what he knew was one of her silkier tones.

The doors opened, and Nova and Greco stepped onto the balcony.

"Fabulous!"

Greco said, "I'll be right back. This shouldn't take long."

"I'll come with you."

"No," he said.

No arguing there. Greco would not allow her to go with him, whatever he was up to.

Greco came back into the living room and went down the hall toward his office or a bedroom. Nova stepped back into the living room. Joe put his head up, then right back down when she saw him.

She strode away from the couch toward the door. He could hear her pacing, probably looking at the furniture, the paintings, whatever.

Greco returned in under three minutes. "See what I said. That didn't take long. Now I shall look in the kitchen for something sweet. And I have just about any liquor you might want."

"While that sounds inviting, you know what I'd really like?"

"And that is…"

Another long silence. Shit! Greco had to be kissing her again.

"That, too," she said.

"You are a delight, Nova."

Their footsteps approached the sofa again. Joe wished he could shrink; the incredible shrinking man, that's what he wanted to be.

Bodies plunked down onto the sofa. Their legs entwined. Nova sure wasn't fighting him off.

In fact, she actually moaned.

He heard the sounds of clothes rubbing together, and then another unmistakably female sigh. Was Greco starting to take off something she was wearing? *Shit! Shit!*

"You said an evening together, right?"

"Yes."

Nova stood. She had to be looking down at Greco. Then he stood as she backed up a step, as if she'd maybe pulled him up from the sofa.

"Then let's make it a whole evening. You're a local and this would be a perfect opportunity for me to sample the nightlife. You know the club along the Amalfi drive. The Volcano. I understand from my host that they have dancing."

"Of course. I go there often. Hottest place on the coast."

"Would you take me there? Please. Let's go have some fun. First."

"Are you sure you wouldn't—"

"Please."

Joe knew that *please.* Knew the beguiling smile that went with it. If he had to bet his life at this moment, he'd bet that Greco would fold. Hell, every cell in his body was urging Greco to fold. Greco had to be out of the condo. And Nova out of his arms.

Another long, agonizing silence. She was *way* over-doing this!

"Okay," Greco said. "Dancing first."

"Thank you, thank you."

They crossed the room, the door opened, they left.

Joe continued to lie on the floor for another minute, imagining those kisses, turning the images at different angles in his mind.

He finally pushed to his feet. Nova was out dancing with Fabiano Greco, arms dealer and sworn member of La Cosa Nostra.

Dancing.

Chapter 19

With Fabiano holding her elbow as if he owned her, Nova stepped out from the Volcano's booming interior into the stillness of the balmy Italian summer night. Still overheated from dancing, she lifted her hair off the back of her neck and let the soft zephyr off the water kiss away some of the excess fire burning in her blood. Fortunately, the skimpy silk top let her body heat rush away.

Fabiano's driver, seeing them exit, rose from a seat he'd taken close to the door and hustled off to fetch the Jaguar.

Fabiano slid his arm around her waist, bent and kissed the back of her neck. Up close, he smelled subtly of a cologne that reminded her of her father's Old Spice—fresh and nutty. She knew he was no good, a thief, a crook, a seller of weapons and possibly willing to sell the formula for a deadly virus to the highest bidder—but she didn't mind the kiss. Such was the strength of sexual chemistry. Were he not a sleaze, she would gladly begin an affair with Fabiano Greco, no doubt to be crushed when he wearied of her.

Fortunately, she would be spared that anguish since her knowledge of his business kept rudely intruding every time she felt another rush of pleasure from his voice or touch or the sight of his sensual face. And she had learned as they moved together on the dance floor, hips pressed close, that he kept his body as lean and flexible as the wild cat for which his car was named. That too had worked to seduce her.

The Jaguar pulled up. The Volcano's parking attendant opened the door and she slid into the backseat, followed by Fabiano.

He said, "To the condo."

She thought, Well, hell. *Now is when things get unpleasant.* "I've enjoyed one of the best nights I've had in a very long time, Fabiano. Truly, I am a happy woman. But I'd appreciate it if you'd take me, instead, to my apartment." To the driver she spoke a bit louder. "My apartment is at 36 Via Cremona in Positano."

Fabiano said, "I assume you don't really mean that. Surely your rented apartment cannot be as…comfortable as my condo. And did you not say that your partner is sleeping there?"

She put her hand on his leg. Perhaps the gesture might soften his anger. "I do mean it."

"Then I truly don't understand."

"It's not you. It's me."

"Exactly what does that mean?"

They had pulled onto the Amalfi Drive. The driver said in Italian, "Where do you want me to go, Mr. Greco?"

"Back to Amalfi," Greco snapped. To her, he said, "I expect you to return to the condo with me. We'll have an after-dinner drink and listen to some softer music than what the Volcano offers."

"I know what you expect. And, unfortunately, I can't oblige."

"Like hell you can't."

He was so angry that for a moment she wondered if his otherwise charming exterior might cover a man inclined to be violent.

"Don't pretend to be naive," he said, softening his tone slightly but still firm. "We've spent an enjoyable evening together. I want you to come home with me."

She waited him out.

"I rarely spend a night in bed alone, and I don't intend to spend this night alone."

"I'd rather not have to explain. Can't we just agree that we've had a wonderful evening and let it go at that?"

"No. I can read women's signals as well as any man can, and I know you are as attracted to me as I am to you. And neither of us is a child."

They were now on the outskirts of town and would quickly need to make a turn if Fabiano were to let her off at the apartment.

"Okay, then, here's the truth." She thought— hoped—that she had read him correctly. "I *am* powerfully attracted to you. And if we go to your place, even for drinks, you will of course be expecting that·we'll go to bed. But I don't go to bed with any man who won't wear a condom. And, well, my instincts and things you've said tonight tell me you won't."

He leaned away from her, scanning her face, stunned. Then he nodded slowly. "You know, I don't. But for you, Nova, I will if that's what you want."

It was her turn to be stunned. Hell. What to say now?

The driver said, "Shall I turn, Mr. Greco?"

"Stop the car," Greco ordered. They pulled to the curb.

She and Greco sat in silence, searching each other's faces. A slow ache began to squeeze her heart. She wanted to go with him. She wanted to spend the night in the arms of a clever, handsome, funny man who would even wear a bloody condom to have her. Didn't she deserve to have a few hours of tenderness followed by passion now and then? Something about the way he danced told her that Fabiano would be an attentive, skilled lover.

He touched her cheek. "Come home with me."

"I'm sorry to make you angry. I'm sorry if you feel I misled you. Genuinely sorry." And she was. "But I want to go to my apartment," she repeated. This was business. All business. To forget herself could be both foolish and dangerous for the mission.

Fabiano turned away from her. He shook his head, as if surprised. But this was not a man to beg. To the driver he said, "Thirty-six Via Cremona."

They sat in silence the rest of the drive. When they stopped, Fabiano made no move to touch or speak to her. The driver came around to her side and opened the door. Not knowing what she could possibly say to excuse having suckered Fabiano, she got out.

She started to walk away, when she heard rustling behind her. She turned as he stepped out of the car. He walked up to her, took both of her arms, looked at her with eyes narrowed and puzzled. He kissed her again, and she melted against him, returning the kiss with one that came from some lonely place deep in her soul.

He let her go. He smiled and said softly, "Will I see you again tomorrow for dinner?"

She shook her head.

"I think something good came my way this evening," he said softly. "And for whatever reason—nothing I can figure out—it is going to escape me." He started to leave, then turned back to her. "And for what it's worth, you just missed the best sex of your life."

He stepped into the Jag and closed the door. The car took off.

Maybe she had. She'd never know now, would she?

As she walked to the door, her thoughts turned slowly to Joe, the safe, the op. Tomorrow she'd know if Fabiano could actually be so crooked, so greedy for his fine life, as to deal in information about biological weapons of mass destruction. She didn't believe for a moment, however, that he'd sell the actual virus.

It was 1:15 a.m. when she let herself into the silent apartment. Cesare and Joe had left a lamp on for her. She nearly popped a blood vessel when Joe said, with heavy sarcasm, "Did you really have to spend the whole night with him?"

Chapter 20

Her spirit, already dragging on the floor, took another blow. Why was Joe still awake? What business was it of his how late she stayed out? She dropped the beach bag onto the apartment's small dining room table and stared at him, the room silent but vibrating with sudden tension.

He rose from the sofa, half a room away, and stared back, still fully dressed in tan slacks and a pale blue shirt. The light from the floor lamp struck him from behind. She couldn't see his face to read his expression.

"I'm tired." She pulled the still damp swimsuit out of the bag. "It's been a long evening."

"Night," he countered. "A long night. It's after one o'clock."

She straightened. "Are you my mother?"

She moved toward her bedroom. He rushed the distance between them and took hold of her arm tightly enough that it hurt. She could smell wine or beer on his breath. Maybe something stronger. He said, "I was worried sick about you."

She stared at his hand. He let go.

She could see his face now, but what she thought she saw in those big brown eyes wasn't worry. It was anger. "You must be kidding. I went dancing with him. It must have been evident to you that he'd bought my cover. Right? So what's to worry about?"

"Oh yeah. His interest was very evident. The guy must be some good kisser."

"How in hell could you tell that?"

Nothing.

"How?"

His bunched shoulders slumped. "Okay, so I couldn't."

"You sure couldn't. I've kissed a lot of toads for the Company."

"I still worry."

"What? That I'd blow my cover after a few drinks? I don't believe you think that for a minute, so I don't know what you're so pissed about."

She started again for the bedroom. Again he took her arm, but gently this time. "I don't like it when you…I hate it when you…." Suddenly angry again, he thrust her arm away. "Why the hell, Nova, do you keep doing this stuff?"

She turned on him full face and shoved him in the chest with both hands. "How in God's green earth do you get off questioning me for working for the Company? I didn't want to be here in the first place."

Only moments ago, she'd wanted to melt into Fabiano Greco and let all of her concerns disappear. "In Costa Rica, I was getting my balance back. I was starting to think about normal things. Like how it would be something special to get married to some guy who loves me and have a couple of kids with him. Invite the neighbors over to dinner. Go on camping vacations where we take only cameras, no guns. You're the one who dragged me into this."

He jabbed both fists into the air as if totally frustrated by a disobedient, willful child and spun away from her.

"What is wrong with you?" she said. Was he jealous? Ridiculous!

He walked to the sofa and dropped onto it like a man defeated. "Yeah. A family and kids would be great. Better than great. Wonderful. You probably think I've never given it a thought. But I have, and I agree that they don't mix with this life. But we make it possible for other people to have that life."

She took a few steps toward him. "If it makes you feel any better, when this op is over, I'm outta here. This is my last. I'm going to go find a normal life. But for now, let's concentrate on Ebola. Did you get into the safe okay?"

"Yes. I've got photos of all papers, but there was no laptop. No disks. Nothing else to copy." Not looking at her, staring at his shoe tips.

So maybe that was it. Displaced disappointment because he suspected Greco might not be Lynchpin. She stepped still closer. He seemed to get a grip on his dejection. He straightened his back, crossed his legs, looked at her again and offered a small grin. "Lots of cash, dollars and euros. Three expensive watches and cuff links set with what look like very costly stones."

She sighed, disappointed too. "I'm bushed. I'm going to bed. I need some rest."

He stood and walked to her and to her surprise, pulled her into his arms in a friendly—just friendly—hug. The smell of alcohol was still there, but this close she also smelled his body odor. She liked Joe's smell, even when he was all sweaty. Other men's perspiration often repelled her, but not Joe's.

He turned her around and aimed them both down the hallway leading to the bedrooms.

"My private life isn't your business," she said.

"I know."

Her door came first. She walked into the room. Joe leaned in with one last question. "Was he a toad?"

"No. He wasn't."

Chapter 21

"Too bad he's not our guy," she announced to Joe the next morning at breakfast.

"Nothing is ever simple, is it? Where's Cesare?"

"Out walking Principessa. I love that dog. When I woke up, she was sleeping with me instead of Cesare. I think it would have hurt his feelings. Fortunately, he was still asleep so I returned her. He'll never be the wiser. Coffee's ready."

"Right. Smell got me up."

He rummaged through the fridge. "What time is it?"

She checked the microwave clock. "Nine-thirty. You can't call Sorokin until at least ten o'clock when his office opens."

"Right."

At ten o'clock, Cesare returned. Nova informed him

that Greco was clean, at least as far as being the seller of Ebola virus information. Cesare checked in with Provenza.

Nova said, "Ask him whether anyone has found the electrician informant who knows who Lynchpin is."

When he had hung up, Cesare said, "No leads from the CIA yet, but Interpol says the man's neighbors claim the electrician and his sister were going to the Caribbean. So along with Interpol, SISMI has diverted as many resources as they can spare to contacting every tour to that region leaving from Italy, as well as contacting every major tourist hotel destination from Freeport in the Bahamas to Grenada in the Lesser Antilles. Needless to say, that's an impressively long list to cover."

"Okay," she said to Joe. "It's time for you to hit up our target B."

Joe punched in Sorokin's number at the office of his import/export company in Ravello. The secretary informed him that Signore Sorokin was out of the office and not expected to return until after two o'clock that afternoon.

Nova said, "No moping. I want to go swimming again."

Cesare started extracting items from the refrigerator. He had become their de facto cook, another something at which he excelled.

Joe said, "I want to go parasailing again."

"We can do both," she agreed. "Let's hope we get Sorokin at two o'clock."

Joe started to have a second cup of coffee.

She said, "First, before we swim, let's get cappuccino."

He grinned and returned the pot to its warming stand. "Fine. But we can't kill the whole day only with cappuccino and swimming."

She moved the beach bag to the kitchen counter pass-through and took out her camera. "For our cover, we should take photos of houses and stuff—do a big public shoot at the cathedral. But then, this morning I woke with a new itch. This coast, in fact, has some of the most breathtaking vistas I've ever seen. I'm thinking of maybe starting a genuine photo project along the lines of 'the ten most beautiful coasts in the world.' I already have a set of shots along Australia's southern coast that will be perfect. They take your breath away."

"I would buy such a book," Cesare said.

She walked around the counter into the kitchen and gave him a hug. "You are one of the most positive people I have ever met. I simply can't think of you as an agent, as part of the intelligence world."

"Ah, yes." His smile lit up his face. "Did I not tell you from the beginning? That's my greatest asset."

After Cesare's brunch, she and Joe drove the SUV into Amalfi to the Piazza del Duomo—Joe driving—and found a seat outside a café so they could watch the tourists streaming into and out of the Cathedral of Sant'Andrea. Afterward, she spent forty minutes photographing the cathedral, concentrating on the portico and the bronze door, Joe lugging the camera bag and changing lenses like a pro. Actually, he now qualified, in her view, as a first-rate photographer's assistant.

By the time they had finished checking out the old Capuchin monastery's beautiful cloister and view, it was slightly after two o'clock.

They picked a quiet spot on the hotel's terrace and Joe again called Sorokin. He quickly nodded his head and grinned at Nova.

"Yes, Mr. Sorokin. I'm a friend of an American who has moved back to the U.S. He owns a Ferrari Berlinetta Lusso. He didn't want to ship it over. He wants to sell it. Cesare Giordano, who once decorated your home, told me that you like classic Ferraris."

A bit of silence as Joe listened.

"Yes, sterling condition. He's asking only 310,000 euros. I would be glad to show it to you. Take you for a drive. Let you drive it, if you'd like. I'm staying in Positano right now. I'd be glad to pick you up at your home."

Pause. She realized she was holding her breath. She let it out and drew in a deep one.

"Well, tomorrow would be ideal for me."

From the Sorokin file, she knew their family schedules. His wife attended some class every afternoon of the week. Monday yoga. Tuesday painting. Today, being Saturday, she should be having lunch and then shopping with her closest friend. Tomorrow, Sunday, was her spa afternoon. Nova had more than once thought how great it would be to have such a life of leisure that every Sunday afternoon you could go to a spa, work out, have a facial and pedicure, and get an hour-long massage. What a life.

Their ten-year-old daughter, under the constant care of a tutor who doubled as a chaperone, had an equally busy schedule. When the girl wasn't in school she was off to riding, ballet or flute lessons. Tomorrow, Sunday, she would be riding. Sunday would be a fine day for their op.

Nova nodded her head, grinned at Joe and gave him a thumbs-up.

"Oh, really. Then perhaps Monday would be better for you?" Long pause. "Well, fine. Tomorrow, then. I'll pick you up promptly."

When he got off the phone, she said, "What's this about trying to shift to Monday? Tomorrow is perfect."

"Not so perfect. Not impossible, but the mom and daughter will be at home. I still think it has to be a go."

"What!"

"Sorokin's delighted to have an excuse to get away because his wife is throwing a birthday party for the girl and fifty of her friends. They will be out of the house, though, on their big front lawn. You can still get in and have the run of the place, although we'll have to check whether they'll provide a restroom cabana outside or not."

"I don't like it."

A sudden jolt of the floor caused her to step backward and fling out her arm. It was followed by two more slight tremors.

"Quake," Joe said. "The volcano god reminds us of his presence."

Being from California, quakes, especially little ones, barely registered with her. "Why not Monday?"

"He made clear that if it wasn't tomorrow, he would be away until next Thursday. Thursday is too long to wait." Joe grinned. "Besides, I don't want to have to wait until Thursday to get my once-in-a-lifetime chance to drive this car. It's fabulous, Nova. You're definitely getting the raw end of this deal."

She stared at the view of the bay, not really seeing the water or the shore. "What time?"

"One o'clock."

"One o'clock is good. Okay. We're on for tomorrow. Terrific."

They were silent for a moment, Nova still digesting the news and arranging things in her mind, given those fifty kids on the front lawn. Finally she said, "We'll take a swim, and then I want to shoot photos at sunset at two places north of here."

They headed for the SUV. She felt good that they would get a look soon at Sorokin's safe. But she didn't like it at all that Sorokin's wife and daughter and fifty kids would be roaming around the property when she was rappelling down that sheer cliff onto the mansion's roof. Kids were notorious for seeing things adults didn't intend them to see.

Chapter 22

"Your family will not know exactly how you died," Ahmad said to Ali. "But they will know you died with great courage and great honor."

Ahmad handed an AK-74 to the boy, showing him how to hold it across his chest, resting it on his left arm, its barrel pointing up at an authoritative angle. He felt Ali straighten his back and heard him suck in a sharp breath.

The boy wore a camouflage suit, although during his travel throughout Italy and into Europe he would at first wear the same dust coat and stylish garb as Khangi and the bodyguards. On the second day, they would all change into common streetwear. But for Ali's families' sake, Ahmad felt the camouflage suit seemed best for this last, farewell message. Also, it was how Ali had said he wanted to be remembered.

Mohsin waved his hand. "Have Ali stand just a bit more to his left. The light from the side is better there."

Ali moved, and Mohsin tinkered with the tripod holding the video camera, then said, "That's good."

Khangi returned to the safe house's living room from the kitchen with a second helping of spaghetti. He dropped into the apartment's second most comfortable armchair, leaving the best for Ahmad.

The five other soldiers, filling themselves with pasta, occupied the sofa, another chair, and handy spots on the floor to watch the filming. The entire team was in place on time, and Ahmad considered them ready.

"This is your big moment, Ali," Khangi said. "Tomorrow at three o'clock, when we all meet back here again, you will be the most dangerous man in the world."

Ahmad joined in the laughter. Though he might be brave, Ali was skinny and looked even younger than his sixteen years. He hardly looked the part of "the world's most dangerous man."

"Do you remember your lines?" Ahmad asked, taking his seat.

"Yes," came the answer, firm and sure. Ali had been carefully chosen in Palestine for determination, courage and motivation. His was not a faint heart.

"Let's begin, then," Ahmad said to Mohsin.

A blinking light on the running digital camera indicated the moment filming began. Mohsin waved to Ali.

"My name is Ali Yassin, and this is my final testimony, to be delivered to my family in Palestine. Tomorrow, I undertake a mission to strike at the heart of Western infidels, to humble them, to terrify them, to make them pay for the lives of Muslims they kill so eagerly. When you receive this, I shall—"

The sound of a soft but clear single thud had emerged from the bedroom. At least Ahmad thought it was their bedroom.

Every man straightened and looked toward the bedroom door. Ahmad jumped to his feet, as did Khangi.

With Khangi right behind him, Ahmad rushed through the door to find the room empty.

"Do you think it came from here?" Khangi asked.

"I don't know."

The other men clustered around the door. Ahmad waved to silence them. He strained to hear if another sound would come from the apartment above. As he listened, he noted that the bedroom window of this first floor apartment was open.

Hearing no further noise, he went to the window and looked out. Nothing but plants and grass and cars on the street.

"Was this window open this morning?"

"I think so," Khangi said. "It was hot last night." Both of them looked toward the door. Two of the soldiers nodded.

Ahmad listened once more. Hearing nothing, he turned. "Let's finish the taping."

The noise must have come from above them. He was simply overcautious, now that the time for action was so close. He had seen to it, and double-checked, that all tracks had been covered with skill and care. No one could suspect them.

Chapter 23

The sheer seventy-foot cliff behind the Sorokin mansion had its good features and several bad ones. On the plus side, shrubs and trees cloaked the top, so Nova felt little danger of anyone seeing her fix the climbing rope to a rocky projection of what appeared to be a well-anchored, suitcase-sized boulder.

But on this lovely Sunday morning—ideal for an outdoor birthday party—as Nova started a quick rappel down the cliff, she was keenly aware of its worst feature—any of the fifty adults and kids on the Sorokin front lawn looking at the cliff within the next ten seconds would likely notice her movement.

They would have to stop and take a second and maybe third look, though, to recognize that the movement was a human climber because she wore a tight-fitting, camouflage jumpsuit, the material of which had been chosen to match the colors and tones of the rocks and shrubs on the cliff face. Cesare had seen to it that the suit, originally tailored for Joe, had been shortened, tightened and let out in all the right places for her body. Even her face was smeared with streaks of soft brown and green.

She let herself down at quick speed. At the last bit of the drop, she had to push off against the cliff face in order to jump a four-foot span between the cliff and the back of the house.

On the roof now and hidden from view from the lawn, she breathed easier. She listened a moment to the sounds of carousel music and laughter. No one appeared to have detected her if the continued normalcy of the sounds could be trusted. Cesare had determined that a restroom cabana had been ordered; the house should be all hers.

The Sorokin den, her first objective, lay at the extreme east end of the single-story house. She sprinted to the den's chimney. She'd strapped what she thought of as "the magic laptop" under the jumpsuit against her chest, and she wore the safe break-in kit flat against her back in a special pocketed pouch.

She shrugged off the second climbing rope, attached it to the chimney by looping it around the base and securing it with two prongs of a trident hook. A firm pull assured her that the trident would not give way. Since the break-in must be undetected, breaking a window wasn't an option. Besides the windows and exterior doors were wired. If by any chance Mrs. Sorokin decided to activate the security system while attending to her party on the lawn, messing with a window would cause all hell to break loose. Joe, Nova, Cesare and finally Provenza had agreed that the large, old chimney was the way to go.

She removed her climbing gloves and from one of the jumpsuit's leg pockets she fetched the specially modified, shortened crowbar and a screwdriver equipped with heads of several sizes. The chimney cap, designed to keep out debris and animals, held two chimney pipes and only two screws held it in place. It came off easily, exposing a top-mounted damper.

From plans of the house, she knew the flue dimensions to be twenty by twenty-six inches. A tight fit for her, and a really tight fit for Joe, given his broader shoulders, but not impossible. The mansion was old, constructed in the early twentieth century, with a fireplace opening four feet wide and three feet high.

She set to work removing the four screws holding the damper in place; in less than a minute, she stared down into the dark, filthy mouth of the twenty-foot length of soot-filled flue. After donning a surgical mask, goggles, and her gloves, she let the rope down, eased herself over the edge and dropped inside.

Despite the mask, she held her breath as she shimmied down. Once down and squatting just inside the fireplace, she took out a folded sheet of four-by-four plastic from one leg pocket, opened it, and spread it over the marble hearth.

She stepped onto the plastic and removed her gloves, mask and goggles, and unzipped the jumpsuit. Under the suit, she wore a full-bodied black leotard. After stripping off the climbing shoes and jumpsuit, she stepped barefoot onto the wooden floor of the den.

Drapes at the two windows were half closed, the room suffused in dim light. The door was slightly ajar. The house seemed almost eerily silent. Only a standing clock ticked away softly, like her heartbeat. She sent thoughts for good luck to Joe, who was at this very moment enchanting suspect number two with a magnificent old Ferrari.

The Sorokins employed only one full-time servant who doubled as cook and maid. She, along with Mrs. Sorokin, should be fully engaged in either the kitchen or the front lawn for the next three hours or more. Just to be on the safe side, though, Nova crossed a couple of oriental carpets to the door, closed it, and propped the edge of a straight-back armchair under the knob. She placed the laptop onto Sorokin's desk and slipped off the straps of the safecracking kit.

Tapestries, thick rugs and dark walnut furniture upholstered in soft green and brown tones gave the room a cozy feel. It took her less than half a minute to find the safe, amateurishly hidden on the floor under an inch-thick red-and-gold Saurek rug that looked like a masterpiece. Her toes reveled in the carpet's feel even as she was thinking that Sorokin would be a fool to hide something illegal in such an easy place to find. But then again, sometimes arrogance led to over confidence which led to the mistakes that allowed authorities to catch people. Maybe Sorokin suffered from such over confidence.

She sighed. The safe was a Bergan-Soffit, the model with a three-number combination, and not electronic.

Using the laptop was out. She'd have to do this the old-fashioned way.

Praying that Sorokin would make it easy, she began with the safecracker's standard method number one, a systematic search of the desk's contents and drawers. People could never be sure they would remember a combination and so they almost always wrote down the number. And being lazy, they usually left those numbers in the same room as the safe. Just a series of three unidentified numbers, that's what she needed to find.

Fifteen minutes later, after finishing a search of the bookshelves, she straightened and sighed again. If he'd hidden the combo in this room, he'd done a good job. More time spent looking would be a waste.

A cracking sound in the room's far corner triggered a freeze reflex and a skipped heartbeat. She turned her head, held her breath, then let it out when she realized the sound was the house itself, creaking with old age.

Smiling sheepishly, she went back to the safecracking kit and pulled out the stethoscope. She was already wearing latex gloves. Later she would need pencil and graph paper.

"Patience," she muttered. First, using the stethoscope and carefully listening as she turned the dial, she had to determine the contact points on the drive cam. Next, she turned the dial to park all three wheels in the wheel pack at zero, listening again to determine the right and left numbers, indicating a contact area. Working around the entire dial, she reset the lock then reparked the wheels at three number intervals. She repeated the process again and again, tediously graphing, for each contact area she detected, the numbers of its right and left side. Every time she reparked the wheels at a different number on the dial, the contact areas she detected changed slightly. In the end, the graphed points of all the contact areas gave her the numbers of the combination.

As the minutes ticked away in her subconscious and in the heart of the big old clock, she resisted the urge to check the time. It would take however long it would take. Twice more, the house creaked, and she jumped and froze both times.

"Got it!" she finally said with satisfaction. She glanced at her watch. Thirty-eight minutes after one. Only an hour and thirty-five minutes had passed. Excellent, really.

She opened the safe.

Remembering her lessons, she took care to remove and then place the items in order so they could be returned with no one the wiser. She ignored the usual jewelry and cash, some gold coins, some bonds, and a will. No laptop or disks here either. Just some business papers.

She sat quietly a moment, thinking and chewing her lip. This was not good. Two of their three suspects were *not* Lynchpin. This left only Ya Lin. If Ya Lin turned out to be a negative, then as Aldo Provenza once so colorfully had said, this op was screwed.

She had no way to know if SISMI and the Company or maybe Interpol were working other leads by now. That information would be on a need-to-know basis only. But she had, for some reason, thought that Sorokin would be the one. The truth was, hunches didn't always pan out. Although it was certainly nice when they did.

She wondered for a moment if perhaps what they were searching for might be elsewhere in the house. But Provenza, relying on specific information from the informant, believed that the "stuff" was in Lynchpin's home safe. She had no instructions to make any other searches, and they certainly hadn't made any time allowance for it.

She returned the items, bundled up the computer and put the break-in kit back on, took the chair from the door, then, everything again secured, she stepped onto the plastic and into the jumpsuit. She zipped it, put on the climbing shoes, and then, squatting, backed into the three-foot high fireplace opening, and gathered up the plastic.

A sound—someone humming—nailed her in place. A woman had entered the room, and Nova could see her black skirt from the waist down. She walked toward the fireplace. Were Nova to be caught crouching inside it, Nova imagined that the woman would scream loud enough to be heard for a mile in all directions. And Nova would have to silence her quickly.

Nova tensed, ready to leap out. The woman moved to Nova's left toward the bookcase. She halted briefly, then turned and left the room. Nova resumed breathing. She would never know what the woman had been sent to get, but my God, had the timing been fortunate, for Nova and the woman, who doubtless would not have enjoyed being knocked unconscious.

The plastic had done the job. Nova had a damp cloth in case some soot escaped the plastic onto the marble or wooden floor, but there was no need to tidy further. She realigned the iron log holder, which she'd inadvertently moved out of place.

The climb back up the chimney on the knotted climbing rope was dirty but easy. *I should send them a bill for chimney sweeping.* The expression *light a fire under you,* popped into her head, one of her mother's many such sayings. At one time, perhaps the late 1800s, in places like this in Europe, small people, often women and especially children, had been put to work climbing up chimneys to clean them out. Often their rather tyrannical bosses burned something in the fireplace to make their workers hurry. A pretty grim origin for that particular saying.

She gathered up the rope, slung it across her chest, and collapsed and pocketed the trident. Even though she knew she couldn't be seen from the lawn, she stooped as she ran to the spot on the cliff face where the climbing rope still dangled. The rappel down had been fast. The climb up was going to be slower, longer, providing a greater risk that someone might look up and see her.

She grabbed hold, started climbing, and ascended no more than four feet when the cliff started shaking. The rope snapped her against the cliff face. Her cheek slammed up against rough, cold granite. By sheer reflex, her grip on the rope turned to iron, as if her fingers were welded to it.

The cliff and rope continued to collide, and she heard the deep rumble of the earthquake just as the rope gave way. She dropped. Straight down. Hit feet first. A hot poker of pain jabbed through her left ankle. She toppled backward, cracking her head against the stone house.

Her vision swimming, her ankle throbbing and on

fire, she sat stunned with her back against the house wall. Rocks and dust from the cliff continued to rain down. She shrank together and covered her head.

Finally the shaking ceased. She put her hand to her temple until the spinning stopped, but the pain in her ankle didn't let up. She bent her leg, ran her hands over her ankle. She wiggled it. It didn't seem to be broken.

The climbing rope lay in a heap all around her and around the fallen boulder, the size of a beanbag chair, to which it remained attached. The boulder had avoided hitting her by a scant inch. She looked up the face of the cliff. If she was in good shape, she could easily free-climb out of here. She wiggled the ankle again and bit her lip against the sharp jolt of pain.

She could try to free-climb out with a bum ankle, which would take thirty or forty minutes or more if she could manage it at all. Her only other alternative was to take off through the party on the front lawn.

Chapter 24

"So how bad is it?" Nova asked, staring at her ankle.

She put weight on it, slowly. It hurt, but she could walk. Climbing a cliff face, however, seemed a distinctly bad idea.

She gathered the climbing rope, then ducked around the side of the mansion. Near the front of the house, she heard the voices of children and adults screaming.

Wanting to get away quickly, she started a limping jog toward the crowd clustered around something on the opposite side of an overturned long table. No one even looked her way. A woman kept screaming "Angela! Angela!" over and over. Angela was Sorokin's daughter, the birthday girl.

Good sense said to use the confusion to slip away

unnoticed, but the terror in the woman's voice yanked Nova to a halt. She caught a glimpse of a body on the lawn and blood across a white dress.

She shoved her way through kids. On the ground lay Angela and beside her, still shrieking her name, crouched her mother, her lap covered in blood. From the girl's neck came a stream of blood.

Nova rushed to the woman, pulled her up and away from Angela. She shoved the mother into the arms of a woman right behind them. In Italian she commanded, "Please keep her away."

She fell to both knees beside the girl. The table had fallen. Somehow, the glass of a huge punchbowl had shattered and struck her in two places, the most obvious wound being to the jugular vein that pumped Angela's life away at a rapid clip. Another wound, on the girl's arm, needed attending.

Nova pulled the white tablecloth under Angela's neck for support, then pressed, hard, above and below the cut vein. The bleeding stopped at once.

"You," Nova said, looking up to another woman. "Get down here and put pressure on the arm where she is bleeding."

The woman responded quickly.

Searching the faces above her, Nova asked, "Has anyone called for an ambulance?"

"Yes, yes. I did," said a woman, the front of whose dress was also blood-soaked. "They are coming."

"Did you tell them that the girl has a bleeding jugular vein?"

"I—no."

"Call them back. Tell them she is bleeding from the

jugular vein and they have to be here *now* if they are going to save her."

"Yes. I will." The woman pulled her cell phone from her purse and stepped back.

Angela's mother, frantic but no longer hysterical, knelt beside Nova. "She will be all right, yes?"

Nova said nothing. She wasn't in the habit of making false promises. She wouldn't have survived killing her stepfather or the years in prison if she'd believed in false promises, so they never came easily, if at all. In what she guessed was no more than two minutes, an ambulance rushed into the yard, siren blaring. A forty-something man with big shoulders traded his hands for hers on Angela's neck.

Nova stood, her legs shaking. Her hands and arms were covered in blood, her jumpsuit filthy, her own face streaked with green and brown camouflage paint and soot. Half the crowd watched the medics moving Angela. The other half stared in stunned amazement at Nova.

She limped across the lawn and out onto the street. From yet another jumpsuit pocket, she pulled out her cell phone and dialed Cesare.

He picked up and she said, "Big mess, Cesare. I am out here on the street loose, covered in soot and blood. You've got to come pick me up and quick. I'll go three intersections down from the Sorokin mansion and hide behind a bush or something until you get here."

"I will be there at once," he said, and rang off.

God, what madness.

She hurried her pace to just short of jogging. A red Ferrari approached—Joe and Sorokin.

As the car passed her, heading for Sorokin's place, Joe twisted in the passenger seat. The wide-eyed look on his face was priceless.

Chapter 25

The Laforza SUV pulled to a stop at the corner, and Nova scrambled up. She'd hidden behind the only bush she could find. She limped to the door and climbed in.

"My God, what a fright you are," Cesare said. "And you are hurt."

She sighed and leaned her head back against the seat. "I need to get ice on my ankle as quickly as possible. It's not broken, but it hurts like hell, and it's going to start to swell."

"I know just the place."

He jolted the van into motion. She'd thought his driving erratic before, but now she clutched the armrest in a death grip to keep from rocking back and forth as he took the turns at what she figured was as fast as you could go in an SUV without overturning.

Up ahead a small market appeared on the opposite side of the street. "Hide," he said. "Lower the seat and lie down." He swerved into the single-row parking lot, hit the brakes and was out the door as quick as quicksilver.

Principessa, who had been in his lap, put her paws tentatively on Nova's seat, her nose quivering with each breath as she took in these strange, strange smells. She was not so foolish as to climb into Nova's lap. Much too fastidious was Principessa.

"You should have been there," Nova said, smiling faintly while resisting the urge to pat the beautiful white fur with her bloody hands.

Cesare returned and tossed her a plastic bag. He returned them to the road as she pulled from the bag a packet of four white dishtowels and a sack of ice cubes. She put the seat upright and set to work, first washing her hands a bit by swishing them among the cubes and then using a towel. Then she fashioned an ice pack using ice and two more towels, which she tied around the ankle.

"What happened?" he finally asked when she laid the seat down again and took a deep breath. "All that blood. Where are you most hurt?"

"The blood's not mine. The earthquake brought down the climbing rope and me. I landed on fresh-turned soil, thank God. It was a two-story drop onto what could just as easily have been cement. I only twisted my ankle. Obviously I couldn't climb back up and had to leave on foot. Ran right through the birthday party. The quake had turned it into a nightmare. Somehow Sorokin's daughter got cut. The jugular."

"*Madre di Dio.*"

"I think I may have saved her life. She was alive when the ambulance arrived."

"Nova, please forgive me. Don't think me crass. But what about Sorokin?"

"Bad news there. He's not Lynchpin."

As soon as they reached the apartment, Nova insisted that Cesare call the hospital.

"They may not know anything for sure yet," he protested.

"Just call."

When he snapped the cell phone shut, he said, "She's in intensive care but stable."

"That's a good sign. The gods be praised the ambulance got there quickly."

"Probably her family should be thanking the gods that someone with the knowledge of what to do when someone has a cut jugular had been breaking into their safe," Cesare replied dryly.

Wanting to keep the ice against her ankle as much as possible, Nova showered quickly, pulled her hair into a ponytail, slipped into casual khaki slacks and a green tank top, and threw herself onto the sofa.

At two-thirty Joe called asking Cesare to pick him up at the home of the owner of the Ferrari. At three-forty Nova greeted them from the sofa, her foot propped up and her ankle surrounded with ice.

Joe strode to the sofa and squatted beside her.

"I will fix us all a bit to eat," Cesare said. He and Principessa disappeared into the kitchen.

Joe gave her one of his warmest smiles, his old melt-ing-women's-hearts-on-contact one. "You don't look much the worse for wear."

"I'm just keeping the ice on for sympathy. I tried the ankle ten minutes ago and it's better."

He laid his warm palm on her thigh. Chills ran up the skin of her chest and throat.

He didn't say anything, just let his hand rest there as his gaze searched hers.

Unable to bear the silence and aware of a sudden warmth that indicated, beyond question, sexual arousal, she said, "Really, I'm okay."

Finally looking away, he slid his palm down toward her ankle. She'd been unconsciously holding her breath and now drew a deep one. Her feet were bare. He stood and went to the end of the sofa and took the foot with the bum ankle into his hands, rubbing the sole and then the arch.

She couldn't bring herself to protest—if for no other reason but that the warming rub did somehow ease the pain. He was rubbing the other foot similarly when Cesare rejoined them with a tray of sandwiches, cut apples and pears, and a strong-smelling cheese. The moment of intimacy was over. She still felt agitated and breathless.

"I'll get a beer," Joe said. "Anyone else want one?"

"Yes," Cesare said.

"I'll pass," she said.

Principessa leapt onto Nova's stomach and settled down. "Sorry, love," Nova sat up. "I'm starving. You'll have to settle for my lap."

Joe returned and she told them about the safe. Since Cesare had already told Joe that no incriminating evidence regarding Ebola had been present, Joe was much more interested in her recounting of the accident with

Angela. "Man, you must have freaked those people out totally. When I saw you on the road, I thought I was hallucinating. The Sorokins will be talking about this birthday party for the rest of the girl's life. Who, they will always wonder, was that strange female creature to whom we owe our daughter's life? It was like a damn comic book—Sootwoman saves the day."

He rhapsodized a bit about driving the Ferrari, and then they turned their attention to tomorrow's op, getting into Ya Lin's, their last chance at Lynchpin. It wasn't much past four when Cesare's cell phone rang.

"Cesare Giordano," he said.

"No!" he exploded almost at once.

"No!" he said again.

She watched Cesare's eyes widen, his face darken. Something was terribly wrong. He listened and listened until she felt like bursting with the need to know. Finally he hung up.

"Friends," he said, "we've been overcome by a disaster. Interpol found the electrician informant. We know who Lynchpin is. It is Ya Lin."

"I don't get it. That's good," Joe broke in.

"Lynchpin is Ya Lin, but the date of the sale somehow got botched up. The informant gave Provenza the wrong date when he was interviewed. The date for the sale is, was, today."

Nova jerked upright, spilling Principessa off her lap. "Today!"

"Shit!" Joe said.

Cesare nodded. "Today. The sale may already have happened. The local police are at this moment seeking a search warrant."

Nova stood and tried the ankle. Some pain, but sturdy nevertheless. "We can be at Ya Lin's in under twenty minutes." She grabbed her khaki jacket, a jacket handy with pockets and able to hide a shoulder-holstered gun if the need should arise. They had arms in the SUV—Glocks for all three of them—and unfortunately the time of need was now.

Chapter 26

Joe, also wearing a jacket and armed with a Glock in a shoulder holster, again took charge of the driving. Cesare said he didn't think they would need guns and so remained unarmed, but he didn't try to stop her or Joe from carrying.

Nova took the backseat so she could keep her ankle elevated. She no longer limped, but the joint still twitched in pain if put under pressure.

"Call Provenza, Cesare," she said as they turned from the side street onto the Amalfi Drive. "Find out whatever you can from SISMI's surveillance. Find out where Lin has been all day. Is she at home now? Do they know if the sale actually took place?"

Cesare called and asked Nova's questions plus a few of his own, including what SISMI expected of them. He did a lot of nodding.

Finally he rang off. "Provenza says he has someone talking right now with the people who have been doing surveillance on Ya Lin and he'll get back to me."

They drove in silence until they approached Lin's property. Cesare checked with Provenza again and reported, "She is at home and has been all day. She had three visitors, the first very early, at seven-fifteen this morning. Provenza says the electrician is wavering, saying he's now confused, and the sale really could be next Sunday, the twenty-second, not today. As for what we should do, Provenza says we should wait and let the local authorities go in with a search warrant."

Joe glided the SUV to a slow, careful stop opposite Ya Lin's gate. Through its fine wrought iron, Nova could see the mansion's ornately carved front door where the same two guards who had accosted her and Joe stood on the porch. "Those guys look very business-like to me," she said. "What do you think, Joe?"

"I get the same feeling. Why should they be standing that way if they aren't on alert? Why not sitting?"

More silent thinking in the SUV.

Finally Joe said, "If the sale has been made, the buyer will be getting away."

"Right," Nova agreed.

"Every minute that passes, the buyer would get farther away with the information to make a deadly virus that, if let loose, could kill thousands if not more."

"Right."

"So the sooner we know whether there has been a sale or not, the better our chances of catching him are. So you're thinking what I'm thinking?"

"Right," she said. "I say screw the warrant. Let's go in there and do our own search. We play it from there."

Joe opened his door at the same time she opened hers.

"Wait! Stop! Are you insane?" Cesare blurted out. "You must not do that."

"Yeah, we must," she said.

"It will be an illegal search. We can't operate that way."

"SISMI can't."

She felt Joe's solidarity and knew her back was covered. They were of one mind. Letting the Ebola information get into the hands of terrorists, if there was any way to stop it, was unacceptable, and bureaucracy be damned. The potential risk was just too great.

They strode across the two-lane road together to the gate. Cesare hopped out, leaving Principessa in the van, and hurried to catch up with them. "What is it you're going to do? What shall I tell Provenza?"

She gave Cesare full attention. He deserved that. "We're going to get inside and confront Ya Lin. You can tell Provenza whatever you wish. Do you seriously think he'll object? We're just not going to wait. Tell him SISMI will be clean. They can lay it all off on the CIA if necessary. Or on Jane and James Blake. I don't really care. Nice and neat isn't the thing here, Cesare. My gut says, 'Do it now.' And I always listen to my gut."

Joe went to the gate for pedestrian traffic, tried it and found it also locked. "The two heavies are both at the front," he said. "Remember the place on the side? It's completely exposed, but we can climb over the wall there easily enough. There's the big tree."

She patted her cell phone in her pocket and smiled to reassure Cesare. "We'll keep you posted, I promise."

Without looking back, she followed Joe as he trotted along the road beside the wall and then turned to follow along the wall's west side. The big oak was easy to climb. Joe jumped the three feet from the tree to the flat, bricked top of the wall and turned to her. "How's the ankle? Can you make it?"

"Sure," she said, not sure at all.

She sprang off the branch, her ankle protesting as though someone had stuck a white-hot glowing steel rod into it. She landed beside him, and he hugged her to him to steady her. He immediately released her, jumped the seven or so feet to the ground, and turned to look up at her. "Jump into my arms. Let me take the weight off the ankle."

"Right," she said.

He caught her in a tight embrace and they held each other just a heartbeat longer than necessary. She felt strength and comfort in that moment, the comfort of not being alone.

As they trotted back toward the front, she said, "I say we should take out the big guys so they don't end up surprising us."

"Roger."

At the mansion's front corner, they slowed to a walk and, side by side, rounded the corner and strolled casually toward the entry. When the two men spotted her and Joe, both stiffened and put their right hands inside their beautifully tailored suit jackets. Bald Head said in Italian, "You are trespassing."

She and Joe walked up the steps to within striking distance, no more than five feet from both men.

Again Bald Head protested. "I told you yesterday,

no photographers allowed. No one. Get out or I will—"

She and Joe charged. She slugged Baldy with her fist in the solar plexus. He doubled over, and she gave him a left uppercut to the nose, followed by a knee kick to the groin. He went down, the only noises being the *uugh* as he lost breath, the crunching of his nose and the thud as he hit the beautiful gray marble entry tiles. He might be able to take on paparazzi, but not a trained CIA agent.

Joe's target crashed down beside Baldy. Nova lifted Baldy's gun, a 9mm Beretta, a weapon she knew well, and tucked it in her slacks' waistband at the small of her back. Joe also relieved the other guard of his gun, the same make of Beretta. They used the guards' socks and belts to hog-tie them.

Joe tried the front door, conveniently unlocked. They strode inside and Joe closed the door behind them. The elegant interior decor ranged through various Chinese dynasties. "Direct approach," she said.

"Agreed."

From the second floor, reached by a curving marble stairway with gilded banisters, Nova heard the bang of a door closing or perhaps a drawer being shut.

"Miss Lin," Nova called out, the sound feeling especially loud in the cavernous house.

She received no response, just another banging sound. They climbed the stairway. Another bang drew them down a long hallway to the door of a master bedroom the size of Nova's entire La Jolla condominium. Ya Lin stood with her back to them. Three suitcases lay on a massive four-poster with carved teak headboards and footboards covered in dragons, the Chinese symbol for luck. Ya Lin turned from a chest of drawers, her arms full of lingerie. Seeing two strangers in her house, she screamed and dropped the silky garments.

"It's okay," Nova said in Chinese. "We're not going to hurt you." *We should have hidden the guns.*

"Who are you? Get out!" the actress said in English. Something about their dress, or perhaps Nova's accent, had cued her to their native tongue.

Joe said, "Are you leaving?"

The beautiful woman's eyes were large with terror, her hair unkempt. "I want you to get out of my house," she screamed.

Nova pulled out her badge identifying her as Jane Blake. She doubted that Ya Lin would read a word of it. The woman was gripped by panic. "Ms. Lin, we're government agents. We know you are a spy and that your code name is Lynchpin. And we know that you are in possession of dangerous information."

Fear on Ya Lin's face turned to bewilderment. "How can you be government agents?" And then Ya Lin broke into tears. "I am so so sorry," she said. She searched Nova's face as if Nova could somehow forgive her.

"What is it, Ms. Lin?" Nova said. She stepped closer to the weeping woman.

"I cannot believe what I've done. But how could I know? It's insane. Crazy."

Joe said, "We believe you intend to sell information about the Ebola virus to terrorists. Is this true?"

"They…they lied to me." Ya Lin's words now came out choked and through sobbing tears. "I swear it. And now we must get out of here, get out of Italy. Right now."

Nova walked her to the bed and sat her down. "Ms. Lin, have you already made the sale?"

"Yes. This morning."

"If you're sorry, help us by telling us immediately who you sold the information to so that we can find and stop them."

"Oh, no. It's much too late. And that's why I've decided to leave Italy, even though they claim I will be immune. So many people are going to die. And maybe they lied to me."

A chilled hand brushed across Nova's heart. This woman wasn't just sorry she'd sold some dangerous information; Ya Lin was petrified.

Joe beat Nova to the question. "Why will people die?"

Ya Lin clenched her bedspread in both hands and looked at Joe. "They lied to me. I thought there was just supposed to be some disks, a laptop containing information on how to modify the virus, but along with those were vials of the virus, already changed. They told me no one would get paid if the package was opened before the sale. The man opened the package here. To be sure he was getting what he paid for, he said. Only then did I know that there were vials inside containing the virus."

The chill over her heart spread to Nova's guts and she held her breath as Joe asked, "Is that why people are going to die? Is that what you're saying? He intends to unleash the damned virus."

"He has already done it, I'm sure."

Not possible. Good God! "How?" Nova asked. "Where? Please, Ms. Lin. Take a deep breath. Be clear. Tell us everything you know."

The actress let go of the bedspread, took a breath, pressed her palms to her eyes and then clutched her hands together in her lap. Collected, at least a bit, she said, "I cannot tell you who he really is. We only met in person this one time. I'm sure the name, Mohammad Kanzi, is not his own. Before he left he said that he was going to save me by telling me what was going to happen. He said that today he was going to inject a brave volunteer with the disease and the volunteer would become contagious by late this afternoon."

Nova tried to listen to Ya Lin and at the same time absorb the stunning meaning of what the woman was saying. Upon contact with the virus, an infected person became moderately contagious within two hours, and fully, devastatingly contagious within six. She knew from the files supplied by Provenza that the CDC had a limited supply of vaccine against Reston, but there was no antidote. And because so few infections by this strain had been recorded, no one know the actual survival rate. Once infected, you either survived or death came to a victim horribly within days.

"He said they were going to make this volunteer a carrier. I don't exactly know what that means, except he can go around giving it to other people for days and days. Hundreds of people. Maybe thousands."

A carrier! Nova imagined a faceless man walking in St. Peter's Square, surrounded by hoards of tourists. *They're going to create a carrier!* No, if Ya Lin was right, they had already created one. Thousands of people might be killed! "You're quite sure he said they were going to create a carrier?"

"Yes. Oh, yes." Ya Lin wiped tears, rubbed her eyes.

Joe asked, "When did he leave?"

"I think, yes, no, I don't know. Early this morning. I should have left at once, but I didn't believe it was true. Not really. Not until I started running a fever."

If Ya Lin had started running a fever then, clearly whatever she had taken was having an effect. It might be a vaccine. Nova had once been vaccinated against cholera and she had run a fever as her body started making protective antibodies. Running a fever was not uncommon after all sorts of vaccinations. And why would the buyer have lied to Ya Lin? He really would have nothing to gain by doing so. Nova decided that it was, in fact, likely that he had given Ya Lin a vaccine.

Joe pulled his cell phone out and punched a number as he walked toward the room's windows. He started talking to Cesare.

Nova crossed her arms to ward off the chill spreading over her skin now. People in Rome would get on buses and trains and then planes, and if they were infected, they would be a hazard to every other person they met. This nightmare would spread like a wildfire in a high wind after a hundred-year drought.

Maggie. She snatched her cell phone from her pocket and punched in Star's number.

The usual long wait for the international connection became a wait that felt like infinity. *Be home, be home,* Nova repeated in her mind, over and over.

Finally the number rang. Star's answering machine came on. *No! Please no!*

"This is the McDonald residence. Please leave a message. For Maggie's friends, Maggie is in Italy and won't be back for three weeks."

"Star, this is Nova. It is urgent that I reach you. It's about Maggie, and though I'm sorry to have to scare you, it's life and death. I want you to call me the second, not the minute but the second, you get this message. You have my number."

She punched in her mother's number. During another long agonizing wait, Joe had finished his explanation and was now listening to Cesare. Ya Lin had picked up and packed her lingerie and was throwing slacks into a suitcase.

Finally Nova heard her mother's voice. Thank heaven.

"Hello, sweetheart. It's so good to hear your voice."

"Hi, Mom. I love hearing yours, too. I'm calling because I urgently need to get in touch with Star. Do you know where she is right now?"

"Yes. She and William are on the boat in Catalina, along with the boys."

Nova imagined Star snorkeling or hiking or sailing. It might be quite some time before she checked her messages. "I'd also like to get in touch with Maggie. Do you, by any chance, know how to contact Maggie or the Robertsons in Italy? Perhaps you know the name of the tour group they are with."

"No, dear. Sorry. Are you still in Costa Rica?"

"No. That tour is over. And I wish I could talk longer but I'm with another group and right at the moment I'm really busy. I will call back later."

"You sound terribly stressed. Is anything wrong?"

"No, Mom. Don't worry."

"Please take care of yourself. You are always doing such dangerous things on those tours."

"Yes, I'll take care. I love you."

"I love you, too."

Nova hung up, her hands trembling slightly. Now she had to concentrate. She checked her watch. Five-ten. *Think.*

Joe said, "Well, major shit has hit the fan. Cesare says they have to try to figure out what to do without causing a monumental panic. We should meet him at the van." Ya Lin had disappeared into her closet. "He says the authorities are approaching the front door as we speak to arrest Ya Lin."

Nova walked to the door of a closet roughly the size of her dining room and called to Ya Lin. "I want to thank you from the bottom of my heart for being honest with us."

She joined Joe and they headed for the bedroom door, but Ya Lin burst from the closet. "No, no," she yelled. "You can't leave. I want to help you. If I don't help you, you'll die, too."

Chapter 27

"Maybe he didn't lie to me," Ya Lin said, her face flushed with excitement and fear.

Nova turned back to see the actress throw the skimpy dresses she'd brought from the closet onto the bed. Her face still stiffened by urgency if not panic, Ya Lin hurried on. "Why would he lie such an elaborate lie? I'm still leaving Italy. I'm taking no chances. But I want to help if there is any chance you can stop him."

What the heck is she talking about? Absolutely baffled, Nova waited.

Ya Lin rushed to her bathroom and returned carrying a leather cosmetic bag embossed with her initials. She laid it on the bed next to the half-full suitcase and opened it. Lying in the center, something had been wrapped in white tissue paper. Ya Lin stripped back the paper to reveal three vials, each of which was topped with a stubby, capped needle.

"He gave me six. He said that if I injected one under my skin it would make me immune within two hours."

"IMMUNE!" Nova gasped in unison with Joe.

"If the man is right. If I took the drug right. I don't want to stay here in Italy and find out. But I give these to you." She picked up the three vials and pressed them into Nova's hand. "You can use them, and then maybe you will be immune. And that might help you, or at least save you, if you try to stop him. Then perhaps I can feel less guilty."

Ya Lin was right. If the drug conferred immunity within a matter of hours, even partial immunity, the chances of stopping these madmen would be tremendously increased. Otherwise, approaching them without wearing bulky and confining HAZMAT gear would be a death sentence.

Joe said, "He told you it takes two hours to work?"

"He said it would help right away, and for certain I would be safe in two hours. I didn't feel he was sure himself."

Nova grabbed the actress. "Thank you."

She heard steps outside the bedroom and then three men appeared at the door, two in uniforms and one plainclothes. They nodded to her and Joe. The last thing Nova heard as she and Joe bolted down the curving stairway was one of the officers informing Ya Lin that she was under arrest.

The moment they reached the van, Cesare said, "Surveillance says the guy who visited Ya Lin this morning around seven is a fish dealer from Positano. Ahmad al Hassan. We have an address. Get in. We'll drive and by the time we get there, maybe SISMI will have decided what in the name of all the saints they want to do or can do. There is talk of immediately putting a quarantine on all of southern Italy, if you can believe that. Imagine the chaos. Oh my."

"Wait, Cesare," Nova said. "See these." She showed him the three vials and began to explain that they would presumably provide immunity. As she was talking, she popped the cap off one vial. She had already decided. Without immunity or without wearing HAZMAT gear, approaching these men, one or more of whom might be a carrier, was a death sentence. Immunity would give her mobility. Freedom to act. Better odds for success in stopping them.

"What are you doing?" Cesare said.

She looked at Joe for a moment, and then slid the needle under the skin on her inner left arm. The thing self-injected the contents. Only a drop of surplus clung to the bottom, something the CDC could use for analysis. The site of injection burned like hell. She caught her breath.

Cesare exploded. "What have you done?"

Joe took a second vial from her and injected it similarly.

"You two are crazy. You are out of control. You have no business, no right, to do that," Cesare yelled.

"There is one last vial." She offered it to him. "It will be quite a few hours before we're likely to get any vaccine over here to Italy from the CDC. Until we do, any contact with these bastards will be deadly."

"I don't…I don't know."

Joe, man of action, shook his head at Cesare's dithering. "If we get over to Positano and this Hassan bastard is contagious and is still there, you know what's going to happen to you if you don't at least try it."

Gingerly, Cesare took the vial, looked into her eyes. She said, "Burns like the devil."

He gave her a weak smile, then injected.

She took back all three vials, wrapped them up and, after the three of them climbed into the van, put them into its glove compartment for safekeeping and for analysis as soon as Provenza could arrange for it.

Joe said, "It's half past five. By half past seven, we should have full immunity."

"That's the theory. I can understand why Ya Lin kept saying she wasn't sure the man hadn't lied. Maybe we'll have immunity. Maybe not. The 'maybe not' possibility is very, very scary."

"Do you think this Ebola affects dogs?" Cesare asked as Joe burned rubber.

She ignored Cesare, thinking now at double speed about what they might find in Positano. And what, if anything, they were going to be able to do to stop a nightmare from being unleashed.

She pulled out the cell phone and punched in Star's number. Again, only the answering machine.

"Who?" Joe said.

"Remember my niece?"

"Oh, shit. Sorry I didn't think of her sooner. Where the hell is she?"

"I don't know. And I can't reach Star."

Chapter 28

Traffic on a Sunday afternoon on the coast drive sometimes could be not just bumper to bumper but stalled. The traffic gods favored them, though, and they made it back to Positano in quick time.

SISMI had taken control of the situation from local police, and when Joe drove up to the apartment house at the address Provenza had given Cesare, the place where the fish dealer had gone after leaving Ya Lin, they found it surrounded, after a fashion. Four large white vans the size of small moving trucks, presumably from city gas services, sat outside, two in front and two in back, but there wasn't a man in sight.

In fact, there wasn't a person in sight. Cesare was now in almost constant contact with Provenza, and Provenza informed him that SISMI had already arranged that no foot or car traffic be allowed into the area

within a four-block radius. Guards only allowed the Laforza to join up with the SISMI teams in front of the
suspect location after all three of them had shown ID
at the blockade. Cesare was immediately recognized as
being top on-site command.

A trim mustached man of about forty wearing a special ops all-black jumpsuit stepped out of the back of
one of the two vans at the front of the house. He gestured for Cesare to come to the customized special ops
transport. Nova, Joe and Cesare climbed inside.

"Serge Alonza," the special ops guy said, introducing himself to Cesare.

Four other men sat on jump seats. HAZMAT gear
hung on pegs along one sidewall but all of the men still
wore only black special ops suits.

*If it were me and I were in their shoes, I'd be wear-
ing one of those damn bubble bags no matter how awkward or uncomfortable they are.*

She checked her watch to find out how much time
had passed since she had injected the vaccine. Roughly
forty-five minutes. Long enough to give her some protection from whoever might be inside the house, but not
long enough to be safe—assuming, of course, that Hassan had not lied to Ya Lin.

"Here's the deal," Alonza said in English, presumably for her benefit and Joe's, working on the assumption that like the majority of Americans he met, they
didn't speak the language. "Headquarters still hasn't
given us the go-ahead to enter the premises. The sight
of HAZMAT suits on the street would set off a flash-
fire of questions and attract immediate media attention. We expect to get instructions pretty quick to wear

normal gear to clear all civilians off this block, and then, when there are no witnesses, we can go into the house in the HAZMATS. For that matter, we still don't know if there is anyone inside."

Alone and depressed, Ahmad sat slumped on the sofa of the apartment house, elbows on knees, chin propped in his hands, staring at the news channel on the television. Everything so far with Operation Awesome Vengeance had moved perfectly on schedule and with no hitches. But he could not find Saddoun, and something ominous roiled in the pit of his stomach.

He had picked up the Ebola and the vaccines from the extraordinarily beautiful Ya Lin as planned. He had injected himself with the vaccine, as had all the bodyguards. He was now safely immune. Ali had been given the slightly weakened version of the virus that triggered a partial immunity. An hour later, he had been given the full dose that turned him into a walking carrier of death and by now he was exactly that—and carrying vengeance into the heart of Italy. In ten or twelve days, however, he too would die. This was his sacrifice.

The thing was, Mohsin had called right after they injected Ali to say that he had taken Nissia and the girls to the airport and they were safely out of Italy, but that Saddoun had not been with them.

Ahmad had spent the rest of the morning and all of the afternoon searching for Saddoun. None of his son's three friends had seen him or knew where he might have gone. Ahmad had checked the closest soccer field and two others more distant. He'd checked for over an hour at the mall.

He could not imagine why the boy had disobeyed so outrageously. The punishment, when Saddoun was found, must be severe. But the horror twisting Ahmad's gut was that if Saddoun extended his rebellion beyond today, perhaps fearing how severely he would be punished, he might hide out for, say, three or maybe four days.

Three or four days, and he could contact someone infected and then die himself.

The cell phone rang and Ahmad jerked upright so hard he felt a sharp pain in his lower back. *Mighty and merciful Allah, I beg You to let it be Saddoun.* "Yes," he said. "Ahmad al Hassan."

"This is Alberto," said the familiar deep voice of his contact with La Cosa Nostra.

The usual anxiety this voice always evoked got mixed with crushing disappointment that it wasn't Saddoun. Ahmad could barely get out, "Yes."

"This is a warning. We have information from Rome that something big is happening in Amalfi, and that the authorities will be on your doorstep in minutes, if they aren't already there."

The phone went dead.

Ahmad leapt to his feet. His thoughts reeled. He must get home at once. And do what? No, he thought. *I must not go home at all. I must go someplace. But where?* What authorities? What do they know? *Should I call Khangi? And tell him what?*

He was very confused, that he realized, but he wasn't so confused that he would forget to take the tape Ali had made. He ejected it from the VCR, put it into a Ziploc bag and into his jacket pocket. He shrugged into the shoulder holster carrying the Beretta semiautomatic. He did not intend to be taken alive.

He put on the jacket, looking around the clutter of the room with its pizza boxes and miscellaneous debris from having men living without the care of women for nearly three weeks. No time now to sort through it all. He could think of nothing incriminating, even if the authorities were to find the place. He had the tape. That's what counted.

Chapter 29

"**B**oss," the special ops man in the van's driver's seat called out in Italian. "Someone's coming out of the house."

Nova and everyone else in the back of the van looked out the one-way glass windows. "That's him," Serge Alonza announced.

Cesare asked the question everyone had to be thinking, the question that had them all momentarily paralyzed. None of them had put on HAZMAT gear, and no one was eager to die. "Do you think he's contagious?"

Ahmad al Hassan dashed through the gate in the wooden fence toward a car parked directly in front of the house, directly across the street from the van. He jumped inside, and Nova gingerly got to her feet, still being careful of the ankle. She bent over Cesare, stuffed her hand into his pants pocket and fished out the La-forza's keys. Hassan pulled into the street as Nova's feet hit the pavement.

Limping slightly, she ran for the SUV. If this guy got away, they might lose their only chance to stop this monstrous machine of death before it could reach out to all of Italy. To all of the continent. To Maggie.

She slid into the driver's seat and burned rubber as she spun the van in a U-turn up onto the tiny front lawn of the apartment house, taking down the wooden fence. Principessa barked twice. Nova passed Joe. No time to stop and pick him up. No time to stop and let Principessa out.

Hassan crashed right through the wooden saw horses and tape that made up the police barrier intended to keep the public out, and clearly inadequate to keep Hassan in. Nova kept tight on his tail.

She glanced into the rearview mirror and saw several policemen scrambling toward their car doors.

To pass a tiny Smart car, she swung the SUV into the oncoming lane and nearly ran headlong into a lime-green Volkswagen. The squealing of her tires and the tires of the VW apparently reached even Hassan because she saw him checking her out in his rearview mirror.

At the next intersection, he made a hard, fast right, and when she followed, he stepped on the gas still more, swerving into the oncoming traffic to pass a red car in front of him. She glanced to the passenger seat. Principessa had curled up into a tiny white fluffy ball, her nose hidden under her haunches. Smart dog.

They wove downhill, in and out of traffic, until he

took a sharp left. They were leaving the relatively un-populated suburbs, getting closer to the heavily popu-lated center of town. Time to stop him.

She swung into the passing lane.

He swerved left and blocked her.

They both swung back into their lane, she behind him, as three cars passed. An intersection loomed ahead. She made her decision, gave the Laforza gas right into the oncoming traffic. Cars ran off the road into parking lots and onto sidewalks as she zoomed up beside Hassan's sedan.

He gave his car more gas and they raced through the intersection. Cars were still dodging her. She was ei-ther going stop Hassan or kill herself, and maybe a lot of other people.

Just short of the next intersection, she turned the car across the bow of the sedan. "Hang on, Principessa. This guy is going down."

Metal screeched, the wheel jerked in her hands, but she kept control.

Hassan slammed into a sidewalk vendor. Pottery shot into the air and crashed onto the sidewalk and her windshield. She braked just short of ramming into a dress shop, jumped out, grimacing with pain as she slammed the door to keep Principessa inside.

Hassan was already running.

She pulled out the Glock. *"Basta!"* she shouted, as she raced after him, her ankle screaming in agony. She shot into the wooden storefront to Hassan's left.

A woman and a girl about Maggie's age had stepped out of the shop just before Nova fired. Hassan grabbed the girl and whirled around, holding the girl with what looked like a Beretta semiautomatic in his right hand aimed at the girl's head. Her mother started screaming.

Alive. Need him alive.

Nova stopped, took aim at his right shoulder and fired.

His arm jerked. The Beretta went off twice, but neither shot hit the girl or her mother. Nova had only a moment to feel a rush of gratitude that her risk of the girl's life for Hassan's capture had paid off. This game was for high stakes.

He clutched his shoulder and moaned. Nova rushed him, kicked the Beretta out of his hand. Kicked him again, this time on the side of his right knee, a hard blow that if delivered right was guaranteed to bring him down and probably cripple him.

Screaming, he fell onto the cement on both knees.

"You shitty bastard," she muttered in English.

Hearing her, he spat out, "Go ahead!"

With a squealing of tires and the accompanying smell of burnt rubber, one of the SISMI vans halted beside them. All traffic had stopped. The mother grabbed her daughter, and both ran back inside the store.

Joe jumped out of the SISMI van and grinned that oh-so-cocky grin. "You know, babe, it's you and me against the world. For better or worse."

Babe. Joe had never called her *babe* before. Did she like it?

Yes, she did.

Joe pulled Hassan to his feet, and grabbed something out of Hassan's jacket pocket. A closer look revealed a videotape. He said, "Let's get back to Cesare and to the apartment house. Maybe there will be a VCR there and we can see what's on this tape he thought so important to bring with him."

"You know what?" Joe said to Hassan as he marched him toward the SISMI van, which presumably came equipped with handcuffs, "It's too bad we need you alive. I'm a connoisseur of scents. Perfumes and such. Bad odors are something I hate, something to be disposed of as soon as possible. And you are one of the worst stinks I've ever smelled."

Chapter 30

Joe marched Hassan into the apartment's living room and they immediately became the center of attention. Cesare and the SISMI team were already inside, all dressed in HAZMAT gear.

Cesare said, "Is he talking?"

Nova answered. "No. And I wouldn't trust anything he says anyway."

"Then we will keep on this gear. Provenza says that the Centers for Disease Control in Atlanta is fairly certain that the Reston strain most likely involved in this mess can only live outside a host for ten or twenty minutes. In twenty minutes, if we left it empty, the house would probably be safe. But if Hassan is either infected or the carrier, this place is fatal at present for the unprotected. And for now, I'm considering myself unprotected." His tone changed from commander to worried man. "May I ask, I almost fear to ask, where is Principessa?"

"She's okay, Cesare. I left her in the SISMI van."

"I do thank you, love. Really I do."

Joe held up the videotape. "He had this on him."

"Then we must play it at once." Cesare lifted the tape from Joe's hand and turned to the VCR and TV.

The six SISMI guys had apparently already done a thorough job of searching everything in the living room. All except their team leader, Alonza, shambled into the bedrooms and bathroom.

Cesare said, "While you were in pursuit, we interviewed the neighbors. It seems that six to eight men have been living here, and they left together around three-thirty this afternoon."

Nova pressed the buttons on the VCR. After a few seconds of white static, the face of a young man appeared on the screen. A date and time stamp indicated that the tape had been made yesterday, Saturday.

"My name is Ali Yassan," he said in Arabic. She watched in horrified fascination as this young boy— maybe fifteen or sixteen—explained to his family and friends that the next day he would begin a journey of vengeance against the decadent West, specifically the Italians who persisted in siding with the Great Satan, the United States of America. He would be famous. He explained that he would be well guarded as he made this journey.

They stopped the tape at regular intervals to let her translate into English. Ali proudly said that the money that would come to his family would help them buy a new home. How painfully obvious the look in his face was to Nova, as he smiled at his loved ones, that this money for his family was his great concern. Much more important than the words of glory he was reciting. And finally, he said that his family should not grieve even though, in the end, the journey would take his own life.

"Allahu Akbar," he said, his tone triumphant, his eyes bright with youth. "God is great," she translated. These were the first words a Muslim child hears upon entering this world, the father making the call to prayer in the child's ears as the welcome-to-this-world message. The same call heard wherever there are Muslims, five times a day. The last words his family would ever hear from him.

Nova felt sick. She stood and went into the kitchen and, loath to use any utensils anyone in this house had used, cupped her palm to take a long drink from the tap. So this was the face of the carrier, not the coward of middle age, al Hassan.

She walked back into the living room and to Hassan. In Italian, she said to him, "I cannot tell you how much I loathe you old men who send young men to die and to kill others."

"You don't know what you're talking about, woman."

She turned away. She checked her watch, now showing six-thirty. "Looks like you and your guys can take off all that gear," she said to Alonza in English. "I'd bet Mr. Creep here took the same vaccine Joe and I and Cesare have taken and he took it hours ago. He's not the carrier, and he's also not infected."

"I agree," Cesare said.

Joe said, "It's half past six. My guess is that this Ali Yassan probably injected early this morning, as well. In which case, he'd be fully lethal right now. The question is, where is he?"

Alonza strode to the dining room table where the SISMI team had spread out items found in the house in neat order for cataloguing. "Take a look at this," he said.

She, Joe, and Cesare joined him. He held a crumpled brochure, now smoothed out again, that looked as if it had been retrieved from a wastebasket, an advertisement for a rock concert starring the dark, edgy, duster-coat-wearing rock band Doomsday. It was to be held in Rome, outside the Coliseum, this very evening. Time, 20:00. Eight o'clock.

"Well, well," she said.

Joe added, "I can't imagine a much better, or more symbolic, opportunity to infect as many Italians and spread the disease any faster than attending a rock concert by a group like Doomsday."

Terrorists like Al Qaeda loved symbolism. The tragic attack on the Spanish train had come on 3/11, two years and six months exactly after the infamous 9/11 attacks in America. They would love the symbolism of a rock band with a name like Doomsday, and had probably picked the Coliseum event precisely because of the band's ominous name.

Cesare pointed to several badly copied white sheets. "Look at the train schedules. See, this one has a pencil mark beside Rome. I would say that they are making for the city by train. Let's see. If they left the house at three-thirty, they might have been in Naples to catch the direct Eurostar for Rome at five-thirty or six. Not sooner than that. But in any event, they may possibly already be in Rome."

Nova could not stop the thought of all the people that Ali Yassan had already doomed as he traveled to Naples, and then to the capital. "You have to tell Provenza, right now, to quarantine all of Italy," she said to Cesare. "Panic or not, you guys can't let this goddamn germ escape this peninsula."

She strode back into the kitchen and punched in Star's number. Mercifully, Star answered.

"It's me. Nova. I've left you message after message."

"We just got back from dinner at the Isthmus. I haven't picked up my messages yet."

"Star, where—exactly where—in Italy, is Maggie? Don't I remember you saying that they were going north? Portofino?"

"Yes."

"I don't want to alarm you excessively. But I am in Italy now. I'm on a tour and we have a tour member who is…who is a government insider. And he tells me that something really bad is going to happen here soon. I can't say just what at the moment. You just have to trust me, okay? You have to call the Robertsons and tell them to cut short their trip immediately."

"What in the world are you talking about?"

"Listen to me, Star. I don't mean they should cancel their trip tomorrow. I mean you must call them as soon as we stop speaking. And you must tell them to go immediately to the nearest airport and buy tickets, no matter what the cost, and leave Italy. Frankly, they should not stop to pack."

A dead, eerie silence fell between them.

Finally, from half a world away, "You are scaring me shitless, Nova."

"I'm sorry. It's important that you must believe I know what I'm asking, and that it's every bit as important as I say it is. Do you believe me?"

"You've seldom been wrong, except about men." Star chuckled, not very strongly.

"Will you do what I ask and then call me back when you have reached them? I don't want to spend time talking. Time is too valuable."

"I will do exactly as you say. It may take some heavy-duty convincing."

"Convince them, Star. You must."

"I'll do what you say, love."

"Then I'm hanging up. I love you. And I adore Maggie."

She hung up.

When she entered the living room, Cesare looked at her with narrowed eyes. "Who did you call?" he asked. "You know that this information is classified."

Joe said, "Did you reach her?"

"Yes."

"Good."

"I want to know what's going on," Cesare said, his lips drawn into thin lines, his eyes snapping anger.

"Okay, I called my sister in California to tell her to make my niece fly out of Italy ASAP."

Cesare's face softened immediately. "You have a niece here. I'm sorry. I have an entire family here. And I called them while you and Joe were off catching the creep, as you call him. We say no more."

Alonza joined them from the bedroom. He'd taken off the HAZMAT suit.

"Provenza informs me that this is our status as of now," Cesare said. "The Centers for Disease Control immediately got in gear when they learned that the likely bug was Reston Ebola, and they already have a vaccine against the Reston strain on its way to us. Twenty or thirty doses. But it's like the Salk versus the Sabine vaccines for polio. There can be more than one way to induce immunity to these things, so the vaccine may not be the same as what we've taken. CDC has a limited quantity, but something is probably better than nothing. The first batches should arrive late this after- noon. But the unfortunate truth is that a vaccine is go- ing to come too late to be of much help. This thing is loose now. It's tragic there is no antidote, no antibiotic pill or injection that would cure the disease. What we have to do is stop the carrier and contain the spread.

"Our biggest problem perhaps is that we're not cer- tain it really is the Reston strain. Or, for that matter, that it's Ebola. We're going on the words an informant over- heard outside a window. Until we analyze the samples that Nova gave me, that seems the logical choice. The informant said Ebola and he said 'Rexton.' Reston is airborne. It all fits.

"The virus had to have gotten into their hands some time ago. We may never learn where it came from, al- though CDC is running down possible sources for a Reston leak.

"For now, everyone but us who contacts this carrier has either got to wear a HAZMAT suit or be willing to commit suicide. So we—you and Joe and I, Nova—are going to be taken to Rome by helicopter. We are to find and then apprehend, or even better, kill this Ali Yassan." He turned to Alonza. "Let's get to the van. You can drive us to the airport."

Chapter 31

On the helicopter trip into Rome Nova obsessed about Maggie, expecting to hear from Star at any moment. She found herself several times nervously fingering her gold studs. If Star didn't call, it meant that she had not yet reached the Robertsons and Maggie. The silence kept Nova's gut tightly twisted.

Cesare seemed jittery as well. With deep tenderness, he'd entrusted Principessa to a Positano cop with instructions to take the little Lhasa apso to the contessa for safekeeping until he returned. He kept twisting one or another of his four rings.

The helicopter swung over the great city that had been the center of the world for nearly two millennia, first as Imperial Rome and later as the Holy Roman Empire. The spectacular view of brightly lit monuments even penetrated her fog of worry: St. Peter's Basilica, the Castel Sant'Angelo, The Spanish Steps, the Vittorio Emmanuele Monument, and only, blocks from it, she could see their goal, the Coliseum.

To mark the site of the concert, two searchlights shot beams of dazzling white light into the sky from the piazza just outside the Coliseum, next to the Arch of Constantine.

The helicopter landed on the top of an office building not far from the Vittorio Emmanuele, probably the closest landing pad to the Coliseum. She knew this area of Rome intimately. On her last trip to Italy, she'd spent two weeks in the Eternal City and her hotel had been in this district between the Coliseum and the Central Train Station. Her feet had pounded these streets as she researched their nooks and crannies for many pleasurable hours.

Provenza, the Sicilian who reminded her of an Olympic wrestler, met them. Though still nattily dressed, bags under his eyes suggested lack of sleep and plenty of worry. His dark brown hair looked messed, and his sharp, unpleasant body odor hit her like a brick to the face.

They ran inside the building and down one floor into the spacious hallway of what were probably top-floor offices of someone highly important. Joe handed over the videotape. Provenza said, "We'll have Yassan's face on every news broadcast within the hour. I will e-mail one to both of your cell phones."

She asked, "What will the public be hearing?"

Provenza shook his head. "They are going to be told that this man is highly dangerous. That he is not to be approached under any circumstances, but that his presence should be reported immediately to the nearest authorities."

Cesare said, "So no one is being told he's sick?"

"Not now. Not yet. Everyone still thinks they can avoid panic, or at least they want to try to avoid panic as long as possible."

"What about quarantine?" Nova asked. "The minute you stop travel, people are going to panic. It's unavoidable. But a quarantine is essential."

"All flights in and out of southern Italy have been cancelled. The explanation is that something dire went wrong with the air traffic control system in this part of the country and flights will be resumed when it's fixed. We are also quietly shutting down any sailings."

In truth, she thought they should cancel all flights throughout the peninsula. But maybe if the north was still open, Maggie could get out. "How long will flights be allowed in the north?"

"Two more hours. Roughly the time it might take Yassin or someone he has contacted to reach the northern regions. Fortunately it's night. There's not much traffic of any kind now and it will rapidly drop off even more after twenty-two hundred. The border in the north has been shut down and people there are being detained—to keep them from talking with the media."

"If it were me," she said, "I'd be honest and tell these people what they're facing, and tell them to go into their homes for the next ten or twenty days and not come out."

"Well," Provenza said dryly, "it isn't up to you. Or to me."

Joe said, "There's no way to keep this bottled up very long."

An elevator arrived and the four of them stepped in. Provenza hit the button for the ground floor. "I quite agree. But how the politicians decide to handle the public isn't our problem. Our problem is to find and stop this bastard. And although it's not what I would do, the decision as to how to proceed is a political one, and the decision is for us to keep HAZMAT teams, SISMI, special ops or whatever, from public view as much as possible."

They arrived at the ground floor. Provenza led the way through the lobby, still explaining. "We have a SISMI HAZMAT-equipped van outside. It will take you to the Coliseum. The two men are wearing suits and have been instructed to stay inside. They will drive you wherever you need to go, but that's their limit."

Joe said, "Did you get me the XMSatTV player?" He'd called during the trip up from Positano and asked for Provenza to get him one of the palm-sized satellite TV players.

Provenza pulled it out of his suit pocket and handed it over. Joe punched and BBC News came up on the tiny screen.

"Why do you want it?" Provenza asked.

Joe slipped the player into his jacket pocket. "I want to know what the public is being told in real time, and I don't want to have to call you to find out."

At the door leading out, Provenza stopped again. "Now here's how it's going down. We're not stopping the concert because no one can be certain that's where these men are headed. The decision is again political, not practical. We have three take-out teams—shooter and spotter—already in place in buildings overlooking the piazza there. We also are still letting people into the concert area after the usual search, but no one is going to be able to leave. They will be quarantined. Between them, the take-out teams cover virtually the whole area. They only need to get a fix on the target to hit him. They're instructed to shoot to kill. You'll be in touch with them—headsets for each of you are in the van. Your job is to infiltrate the crowd and act as additional spotters. When they take out the target, two of you should protect the crowd from the body while the third gets a HAZMAT suit from the van. Wrestle the body into the HAZMAT body bag, and get it out of there with dispatch."

"Understood," Joe said. Nova nodded, as did Cesare.

Provenza opened the door and they strode to the van.

Joe opened the driver's door. "You guys get in back," he said to the SISMI men. "You look scary as hell." To Nova, he said, "You want to drive? I'd like to watch the TV."

"Fine. I know these streets."

The two SISMI men moved into the back of the van and Cesare joined them.

Provenza had also provided special IDs to get them past any security personnel plus small, high-powered binoculars, shoulder holsters and Glock automatics. She and Joe flipped their jackets open, indicating they already had their weapons. Cesare took one. Nova slipped a couple of extra ammo clips into the khaki jacket pocket. Joe was also wearing a dark brown jacket that did a good job of hiding bulges.

Seeing Cesare wearing a shoulder holster under his elegant white Armani silk jacket would have made her laugh if things weren't so dire. She just shook her head.

She threaded the van through narrow streets until they reached the Vittorio Emanuele and the broad Via dei Fori Imperiali. She called back to one of the SISMI men, "There isn't going to be any place to park. I'm going to stop the van at the next corner. One of you come up here and drive it off. Keep circling tightly in the area. We'll page when we want you to pick us up."

They hopped out and as the van took off, she tried her special ops headphone: "Ground One to Team Alpha. Do you read?" she said in Italian to establish that she was connected with the take-out teams.

"This is Alpha Team leader. We read you fine, Ground One," came the reply, also in Italian. They would stick to Italian, and she could hear clearly, even over the din of the warm-up band.

She checked out the other two take-out teams, Beta and Gamma. She was firmly connected to them, to Joe and to Cesare.

A crowd of mostly young, tattooed, nose-ringed, black leather-clad revelers packed the street leading to the concert site. For the occasion, the street had been blocked off to traffic. She, Joe and Cesare joined the throng, the whole mass moving nearly shoulder to shoulder.

There is no way we can find Yassin in this mob.

She checked her watch. Seven thirty-five. If Ahmad

al Hassan had told Ya Lin the truth, she, Joe and Cesare were now fully immune.

They showed IDs and passed through one of seven security check stands on the west side of the concert area. Once inside, they had a bit more room, at least this far back from the stage, located in the piazza center. Time to split up.

She took hold of Joe's arm. "See that spot on that fountain? It's up off the pavement, five feet or so. I'm going to perch there and scan from this west side. And let's pray we find this kid and find him fast."

"I'll go east," Joe said.

Cesare added, "I shall go around to the south side."

The two men took off at fast clips. Nova realized she still could only think of their target—this deadly missile—as a kid, not a man. And her job was to help someone blow him away.

Her cell phone vibrated. Given the crowd and the music, she strained to hear Star's voice. "Say that again," she half yelled back.

"The trip to the north, to Portofino, got cancelled. Maggie and the Robertsons are south of Rome, in the countryside outside of a place called Amalfi. They say it's just as nice, if not nicer."

Nova clutched the phone. "Give me her phone number, Star."

She punched the number into her phone's address book. Then she said, "Now I *do* want to scare you. You call Maggie back. They won't be able to fly out. It's too late. You tell her that she and the Robertsons must immediately buy enough food and water to last ten days. Even better, fifteen. Then they're to find a motel or hotel, someplace where they can shut themselves off from any contact with other people but have access to radio or TV, and go inside and not come out."

"My God, Nova. Please tell me what's happening. I don't know if I can reach her. They were just on their way to dinner. She might not take her phone."

"I can't say. But it's a nightmare like you don't want to even imagine, and if you don't reach her in time, she may meet someone who will harm her. Do as I say, Star. I'll explain when I can. Or you may learn from the television, sometime tomorrow would be my guess. I have to go. Please do as I say."

Nova hung up. She climbed onto the fountain, ignoring a number of disapproving looks. Using the binoculars, she scanned the crowd, starting with those closest to the band and working outward.

She wondered where the take-out teams were located but kept her glasses scanning the crowd. *This is nuts! There are thousands of people here.*

Then luck struck. Joe's voice came through her communicator, "Team Leader, I've spotted Target. He's with another man. Both wearing black dusters. They're about 150 feet northeast of Ground One's position on the fountain, heading toward Ground One. Ground Three, let's form up on Ground One's location."

"Affirmative," Cesare said.

"This is Team Beta. I have Target acquisition. Moving too fast for a good opportunity."

Nova paused, scanning the crowd with the binoculars, feeling the beat of her pulse against her eyes.

Then she saw him. A bareheaded kid accompanied by a hefty six-footer with a military-style haircut. The kid was so short she realized the take-out team would have a hard time getting him in the crosshairs in such a tight crowd.

She imagined both men on Team Beta, the spotter and the shooter, with their scopes fixed on Ali, his moving head their target.

Ali moved left toward a stand selling some kind of food and Butch Cut followed.

"This is Team Beta. I've lost Target."

Chapter 32

"I still have a clear view," Nova said. "Target is buying something to eat. Wait a minute. The vendor has a small TV set. Target and his buddy are looking at it."

She zeroed the binoculars onto the tiny TV screen. It framed a face, but too far away and at a bad angle for her to recognize whose it might be.

Ali and Butch Cut, however, remained bent forward, clearly transfixed by what they were seeing.

"Target and buddy—"

She barely got the words out of her mouth. Butch Cut grabbed Ali's arm, spun the kid around, and the two of them took off toward the west entrance, shoving their way through the throng.

"Target is fleeing to west entrance," she said. She jammed the binocs into a pocket, scrambled down from the fountain's decorative rim and pursued, pushing her way past pissed off or bewildered people. Her ankle burned, but she'd bound it with sports tape on the helicopter. Though her ankle protested, it didn't slow her.

"Team Beta, this Alpha Team Leader. Get a shot before he gets away."

"No clear opportunity."

"Take a shot, Beta!"

Off to her right, Joe was shoving his way against the truffic flow and toward the entry. She imagined Cesare somewhere off to her left doing the same.

A gunfire volley shattered the air ahead of her, splintering angrily over the already almost deafening volume of the warm-up band. Six, eight, maybe ten shots from automatics. People started screaming, running, shoving.

"Fuck off," a girl swore at Nova in Italian, and hit her with a purse.

Nova barely noticed.

In maybe eight seconds she reached the perimeter where the security checkpoints had been set up. A wall of Roman police uniforms struggled to hold back a surging mass of people scattering in all directions, including away from the Coliseum. And on the ground lay what looked to be six or seven wounded or dead uniformed security guards and at least five civilians. She thought one of the dead, dressed all in black, might be a terrorist. If not, the terrorists had all gotten away.

She did not see Ali or Butch Cut. Joe reached her side, followed a second later by Cesare.

"What do you think?" Joe asked Cesare. "Would they have transport nearby?"

"If so, God help us," Cesare answered. "But they came by train. More likely, given this enormous crowd, they are on foot."

"The subway," she said. "Let's try it. I know exactly where the nearest entrance is. No more than two blocks."

She took up the chase, praying Cesare's guess was right and that Ali and Butch Cut were on foot.

The subway entrance, she knew, led to both A and B lines. She stopped at the kiosk selling newspapers, tobacco, subway tickets and the like, and whipped out her cell phone. She pressed the buttons that would bring up Ali's photo.

The kid's picture came up, just like on the videotape, only smaller. "Have you seen this man?" she asked the mustachioed Italian.

"Sure," he replied in English. "He and some others just came through here. Into the subway. Crazy-looking bunch. But the crazies are all over the place tonight."

Joe asked, "Are you sure they were all together?"

"At least six."

She followed Joe and Cesare wasn't far behind her as they clambered down the metal stairs. Joe headed for a turnstile. She yelled, "Wait, Joe!"

A university-age woman playing Mozart on her violin stood close to the wall. Breathing hard, Nova gasped out to her, "I'm following this kid. He came down here with others. Did you see them?"

"A bunch all dressed in black?" the woman said.

"Right. What line did they take?"

"Toward Termini Station. It just left." The girl pointed.

Joe changed direction and the three of them leapt over the turnstile.

"Do you know how long before the next train, Nova?" Cesare asked. "You seem to know this area surprisingly well."

"Not that well."

They waited. She thought for an insane moment about going upside so she could use her cell phone to try to reach Maggie, but no way could they risk missing the next train.

Joe stared at the static on the screen of his mini-TV. "My guess is they saw Yassin's picture and are on the run. Like Provenza said, they are still saying he's dangerous and to report him, but not why."

"Right. Right. And I bet that's why they picked the line that runs to Termini Station. They'll take a train out of Rome, and they'll be spreading death with every breath the carrier breathes out."

"Dear Madonna," Cesare said. "When will the damn subway come?"

She felt as though she counted on her fingers every second of the next five minutes. Early in the seemingly interminable wait, Joe said, "Let's go to the street and call the SISMI van to come and get us."

"No," she and Cesare said at the same time. Cesare continued. "We are only two or three stops from Termini Station. The van could never get us there as fast as the train, even if we have to wait another five minutes for it. Street traffic and all that.

"When we get there," Cesare went on, "follow me. I know where the main ticket office for the trains is."

At the Termini stop, they rushed out together and

raced through the tiled tunnel, up the stairs and into the enormous reception gallery. Again, she checked the time. Eight o'clock on the nose. Shops lined both sides of the gallery and ran down the center. Perfume from one of the duty-free shops scented the main area.

"Follow me," Cesare commanded. The speed with which the interior decorator could change his colors to become an extremely competent agent reminded her of the near instantaneous speed of a squid changing the color patterns of its skin.

Cesare walked to the head of a line of eight people, showed the ticket seller his ID and then the picture of Ali on his cell phone. "Have you seen him?"

"Yes. Another man, big guy with short hair, just bought tickets for him and seven others on the Eurostar to Munich. Eight all together."

"Excellent," Cesare said. "When does it leave and on what track?"

"Leaves on Track 11," the man said. "But you're too late to catch him. It took off five minutes ago."

"Shit," Joe muttered.

"Other people were in line," Nova said, leaning toward the ticket seller. "Did they all buy tickets to the same train. The Eurostar to Munich?"

"I can't recall."

"Try," she said firmly.

"Well, certainly not. About that same time, I sold tickets to Geneva and Paris. I believe also to Marseille."

They withdrew to reorganize. "At least we know where they are," Cesare said.

"Assuming they did get on the train," Joe countered.

"I think we've got no reason to doubt that," Cesare

said. "They can't know we are following them." He fell silent, chewing his lower lip.

"You know," she said, "this is the nightmare the world has been fearing. This guy has physically contacted who knows how many at the Coliseum, in the subway, a number of people on four trains and probably as many people as he could here in the station. Maybe we can catch or hold the trains, prevent anyone in the area around the Coliseum from going home or running loose, but there is no way to quickly bottle up the people he contacted in the subway or just wandering around here in the terminal."

Jose said, "Call Provenza, Cesare. Tell him that in our view he needs to do a global quarantine of Italy, ASAP."

Cesare called and conveyed the news, then she said, "Track 11, right?"

"Right."

"Let's go see it."

They walked quickly, three abreast, to the head of Track 11. It was, as the ticket seller had said it would be, empty.

"Look at those." Nova pointed to four off-road dirt bikes lined up on a heavy-duty cart, obviously ready to be loaded soon onto the train on Track 10.

Chapter 33

Nova considered their orders. They were to stop the carrier, alive or, even better, dead. They had been fortunate to find him. They must not lose contact with him now if they could do anything to prevent it.

"Have you had any experience with off-road dirt biking?" she asked Joe.

"Plenty."

"Okay." She turned to Cesare. "I know you'll tell Provenza to put wheels in motion to stop and surround the train. But right now, we need to keep the kid in our sights."

She walked to a group of four light-haired, fair-skinned men standing next to the dirt bikes, Italian Ducatis. The men all looked to be in their late twenties. Joe and Cesare quickly flanked her. She flashed her ID. "English?" she asked.

She got one *"Ja"* and one "Yes."

"We're going to ruin your day. We need two bikes. It's an order, not a request." She glanced again at the bikes. "Give me the keys to the black and red ones."

"Why?" said the guy who had answered "Yes."

"Sorry, no questions. Just give me two sets of keys, unload the bikes quickly, please, and give your name and information to this man," she nodded toward Cesare, "and he'll see to it you get them back or are compensated."

"Do please be quick," Cesare added. He also flashed ID. The English speaker hesitated. "If necessary," Cesare said, "I can have you arrested." He pulled Nova back from the four, who had started to argue in German. "What are you thinking?" he asked. The English speaker apparently convinced his buddies they had no choice. The four men set to work unloading the two bikes.

"Joe and I are going to catch the damn train. Tell Provenza. Ask him to send us plenty of backup. And handle these guys."

Joe added, "Tell Provenza to contact the conductor. He's to tell the conductor to get someone to the back of the train to help us get on board. And he's to tell the conductor that once we are on board, we have full control of the train until SISMI stops and surrounds it."

"Yes. Yes, indeed."

The bikes were down. She turned to the man who spoke English. "They do have petrol, right?"

"Correct."

Without speaking or questioning her, Joe mounted the black bike and she took the red. As the bikes roared to life, she suffered a quick pang of doubt. She hadn't done any off-road riding for more than ten years. She hoped her body would remember all the secrets to not killing herself.

The luggage-toting travelers all around them stopped to see what was happening, to decide if they should flee. After all, in these post-9/11 days, a public place was a potentially dangerous place.

The platform stood four feet higher than the tracks. Following Joe, she sped toward the far end in pursuit of the departed train.

Standing on the foot pegs, knees bent, she did a damn good wheelie, lifting the front tire slightly. The bike soared off the platform. There was a four-foot drop to the ground, and the rear tire hit first. Classic form. Still, when she crashed onto the concrete between the tracks of Lines 10 and 11, she bit her tongue badly enough to draw blood. Swallowing the salty taste, she gave the bike more gas to keep up with Joe.

They raced out of the station just outside Track 11's right rail. She stood, knees bent to absorb shocks. She was surprised when Joe swung right as far as he could, then back hard left, and did another wheelie and a jump that landed him between the rails.

She wondered why, but did likewise and discovered, to her surprise, that riding the ties wasn't bad. It reminded her of being in a speedboat on the ocean. If you went too slow, you slammed into every wave, but if you went fast enough, you simply skimmed the wave tops. That's what they were doing now, skimming the ties, her legs and the bike's shocks cushioning the ride.

The fifteen lines of track rather quickly decreased to

only three feeder lines and then finally there was only one set of rails rolling out in front of them. Up ahead, the tracks started to curve to the left. Outside the tracks, the concrete had changed to dirt.

Joe did another jump, a crazy jump at what seemed to be an impossible angle, that put him outside the tracks. She held her breath and prayed, aimed at the rail, and did a wheelie, clinging to the belief that if Joe could do it, she could, too.

Her rear tire smacked into the rail. She launched and landed in a skid. She used her balance, the accelerator and her leg to just barely keep from going down. When she regained control, her throat was so tight she couldn't breathe. *My God, he's insane!*

They had plenty of room to maneuver for a while on the flat hardpan over which the rails lay, but then the space outside the track started narrowing. She focused tightly to keep on the narrow path between the ends of the ties on her left and a foot-high concrete strip on her right. Hitting the concrete would flip her for certain at this speed and, without a helmet, she'd probably be killed.

Soon, though, they were back on flat dirt. Her thighs were still hanging in there, not tiring yet from standing on the foot pegs to cushion the potholes and bumps.

They were still within the city and going no more than thirty miles per hour. They would have to catch up before the train left the suburbs and increased speed, or they'd lose it.

Twice they had to slow and leave the tracks to zoom around a station, leaving startled Italians in their wake. Her thighs started burning, but when she tried to sit, the jolting was unbearable.

Finally, she glimpsed the train's shiny silver rear end. At this point, the train was passing behind run-down apartment buildings. The tracks were elevated a bit, and a few feet to her right the embankment sloped down four feet into a ditch. Eurostars were Europe's high-speed marvels, especially in France. Italian tracks, however, still couldn't accommodate the one-hundred-and-eighty-mile-per-hour-plus speeds that the trains were capable of reaching. Still, the sleekly streamlined "bullet" trains could move along at a fast clip. She guessed the train was still doing thirty to thirty-five miles-per-hour at the max, a speed they could match on their bikes.

They quickly caught up to the last car, the end trailer.

The last door, on the side and close to the car's rear end, remained closed. No welcoming conductor.

Joe pulled up toward the middle of the last car, next to windows. One by one, people looked out and saw her and Joe. Some waved. Most just looked perplexed.

But no conductor.

Joe gestured, waving his arm and then putting his closed hand to his cheek as though he were talking to someone on a phone—or wanted to talk to someone. Maybe she and Joe couldn't get on.

Then a thin man with a thin black mustache and a dark blue uniform appeared at a window. A passenger next to him pointed to Joe and to her. At the same moment Joe did, she pointed toward the end trailer's rear door, on the side almost at the end of the car.

The conductor or porter—whoever he was—simply stared at them.

She hit a rock; the front wheel of the bike jerked left.

She nearly lost it. She gunned the gas and leaned hard to stay upright. Half a foot more to the right and she would have spun down the embankment into the muddy water of the murky, weed-lined ditch.

The uniformed guy shook his head, lifted his palms up and shrugged in what was probably a universal gesture meaning, "I don't get it."

And then he pulled a phone out of his pocket.

He listened for a few seconds, then he closed the phone and gestured toward the last door and then withdrew into the train, heading toward the rear. He must have gotten the message that there was an emergency, that two agents were to come aboard and take charge.

She throttled back a bit. So did Joe. The silver door at the rear entry slid open revealing the three steps and then the platform of the gangway, upon which stood their thin train employee. Joe yelled in Italian, "I am going to jump on."

With no further explanation, Joe steered his bike onto the ties close up to the door, lifted his outside leg over the seat, and jumped onto the first, lowest, step. With an angry roar, the bike spun off behind him, somersaulting with a great, brown, muddy splash into the ditch.

Her turn.

She imitated Joe's moves, got close to the door, saw him grinning and holding out his arms, ready to catch if she should miss the step or failed to grab the handrails.

She leapt.

Chapter 34

Khangi slid his hand inside his dust coat and rested it on the butt of his Beretta. He felt reassured, and he needed that sense at the moment. Clearly something had gone wrong at some level because Ali's picture had been on the kiosk TV. The announcer had described Ali as extremely dangerous, to be reported at once but not approached. When a guard approached as they were leaving, he and his men had fired. At least four guards had been killed or wounded.

So how much did the authorities know? That was the question.

This Eurostar stopped in Florence and then Milan before going on to Munich. Their original plan called for them to get off and circulate in the stations of all three cities, and then buy tickets to Paris.

Two of the men carried backpacks with a change of clothing for each of them. That's what he'd do next. He'd have Ali and then the others change clothes, discreetly, one at a time, Ali first. Then, in Florence they would get off separately. Buy tickets to Milan separately. In fact, he should probably have them separate right now. Why hadn't he thought of that at once, when they were buying the tickets for this accursed train?

Having come forward from the rear of the car, his second-in-command, Talha, squatted beside him and spoke in Italian. "There's a boy right behind me. He has one of those satellite TV things and he just saw Ali's picture. I heard him say to his girlfriend that the person on the TV is on the train. They are talking right now about who they should call."

Khangi leaped to his feet, Beretta in hand. "He can't be allowed to call anyone. Which one is he?"

Following Talha, Khangi strode to the car's rear. People they passed, seeing the Beretta, murmured in alarm. When he reached a red-headed youth and Talha nodded, Khangi stuck the gun in the boy's face and snatched the mini-TV receiver out of his hands.

Looking around the car, Khangi yelled in Italian, "We are taking over this car. Don't anyone move."

His soldiers all leapt up and drew their weapons, including the four who carried the automatic rifles under their dust coats.

"Don't anyone move," Khangi repeated.

He ordered three of his men, including Ali, to search every person for a cell phone or any other means of outside communication while the other five stood guard.

A man near the rear door leaped up and started to

run out. Khangi shot him in the back. He fell facedown into the aisle.

The passengers sucked in a collective breath. A woman screamed and stood; Talha silenced her by hitting her with his Beretta. She fell back into her seat, unconscious. The man on the floor didn't die at once. Blood oozed out of the entry wound in his light pink shirt. Other women sobbed. Of course, within forty-eight hours virtually all of these people would be dead anyway and he'd given the man a quick and clean death—something they might all soon envy.

"Silence," he shouted. He had to shout it several more times and threaten with the Beretta to get the terrified passengers to shut up.

To Talha he said in Arabic, "Change of plans. They might be waiting for us in Florence. We must take over the train and stop it before it gets there. Get off at a place we choose, God willing. We'll take the whole train hostage. You take two men. Go forward and find the conductor. Don't alarm the passengers in other cars. We don't want them agitated. Any passenger that comes in here, they will stay. No one will go back to the rear. Understood?"

Talha nodded, signaled to two others, and the three of them went forward to find the conductor.

Chapter 35

Nova caught the first step and the handrails, and threw herself into Joe's arms. He hugged her tight. The rear door slid closed behind them.

She clung to him like a tango dance partner, her right leg between his thighs. With the train's gentle swaying, she could feel his every movement as if they were dancing—or making love. She couldn't look at him, but for a long moment she felt and thought nothing else, just his body and that she didn't want to let go.

Joe let go first. He climbed backward up the two steps to the platform, holding her hand to lead her up with him.

In English, their trainman said, "I understand we have a problem. I am to give you whatever assistance you need. What is wrong?"

"Are you the conductor?" she asked.

"No. I'm a porter."

Joe said, "So where is the conductor?"

"He is in the first car, dealing with first-class passengers. Taking their tickets and so on. He said there is an emergency. He instructed me to aid you. Can you, please, I would like to know, what is happening. He said he was told only that we are to do whatever you wish."

"We can't say just yet what's happening," she offered, realizing that would hardly satisfy him.

Joe punched in Cesare's number and asked for an update. When he hung up he said, "We do nothing yet. Just wait for instructions."

"Why isn't the train stopping?" she asked.

"He just said, wait."

"I want some privacy," she said, knowing that Joe would understand that she meant privacy from the porter. She stepped from the gangway through the door into the compartment of the end car and found herself by lavatories. Picking one, she closed the door behind her at the same time punching the number Star had given her.

Maggie's sweet voice answered. "Maggie, love," Nova said. "It's your aunt Nova."

"Auntie Nova! It's great to hear from you. I'm in Italy, you know."

"I've been trying to reach you. So has your mom."

"We just got back from dinner. I was just going to call Mom."

"I'm also in Italy—"

"Oooh. Neat."

"Maggie, hon, I can hardly explain anything, but

I'm going to tell you to do something and you have to do it. No questions. Just do it."

"Sure, Auntie Nova, okay. What's the deal?"

Nova asked where Maggie and the Robertsons were located exactly. It was an inn in a village not far north of Amalfi. They were on the third day of their trip and expected to leave tomorrow to go to the next town. When Nova explained that she wanted Maggie and all of the Robertson family to buy food and water for fifteen days, pay for rooms at the inn and go into those rooms and refuse to come out or have contact with any other living human being until news on the TV said it was safe to come out, Maggie fell dead silent.

"Did you hear me?" Nova asked.

"You gotta be kiddin', Auntie Nova."

"No, love, I'm not. Is Mrs. Robertson there with you."

"Uh-huh."

"Let me talk to her."

When Gayle Robertson came on the line, Nova said, "Gayle, you must do what I say to save Maggie and your family. Literally save them from death." She lied, saying she was on a tour. No choices about that. She still could not tell all. She said she knew someone with inside information in Italy, explained what she wanted them to do and added that it was too late for them to fly out of the country.

Gayle's voice was full of doubt. "I just find what you're asking, well, are you serious? Why?"

"Gayle, do it. Your family's lives depend on what I'm asking of you. I know it's a lot to take on faith. But please, I beg you, do it."

To her credit, and perhaps due to the fact that Gayle had long been an admirer of what she called Nova's adventurous lifestyle, Gayle said solemnly, "I'll do what you say. For Maggie's sake, and for my own."

Nova rang off. Would holing up in an inn provide enough safety? Would they really do what she'd asked soon enough? What more could she do?

You need to stop thinking about Maggie now! Concentrate on what must be done right here in order to save thousands if not millions. Maybe including Maggie.

Chapter 36

"Man, I can't wait any longer," Joe muttered when Nova returned to him and the porter. "I have to know why we aren't stopping. This feels bad."

Exactly Nova's own sentiments.

Joe called Cesare and listened, tapping a finger against the phone the entire time.

"The plan," Joe said when he finished, "is to let the train reach a remote, depopulated area, and then have the engineer stop it. We'll surround it and quarantine everyone until the disease runs it course. They'll also do that with the other trains that recently left Termini Station."

The porter, a distressed wrinkle in his brow, echoed Joe. "Quarantine?"

She asked, "We don't do anything?"

"Not until we're given a go-ahead. About fifteen minutes before the train is supposed to stop, we find the carrier and the thugs and make sure the carrier doesn't escape from the train. That's the main thing he emphasized. We keep the carrier from getting off the train at all costs. Period. His exact words were, 'If you alarm the passengers or stir up anything prematurely, before we can get a quarantine in place, God knows what might happen. We can't risk it.'"

The porter grabbed her arm. "Now! I must know what is happening."

"This is Diego," Joe said, introducing the porter to her officially. "I've told him who we are, Jane and James Blake. I've also explained that we're armed because we're private security guards on vacation who just happened into the middle of some very nasty stuff. We've agreed to leave it at that."

She smiled at the porter, a man with a twinkle in his eye who probably had four kids and a wife who loved him. There was a fairly good chance that he had come in contact with Ali at some point. Maybe not. She hoped not. But then, many people on this train might very well die and there was absolutely nothing she could do about it.

"Well, Diego. We need your help, and I'm opposed to lying to people if I can avoid it. You do deserve to know."

She explained about Ali and that anyone in contact with him could fall deadly ill.

"You can, if you like, stay here at the back for as long as possible. I suppose that's what I'd do."

With eyes now as big as pasta plates, Diego said, "So, you two are going to die?"

"We're vaccinated against it. It's a long story that I can't share."

"Sweet Madonna." The man slumped against the gangway wall. "What about the rest of the crew? Can't I tell them?"

"Not yet," Joe said. "We let them behave normally until my partner and I receive instructions."

Diego stepped as far away from them as he could, probably not even aware of it, and probably because subconsciously he wanted to run as far as he could as fast as he could. But there was no place to run to.

Khangi had cleared passengers out of the front two rows of seats. The conductor in his dark blue uniform, beads of sweat on his upper lip and trickling down his forehead, sat in one of them, in front of Khangi. Talha held the conductor's fingers spread apart on the arm of the chair. From the sheath strapped to his calf, Khangi pulled out a knife with a seven-inch, serrated blade, designed for gutting or skinning.

"If I don't believe any of your answers, I'm going to cut off a finger," Khangi explained, his voice soft, calm, and firm. Given that the conductor had seen and reacted with appropriate fear to the dead man's body, left to lie where it had fallen, Khangi hoped he could easily obtain the answers he needed.

The conductor simply pressed his lips firmly together.

"How many porters are on this train, and do they know how to operate the emergency brakes?"

Those pressed lips failed to move.

Khangi pressed the sharp edge of the blade over the conductor's thumb. "I'm in a hurry. I'm not going to start with your little finger. I'll cut off your thumb and for the rest of your life you'll find out how impossible it is to do much of anything without one."

Rapid eyeblinking from the conductor.

"So I ask again, how many porters are on this train, and can they operate the emergency brakes?"

He pressed down on the blade and a little line of red appeared on the top of the thumb.

"I—I—I'll tell," the conductor blurted, then licked his lips.

"So?"

"There are six, one for each car. Some may know how to operate many things, but only I can order an emergency stop without an obvious cause, and only I have a key."

"A key. Let me have it."

With his left hand, the conductor pointed to one of the keys on a key chain that had already been taken from him.

Assured now that none of the train personnel could interfere with his plan of action, Khangi said to Talha, "Take Faroud with you, and take this man forward. Get control of the engine. Threaten to kill this conductor if the engineer doesn't want to let you into the engine cab. Have Faroud stay in the engine."

Saddoun said, "Let me go with Talha."

Khangi snorted. "Don't be ridiculous. You're too young."

Khangi turned back to Talha. "Once in the engine cab, Faroud is to take orders only from me. You come back and let me know when it's done."

Talha yanked the shaking conductor to his feet, and he and Faroud shoved the man toward the door leading to Car No. 2.

Khangi looked at al Hassan's eager son. Saddoun would have made a fine warrior, much against his father's wishes, but Allah had chosen otherwise. At three o'clock, just before they were to leave for Rome, Saddoun had shown up at the apartment and demanded to be included in the guard. He had simply walked inside. It was he who had listened from the bedroom to learn the time of meeting. There had been no chance to stop him. He had walked in and announced that his father had sent him.

For a moment, Khangi had been so shocked, as they all had, that nothing had been said. But then Khangi found his voice and had almost called Saddoun a liar. Sadness overcame anger however, and tamed his tongue. "You should not have come," he'd said. "And your father did not send you. But now that it's done and cannot be undone, let me explain exactly what is happening."

To his credit, Saddoun had taken his death sentence bravely. He had learned the time of the meeting, but nothing of the actual nature of the mission. "Then I will honor Allah and my father with a martyr's death," he had said.

"I will call him."

"No," Saddoun had protested. "Why anger or sadden him? Let him learn when we have achieved a great success. You can tell him then that I was brave."

Khangi smiled at Saddoun, sitting in his train seat with a sullen pout on his face. "So you want to do something? You get all these cattle," he gestured to the passengers, "to lie down on the floor."

Chapter 37

She had waited with growing impatience for more than ten minutes. Finally, Nova punched Cesare's number. He answered so fast she was certain their tiny electronic lifeline to him must be glued to his palm.

"What's happening, Cesare? We have to *do* something."

"They are trying to stop the train. But there seems to be a problem. I'll get back to you the moment I know something, Nova. I give my word. The train authorities say that the porter can contact the other porters using text message. Have him tell them there is an emergency and for their safety, they must not move about the train. They must sit tight wherever they are currently located. Unfortunately, we can't reach the conductor."

He hung up on her.

They must be very worried, she thought, for Cesare to sound so shaken.

Talha came through the door from Car No. 2 alone and immediately sent Khangi a clenched fist, the hand signal they used to indicate success. He said, "We can stop the train to get off whenever you say. Just tell Faroud and he will make the engineer do it."

Khangi strode to Ali and put his arm around the boy's shoulders. Ali was not a trained soldier, but he was doing his share to guard the passengers and had shown no signs of fear. Khangi admired him. Would have been proud to have a son like him. "We will get off just outside of Milan," he told Ali, sharing in the way of one man to another. "It's not a big change of plans. We will still succeed."

"God's will be done," Ali said.

Nova's cell phone buzzed. She picked up. Cesare spoke quickly, his voice taut and under control.

"We tried to pass word to the train's engineer to stop the train twenty-five kilometers short of Orvieto," he said. "But no one in the engine cab is responding now. And worse, the train will not respond to command directions from central control. It is on manual."

"And that means?"

"It means it will not respond to any automatic shutdown commands that might be sent from central control. The terrorists have, apparently, gained control of the engine car."

"Is there any way Joe and I can stop the train? By pulling an emergency brake cord or something?"

"The conductor has a key that unlocks boxes that have the control for an emergency stop. But we can't reach the conductor, either. Hold the line, please, for just a moment."

She responded to Joe's anxious look by shaking her head. "Not good."

Cesare came back on. "You can find out for certain if you break into a box. The porter can direct you to one. If a green light is showing, then the function is working. If there is no light, the function has been turned off by either the conductor or the engineer. And the bad news is that central control says their instruments indicate that the emergency stop has been disabled. They say the only way to control the train now is from the engine."

"We'll check it out. I'll get back to you."

To Diego, she said, "Show us where the nearest emergency brake box is located."

"It's right there," he said, pointing to a brown metal structure about the size of a big match box on the back wall of the end car gangway.

"Can you break it open, Joe?"

He grinned. "Sure. My pleasure. I'm throbbin' with an urge to break something open."

She smiled back. "Don't destroy it. Just open it."

He used the butt of the Glock. A forceful smack on the right side had no effect. A second forceful smack on the left side and the top of the box sprang open.

She saw a green tab inside on a digital pad—unfortunately not lit.

"So?" Joe asked.

Diego said, "We can't stop the train."

"Is that what they want?" Joe asked.

She answered. "They want to stop this damn thing at a spot twenty-five kilometers before we get to the next good-sized town. But they don't have contact with the engineer. They don't have control of the train."

"Then we need to get to the engine cab," Joe said.

She turned to Diego. "We're going forward. You stay here. It's as far away from harm as you're likely to get."

"This is a terrible thing." The twinkle in Diego's dark eyes had gone out some time ago. "If you need me, you call the number I gave James. I will come to you. If you need anything."

She squeezed his arm in unspoken gratitude.

With Joe leading, they entered the end car and strode forward. Everything seemed almost creepily normal. People reading, several already curling against the side of the car in preparation to sleep, a mother helping her little boy color in his coloring book. In the next car, the same scene. A man she passed had just poured himself a cup of coffee from a thermos. *God, I'd kill for a cappuccino.*

They entered the gangway between cars No. 5 and No. 4. While the noise level here rose noticeably, the closed doors blocked out much of the sound of wind rushing along the train's metal skin and the wheels gliding along the tracks at what she guessed was now about one hundred and forty miles per hour.

In the club car, business was slow; only eight people were nursing drinks.

They entered Car No. 4—and found chaos. The passengers in the last several rows at this rear end were seated, but staring forward. At the far end and even in the middle, people on their feet were exchanging excited gestures and ideas.

The first words she heard clearly, in Italian, were, "It was a gunshot. I'm sure."

Chapter 38

A woman sitting near the front of Car No. 4 was weeping. Another woman held a comforting arm around her. Nova heard someone reply to the comment about a gunshot.

"You keep saying that. Think so? Then what do you want to do?" The question came from a wiry man wearing paint-stained jeans, an equally paint-stained brown T-shirt, and carrying a laborer's hard hat.

She followed Joe past the seated passengers in the back, pulling out the ID Provenza had supplied that said she was a private investigator, Jane Blake. She held it up for inspection by the man who had claimed he'd heard a gunshot.

Joe said in Italian, "We may be able to help. We're private security guards and we're armed. What makes you think you heard a gunshot?"

The weeping woman turned around. Tears were digging rivulets through her makeup base. "My husband went forward after he heard the sound and he hasn't come back. When I tried to go find him, a man at the door of the car said no one was allowed forward. He was dressed funny. He's not a porter."

Sticking to Italian, Nova asked, "Is your husband the only one who went forward?"

The man, about fifty-five, who claimed to recognize gunshots, wore dark brown slacks, an expensive silk short-sleeved tan shirt and a heavy gold cross on a thick gold chain around his neck. His neck made her think weight lifter. Perhaps guessing that Jane Blake wasn't an Italian name and sensing that her Italian was accented, he said to Joe in strongly accented English, "You take my word. I know. Gunshot from a Beretta."

That pretty much convinced her. The boy in the video had been holding an AK-74, but his sidearm had been a Beretta.

Switching to English, Joe asked, "Have you seen the conductor?"

Weight Lifter shook his head. "Nobody come into this car since the gunshot."

She said to Joe, "We need to see whatever we can. I'll go. I look less threatening." This would irritate Joe. It was, of course, true, but he didn't like it that just because she looked less of a threat, she often took point.

The weeping woman grabbed Nova's hand, crying in Italian, "No! No! You really shouldn't go."

"I'll be careful," Nova assured her.

She stepped into the gangway. The windows in the end doors were small—a foot tall by half a foot wide.

All she could see through the window into Car No. 3 was something black.

It moved slightly with the subtle movement of the train.

It was most likely the back of a man wearing black. Most likely the back of one of the terrorists.

He started to turn and she ducked back inside Car No. 4.

She stood still, staring and trying to think fast. What should she tell these people? Calm them? Tell them the truth, which would certainly panic them and was against orders? Joe was searching her face for a clue about what she'd seen.

She grabbed the man with the thick neck and gold cross, pulled him up to the door and planted him there. Even the people from the back of the car were now clustered in the middle and front.

In a calm, firm voice, she said in Italian, "I agree with this man that the sound from the next car may have been a gunshot. And I agree that it would be dangerous for anyone to try to go forward."

Joe looked at the big Italian. "What is your name?"

"Gregorio."

"Well, Gregorio, can you see to it that no one does go forward? And make sure that no one comes into this car, either?"

Gregorio grinned. "Right. No one out. No one in."

Joe raised his hands and gestured. "Go back to your seats. No one is going to come in here."

"We have to do something, now!" shouted the wiry, paint-splattered guy.

Nova pulled the Glock from her shoulder holster.

The effect was as if she'd just sent a thousand volts through the car. Stunned silence. "If someone has a gun, what do *you* propose to do?" Nova countered. "We're going to let the authorities handle this when we get to the next station."

The paint-spattered man's buddy pulled on his friend's arm.

Slowly, and in some cases quickly, passengers returned to their seats.

Gregorio said, "No one in. But how do I persuade them…if I need to persuade them?"

She held the Glock toward him. "Do you know how to use this, and would you want to if necessary?"

He took the gun. "Sweetie, I've fought in Africa and Southeast Asia." He looked at Joe. "I guarantee you and your girl—no one through the door."

Joe took her arm. "We need to confer. We'll get back to you, Gregorio. And thanks."

He pulled her back down the aisle and out the rear door into the gangway, then called Cesare. "We've got a mess in Car No. 4. It seems the terrorists have taken over Car No. 3. Maybe everything forward of it as well."

A pause, then Joe hung up. "Shit. Once again, he'll get right back to us."

Chapter 39

Cesare kept saying "Yes" and "I understand" as Nova explained again that the terrorists had taken over the train, at least Car No. 3, the status of passengers in the other cars, especially Car No. 4, and that the porter had tried but also could not contact the conductor. She ended with, "And since you say they also control the engine, what do the great minds there propose?"

"They are talking right now about landing special forces onto the train, between the engine and Car No. 1. They would take over the engine by force."

She laughed. "You cannot be serious. This is a Eurostar. They don't call them bullet trains for nothing. Every car is sleek and clean, including the engine. Given that you could lower someone onto the top, there's absolutely nothing for a special ops guy to hold on to, on the cars or the engine."

She imagined the black-clad boys slipping like so much grease off the top of a hot aluminum kettle. "They're not going to be able to take over the engine that way. We've picked up speed. We have to be going about one hundred and forty miles per hour now."

"Provenza wants to talk to me," he said. "I'll call you back."

She leaned back against the door into Car No. 5 and sighed.

Joe said, "They could stop the whole thing pretty quick if they blow up the engine."

She imagined the engine exploding in a yellow, red, and black cloud and the cars tumbling off into a desolate cow pasture. "Jesus, Joe."

"Well, it would work."

"Right. Keep thinking."

He crossed his arms and leaned back beside her. They lapsed into concentrated thought.

"How about this?" she said, thinking aloud. "We separate the train from the engine."

Joe didn't hesitate a millisecond. "I like it. Cesare can find out how it's done. Hell, maybe Diego knows."

Her cell phone buzzed.

"Cesare," she said quickly, "what we think will work is to separate the engine from the train. When that happens, Joe and I make sure the terrorists don't bail out when the cars finally slow down enough for anyone so inclined to make a leap. We explain to the passengers beforehand that they have to stay on board to get medical help. Your forces can be there, waiting to secure the train and the passengers and to give medical aid. We can do it. It would work."

"That is good. Wait a minute."

The minute turned into more like four. She timed them.

Finally he came back on. "We can get you whatever you need, coordinate with you, and so on. But the trick is, you will have to act fast because to stop the train in a way that is relatively safe for bystanders, and to subsequently quarantine the whole affair, we've picked a desired spot and have a plan."

"And that plan is…?"

"We will take out the track. Everything will be in place shortly to do it. The area has open fields and will do the least harm to people or property. Also, all the passengers who survive can easily be quarantined in tents in the open area. The train will arrive at that location in twenty-two minutes."

He waited for her to say something. She was going to be in a massive train wreck in twenty-two minutes if she didn't think fast.

"Did you hear me? You have twenty-two minutes. Can you uncouple the engine in that time?"

"We'll have to try, won't we?"

"What exactly will you need?"

"Give Joe and me a couple of minutes to figure out the logistics."

Chapter 40

By the time she and Joe had worked out a plan, Nova's watch indicated that they had eighteen minutes left until the train reached the detonation spot. She pulled out her cell and rang Cesare. "We will go to the end car and open a door. You will pick one of us up. We haven't decided which one yet."

"Me, me," Joe said, batting his eyelashes like a woman wishing to be chosen. She loved that about him. In the worst imaginable situations, Joe was so cool he could manage to keep things light.

Nova continued, "We need to sandwich Car No. 3— one of us will cover its front end and one will cover its rear end as soon as we're cut loose from the engine." She turned to Joe. "What'll we need?"

"Tell him we'll need communicators, special ops

jumpsuits and gloves for both of us. A couple of strong flashlights. Another Beretta to replace the Glock you loaned Gregorio. More ammunition."

Joe went forward, she guessed to let people in Car No. 4 in on the plan. She passed on their needs to Cesare. Cesare offered automatic rifles. She declined. "They spray too much. We'll want accuracy."

He then offered to drop six HAZMAT-dressed Special Forces to work with them to secure Car No. 3. She said, "Only two, one to partner with me and another to partner with Joe. More will just get in our way. Guys wearing HAZMAT aren't going to be able to move very fast in any event."

Joe touched her arm. "I've told everyone in Car No. 4 that we'll be back. Let's go. Turns out that Gregorio's an experienced mercenary."

They rushed back through the train, a surreal experience because life in the other cars appeared to be proceeding pretty much as normal. Once seated, Eurostar passengers tended to remain in their seats or wandered no farther forward than the club car. This whole situation suddenly struck her as bizarre: the train sped through darkness, but the humans on it moved on human time, oblivious to the world rushing by outside.

When they reached the end car, Diego, with a grim look on his face, sat slumped in one of the seats in the car's last row. Joe gestured for him to follow them out onto the gangway. They explained the situation— within minutes a helicopter would be overhead to pick up one of them and drop off one Spec Ops man.

Diego straightened, a spark of hope flickering again in his eyes.

"Okay, Joe," Nova said. "You know I have more experience climbing."

"But I think I've had more experience at insertion and extraction."

"How much? Be honest."

"Honest goes without saying between us."

"So?"

"The usual one course."

"We're tied. Let's toss."

Joe turned to Diego. "Got a coin?"

He handed Joe a shiny euro coin. "Call it," Joe said and flipped.

"Tails, I go," she said.

It landed tails.

Cesare called and while they waited for their gear to arrive, he gave her and Joe directions for how to uncouple a car. They synchronized their watches.

She heard the sound of a helicopter approaching. Fourteen minutes to blowup time.

Chapter 41

The helicopter lowered the gear Nova had requested and Joe fished it into the gangway. Cesare said that as soon as the helicopter lifted her off a different helicopter would lower Joe's HAZMAT-dressed partner. She snatched what she needed and rushed into one of the end car's tiny bathrooms to change. When she came back out in a black jumpsuit and armed with a Beretta, Joe had already changed, as well.

Above the train, the helicopter had backed off a bit but still closely trailed them. Another call came from Cesare. "We have air support ready to pick you up when you give them the signal. They are hanging back so the terrorists can't see them from their position in Car No. 3, but you have a swarm of helicopters on your backside. Do you want communication to be in Italian or English?"

She said, "Tell them I'm ready. And you call the language."

"Provenza says, English. You are Con 1, Joe is Con 2. Con for Containment. Your partners will be Con 3 and Con 4."

Joe took her arm. "The timing is so damn close. As soon as you're in place, contact me."

The helicopter pulled up to the end car. Nova spoke into her microphone, positioned near her lips on the tip of a thin plastic tube that was connected to her communicator's earpiece. "This is Con 1. Ready for pickup."

Holding a handrail, she leaned out. At first, she couldn't see anything but a big moon, scattered stars, and the blur of trees as the train raced forward. Then someone in the helicopter turned on a floodlight. A forty-foot long extraction rope dangled from the aircraft close to the train.

After one failed try, she grabbed the rope with a gloved hand, stepped into the foot loop, latched onto another loop with her left hand, gave the thumbs-up signal for them to lift her and stepped off the train.

The moment she put her full weight onto the rope, the helicopter reduced forward speed. Still, the wind pulled at her, threatening to pluck her off the line and hurtle her to the ground that rushed by below.

They reeled her in and immediately pointed to a guy wearing a white HAZMAT gear, his helmet still off, with the number 3 on his suit's shoulder. "Con 3," he yelled above the motor's roar. "I'll be going in with you."

Seeing him, she still wasn't sure just how helpful he could be given the physical restrictions of the HAZMAT suit, but an extra gun never hurt.

The helicopter pilot took them well away from the train, keeping all lights off. Then they zoomed forward until they were ahead of the engine. Joe and Con 4 would be moving into place in Car No. 4 now.

The pilot dropped back until they were right behind the engine. There was a good chance this maneuver, along with the cover of night, and the train's own noise, had prevented the terrorists from becoming aware of their presence.

She studied the entrance to the gangway between the engine and Car No. 1. Again, a floodlight helped. Cesare had explained how to get the door to slide open from the outside by hitting a big black button midway down on the door's right side.

She leaned close to her new partner's faceplate and yelled, "I'm going first. I'm more flexible."

Con 3 nodded.

Using the same line, the crew slowly let her down the fifteen or so feet between the helicopter and the gangway door.

Whoa! What a difference this drop was, moving in tandem with a speeding engine. For a moment she froze, clinging to the line and feeling paralyzed as wind whipped at her body. After what seemed like fifteen terrifying minutes but was probably no more than fifteen seconds, she came level with the black button, a spotlight from the helicopter holding a jumping beam on it as the train sped through the moonlit night.

She reached out to smack it, and the wind caught her arm. She spun wildly.

She had to stop the spin before the crew panicked and started reeling her back up. She stuck out her free leg, the one with the sprained ankle. Her leg slammed against the car, and a jolt of electricity shot up her leg into her lower back. But her spinning stopped.

She leaned into the wind and reached out, almost but not quite close enough to hit the floodlit black target.

She waved for them to bring her in closer.

It took the helicopter several seconds to maneuver, but the next time she reached out, she banged on the button and the door slid open.

Gasping for air, which the train's forward speed seemed to suck from her lips, she signaled to be lowered a bit more. Three times, she snatched at a handrail; the fourth time, she met with success. She pulled herself inside and onto the second step, quickly kicked her foot free from the loop so she wouldn't get pulled out and fell back against the third step.

"Damn!" she said, her head bowed, her pulse a throbbing lump in her throat.

It was much easier getting her new partner down since she could grab his leg and his arms and then pull him in.

The minute he was inside, she checked time. 8:37. Only three minutes left until they reached the blown-up tracks.

"Con 1 in place, Con 2," she said over the communicator.

"Roger," came Joe's reply. "Con 2 uncoupling Car No. 4 from Car No. 5 now."

Con 3 had already opened the trap door on the floor of the gangway. This opening gave them access to the coupling between Car No. 1 and the engine. The noise from the wheels on the tracks and the rush of wind muffled her head in a blanket of sound.

She studied the coupling. The directions were simple: lift the horizontal bar called a "cut lever"—using the flashlight, she spotted it immediately—to raise the pin that held the coupler closed. Once the pin came up, the coupler would open and the engine, still under propulsion, would pull slowly away from Car No. 1 and the rest of the train. But a full stop would take time, since the back of the train had lots of forward momentum. The stop, everyone hoped, would come well before the train arrived at the blown-up tracks.

"Looks easy," she yelled to her white-clad partner, avoiding the intercom even though she wasn't sure he could hear over the wind and rattle of metal upon metal.

She also located the two lines linked together that operated the air brakes. These she would separate before she pulled the coupler pin.

"I don't know what's taking him so long," she yelled. She checked her watch. Eight thirty-eight and ten seconds. *Come on, Joe!*

At the sound of a loud boom, her head went up and she froze. The new sound mixed with all the noise of wind and wheels on tracks around her, but she could guess that its origin lay ahead. The deed was done.

"They've blown the tracks," her partner yelled. "We either get this thing apart, or in a little over a minute, you and I are going to get a really rough ride on a nasty train crash."

She heard Joe softly in her ear. "Con 1, this is Con 2. We're a go. The train's back half is free. Get us unhooked from the damn engine!"

Checking time, her heart banging against her chest, she forced herself to wait the fifteen seconds they had agreed on between the time he cut loose the back of the train and she separated the remaining Cars No. 1 through No. 4 from the engine. When the cars stopped, they wanted the passengers in the train's rearward section to be as far from Car No. 3 as possible.

Finally, at thirteen seconds, she fell onto her belly and reached down through the trap door preparing to put her hand on the cut lever so she could pull it up at exactly fifteen seconds. She stretched…but couldn't reach the cut lever, let alone the air hose connection. She inched forward as far as she could without falling down onto the coupling. Her fingers still fell a frustrating centimeter short.

"Hold my legs!"

Her partner grabbed her around her calves; she stretched the last bit, pulled up on the cut lever and saw that the pin came up nicely.

The engine immediately began to pull away. The air hose snapped or broke apart on its own. The ground whizzed by in a flickering, dark blur.

Please, please let us stop in time. I don't want to check out yet.

Chapter 42

Nova scrambled to her feet and Con 3 dropped the gangway trapdoor into place. Leading the way, she passed to the far end of Car No. 2. Then, crouching down so as to avoid being seen through the window of the door into Car No. 3, she and Con 3 entered the gangway between the two cars.

"Con 1 in position in the gangway between two and three," she said softly.

"Roger, Con 1," Joe answered back. "Con 2 in position at the rear of Car No. 3."

Now she and Joe would wait and pray. Holding tightly on to the handrail and squatting low on the first step, she opened the gangway door and leaned out of the train enough to watch the south side of Car No. 3. Con 3 crouched with his gun aimed at the door, ensuring that no one left the car before it came to a halt and

the Special Ops teams surrounded it. Joe and his partner, at the rear of No. 3, would do the same, with Joe
watching the car's north side.

The swarm of helicopters Cesare had promised descended. Dark bodies, beating blades and floodlights
jostled each other in the night sky. The horrible thought
struck her that so many helicopters might collide with
each other. With inertia winning over momentum, the
train continued to slow.

Maybe doing eighty now.

On the train's south side, the flat terrain had been
clear-cut to about fifty feet from the tracks, at which
point heavy woods of what looked like mixed beech and
oak trees began. Not really ideal for containment. Way
too easy for someone to run into the woods.

When the train came to a full stop before hitting the
twisted tracks, there would be new problems. The helicopters would disgorge armed Special Ops teams. No
passengers would be allowed to leave their cars until the
terrorists were captured, and she imagined that the terrorists might use the passengers in Car No. 3 as hostages.
The action would get messy. Brutal. There really was no
good way out of what lay ahead for the passengers in Car
No. 3. Indeed, for every passenger on this ill-fated train.

Speed down to about forty now.

A barrage of gunfire erupted from Car No. 3. She
heard the car's door swish open behind her even as she
watched glass exploding outward in floodlit shards
from three car windows. She resisted the temptation to
look behind—the door to Car No. 3 was Con 3's job—
she kept her attention fixed on the outside of the train.

She heard her partner grunting, striking blows as he

struggled with someone. Then all at once, three of the terrorists leaped out of the windows. This was her responsibility—to make sure no one left the train. One of the leapers, she was nearly certain, was the boy Ali.

The terrorists slammed into the ground and rolled. She could see them easily in the moonlight, but floodlights that had been dancing all over rotated and also fixed on the fleeing men. Nova leaped from the train, and she too slammed into the ground and rolled. When she stopped rolling, she lay still, stunned and out of breath. Her communicator had popped out of her ear. She stuck it back in.

Gunfire erupted from helicopters and the train moved away from her. She pulled her arms and legs under her onto all fours, looked to the spot where the three men had jumped. One lay on his back on the ground, probably wounded or dead, but Butch Cut and Ali were already near the trees.

More gunfire from the helicopter, but both men disappeared into the woods.

She picked up the Beretta and took off after them. "Con 1 in pursuit," she gasped out between breaths.

At the point where she thought they had entered the woods, she ran in after them, brushing away low branches and leaping over or dashing around stubby bushes. The noise from three helicopters made it impossible to hear anything.

"Pull up!" she commanded. "I can't find them if I can't hear them."

Immediately, the three aircraft lifted. Ahead of her and to the left, moving in the same direction as the train, she heard the sounds of bodies crashing through underbrush and breaking dried twigs.

Lights—ten or fifteen of them from four choppers—slashed into the woods, crisscrossing, zigzagging, searching.

A tremendous metallic screeching, followed by booms, came rushing through the trees from a distance. She imagined the engineer putting on the brakes, perhaps trying to stop before flying off the blown-up tracks. She prayed the rest of the train would stop in time.

"Ahead of you at eleven o'clock, Con 1," said a voice in her ear.

She spotted two shafts of light aimed at the ground in that direction and followed them. A black movement up ahead gave her visual contact. Was it Ali, her target, or Butch Cut?

It's what you can see. Figure it out later.

The man tripped on something and went down. She strained to take advantage, pushing her legs still harder to catch him, alternately watching the ground and her quarry.

Gunshots rang out ahead of her, and she started zigzagging. A bit of tree bark hit her forehead.

The black figure ran to her left, his body flickering as he raced between one tree and the next. Lights hit him and then lost him.

She braked to full stop, sucked in a deep breath, aimed; the next time a light hit him, she fired off six shots as if she were shooting at moving ducks on a belt at a carnival.

He went down.

As she ran toward him, he started firing again, but way off the mark. She shot three more times.

She found Butch Cut lying in the center of a disk of

light. One of her last three shots had hit him in the right cheek and taken out most of his brains. Blood had speckled and now pooled dark red on leaves, dirt and twigs around his head.

She stopped, listened and heard a noise off still farther to her left.

"About a hundred feet dead ahead," said the voice in her ear. "Now he's stopped, crouched behind a boulder that looks like a Humvee."

The ground sloped slightly uphill. He might be a teenage boy, but she was in top condition. Unless he was in equally good shape, going uphill gave her the advantage.

"He's running again," said her eye in the sky.

She took off after the sound, following the shaft of light.

"You're gaining," came the voice.

From ahead, gunshots rang out again. She ran still harder.

Finally, she saw him. He stumbled, got off three shots at her while his legs kept him in motion. *Catch him,* she said to herself. *Run.*

Suddenly, a clearing opened up ahead. When he ran into the clearing, he'd be naked to the relentless lights. He stopped, hugged a tree, moonlight alone lighting him.

She huddled behind her own tree, an oak with foot-thick trunk.

The teenager leaned against a sturdy birch tree, exhausted, and fired off three rounds in her direction— wild, pointless.

Her hand froze—she didn't return fire.

"You can't get away," she yelled in Italian. Did he understand Italian?

Two more shots was his answer.

He wasn't more than forty feet away and she could see his left leg. She took her time, held her breath, fired.

He spun around and fell, face down.

Lungs burning, she approached.

At fifteen feet, he rolled over in the moonlight, aimed, and yelled, "Allahu Akbar."

She fired off three rounds to his one.

So far Joe had counted six terrorists dead. On the train they had one alive, captive, and very pissed off. That left one more, the carrier, unaccounted for.

"She's about fifty feet ahead and to your left," said a voice in his ear. "Follow my light."

The pissed-off captive on the train was a kid the right age to be the carrier, Ali, but the face was wrong. After a brief struggle in which the young thug had used a knife to cut across Joe's chest, right through the jump-suit and nearly through the skin—two inches higher and it would have been across Joe's throat—Joe had hit the kid's solar plexus so hard that his would-be teen killer fell motionless to his knees. Joe pushed him, facedown, onto the gangway and held him in place with a foot on his back and a gun at his head until Special Ops, dressed in HAZMAT gear, took over.

"More to your left," came his guiding voice from above.

Joe shifted direction.

Car No. 1 and the rest of the train, thank God, had stopped just short of the destroyed tracks. The engine hadn't been so lucky.

HAZMAT-dressed Special Ops teams swarmed

around the cars like busy, white worker ants. Similarly outfitted medical teams were on the way.

Quarantine and isolation now. Every car would be kept separate from every other car, and the passengers from the separated cars would be held in separate tents to await their fate—life or death within two days.

Fortunately, the virus could only live outside a body, in open air, for not much more than ten minutes, so the quarantine and HAZMAT gear would only have to be worn when in contact with the passengers or in their shared environment.

Joe saw Nova, sitting with her back against a birch tree, brightly lit by a floodlight. She seemed oblivious to its glare. Then he saw the body lying next to her. It had to be the carrier.

She looked up at him, and she was crying. Great big tears.

"Cut the damn light," he said softly but firmly into the communicator.

The floodlight moved off, leaving her in moonlight.

Joe had never seen her cry.

She shook her head and brushed at the tears. She wiped her nose on her sleeve. "He was just a kid."

So that was it. "He was willing to kill…he has killed…a great many people. Most of the people on this train, I'd guess."

"He can't be more than fifteen or sixteen."

"Old enough."

"Not so old."

He didn't know what to do. Let her sit there? Make her get up? "Are you okay?"

"You saw the tape. He did it because his family

needed money and some goddamn scumbag said, 'I'll give them money. All you have to do is die and go to heaven.'" She bowed her head and shook it. "Maggie is only a few years younger than he is."

He squatted in front of her, made her look him in the eye. "Are you physically okay?" He didn't add, "You had to do it, Nova." She knew that. He'd not insult her by saying the obvious.

She shrugged. "I didn't feel a thing when my adrenaline was pumping, but right now my ankle is killing me."

"Good. I'm glad that's all." He stood, stuck out his hand; she took it, and he pulled her to her feet.

"Want me to carry you?" he said, letting lightness touch his tone, hoping it would touch her feelings.

It did. She shoved his shoulder in mock disgust. "Don't be ridiculous."

Chapter 43

Moving back toward the train, Nova limped beside Joe, fishing in a pocket for her cell phone. "We took one alive," he explained.

"Good."

She found the phone and punched in the number Star had given her for Maggie. Maggie answered immediately. She and the Robertsons had done as Nova suggested. They were already holed up in the small hotel. Maggie wanted to know where Nova was and what she was doing. Nova explained that she couldn't talk but that she was glad they were safe and that Nova would call later with more explanation.

In Car No. 3 they found Provenza, dressed in a white HAZMAT suit and standing over a seated boy dressed in black. Two Special Ops men also hovered nearby with automatic rifles slung over their arms.

Seeing her and Joe, Provenza said in English, "What about the carrier?"

"He's dead," Joe said without emotion. "You should get a team to go collect his body."

Nova felt a twist in the pit of her stomach, a tightening of the throat. She wished she somehow could have avoided killing the boy. But then, within two weeks or less, he would have died horribly of Ebola. Maybe she should think of herself as an angel of mercy. Wasn't it human nature to always try to put the best spin on your behavior, no matter how bad or disgusting or dishonorable it might be?

"Good job! Excellent," Provenza crowed.

Praise was being heaped on her head; it just made her heart ache all the more.

"You pigs, you infidel pigs," the young terrorist spat out in decent English.

"Well," Provenza said. "So you can talk. And in English, no less."

"For your blasphemous lives and your support of the Great Satan, Allah will punish you by the legions with death."

"Sounds like something you've been made to memorize," Provenza shot back.

The terrorist's young age struck her a fresh blow. So many young people suddenly in her life, and all of them so different: the dead Ali, a boy she'd killed, a boy who wanted to give his family financial support and who had died for a cause that he likely hadn't understood; Maggie, the closest thing Nova had to a daughter, who still might contract this dreadful disease and die from it; and now this ignorant young hater, so filled with stupid lies and venom that he wanted to kill at random—young, old, evil or good—just kill. How could a species so willing to destroy its young, physically or with poisonous ideas, be so damn successful? Or then, again, were the doomsayers right? Were humans setting themselves up for extinction?

Provenza looked at one of the Special Ops guards and said in Italian, "Apparently he doesn't intend to do anything but swear at us. He's not going to tell us if he's immune or not. We don't assume anything. Keep him in isolation. And make damned certain he doesn't get away. We'll know one way or the other by tomorrow."

Taking hold of Nova's arm, Provenza guided her and Joe to the gangway. Once off the train, he kept them walking into a clearing on the train's north side, a good hundred feet away, to a place that seemed almost quiet compared to the small army of HAZMAT-garbed soldiers and medical personnel swarming over the train, disgorged from a couple dozen helicopters. Men were beginning to set up powerful floodlights. She smelled some sweet night flowers, like honeysuckle, in bloom.

Provenza pulled off the HAZMAT helmet. "I'm quite sincere. You've done a superb job. Whatever you two want to do, wherever you want to go, I'll see to it."

"I'm staying," she said. "I'm going to keep the cover of Jane Blair, private investigator on vacation, so that anyone who makes it out of here alive won't be able to link me with SISMI. But I'm going to stay, to be with the dying."

Provenza's eyes widened and he leaned toward her, as if he weren't sure or couldn't believe what he'd heard. "I beg your pardon."

"The people who will come now to help the folks who are going to sicken and die with this miserable thing will have to wear HAZMAT gear. The suits are hateful. Impersonal and ugly, even frightening. And the authorities can't allow loved ones of the dying to come to this site. Right?"

"Well." He stuck his hands in his pockets, clearly not comfortable with the question.

"So I'm going to stay," she added. "I estimate for the people who are infected the virus will run its course here in about ten days. I intend to write final letters for them and hold the hands of those who aren't going to make it. They'll have a person with them. Real flesh. Not a white glove and a face behind glass. And then," she gave Provenza a little smile, "you can count on it, Signore Provenza. I'll hit you up for some really fine reward afterward."

Provenza looked at Joe. "It's a wonderful gesture, but not necessary. Surely you can persuade her."

"Of course it's not necessary. We're staying because it's what we'd want someone to do for people we love."

Joe took her hand and squeezed. She slid her arm under his, as if they were going to take a stroll, and squeezed back. Partners. All the way to the end of the job.

At the sound of crunching footsteps, they turned toward the rear of the train. Moonlight shone on an approaching figure, one not wearing HAZMAT gear.

"Good evening to you all," Cesare said. He must have hitched a helicopter ride. "At least, it's a relatively good evening. The carrier has been stopped. I can tell you that the country is now under full quarantine. It is even possible we might get through this without a disaster of global magnitude."

"What are you doing here?"

"You don't think for a minute that I could resist the need to satisfy my curiosity, do you? I also wanted to be certain that you both were intact. Remember, while you are in Italy, you are my responsibility."

Joe grinned.

Provenza said, "Cesare, they both intend to stay to tend…well, to help the medics with the ill until it's all over here. Quite unnecessary."

"Ah, but what a perfectly sensible thought," Cesare said. "I will, of course, join the two of you. I believe I have the makings of a fine nurse."

She hugged him, her dirty jumpsuit brushing a horrible mess on his while silk jacket.

Provenza shrugged. "Well, crazy or heroic, I don't know which. I myself have to get back to headquarters and start filing endless reports."

They walked him to the helicopter that had brought him to the train and waited until it rose and headed toward Rome. Joe took her hand in his. She didn't pull away.

"Well," Cesare said, "shall we not go and inquire of whoever is in charge of setting up tents where our lodgings will be? And I must make up a list of things I will need."

Chapter 44

"Only one. One must wait," said the jail guard to Nova in passable English.

"No problem," Joe said. "I have no desire to visit the son of a bitch." He nodded to the chairs in the reception room for jail visitors. "I'll wait."

Nova handed her purse to the short, intense-looking jailer.

"Those," he said, pointing to her white porcelain hoop earrings.

She took them off, as well, and placed them, along with two rings and her cell phone, in the tray and then walked through the metal detector.

On the other side, a different jailer said, "Follow me."

Ten days had passed since the train wreck. Ten days of hell for Italy and the world, as people everywhere held their breaths to see how bad and widespread the outbreak would be. The peak of the infection had now passed in the country and, mercifully both the rate of contagion and the death rate were much lower than what the terrorists would have wanted. Of the train's one hundred and eighty-five passengers and crew, only twenty of the forty-two in Car No. 3 and six of those in Car No. 4 became infected, and more than sixty percent of those who'd become infected were still alive. According to experts, everyone still alive now would recover. She was especially pleased that Diego would return to his wife and kids. And to everyone's enormous relief, the menace had been successfully contained within mainland Italy and Sicily.

But among those she'd tended who had died had been the young terrorist, al Hassan's son, Saddoun. That was the reason for this morning's unpleasant visit to Rome's central jail.

She could visit al Hassan because, along with Joe and Cesare, she had a pass entitling her to travel freely anywhere in Italy or leave the country if she chose. The three of them were not only immune, but also weren't manufacturing any of the virus in their bodies, so they were non-infectious. Provenza had also called ahead to let the jail authorities know that two Americans, Jane and James Blake, were to be accorded visiting privileges with the terrorist prisoner.

The guard led her through several barred gates until they reached a simple white visiting room with two chairs. A bare wooden table sat in the center.

The guard indicated the chair she should take. The chair on the table's opposite side had a metal ring in the floor beneath it. A sign on the wall said, "Visitors, be informed that you are being watched and, unless you are a lawyer, your conversation may be tape-recorded."

Ahmad al Hassan shuffled in, wearing a bright yellow jumpsuit and leg and wrist irons. His guard sat him in the chair, attached his leg irons to the ring in the floor, and left the two of them alone.

The man sat erect and defiant, offering only a sullen glare to the woman who had captured him.

"You're not curious as to why I'm here?" she asked.

Silence. He looked away, instead gazing at the wall behind her.

"I bring a message from your son, Saddoun."

His gaze snapped at once to her face. "Saddoun?"

She took a deep breath. She should hate al Hassan, this mass murderer who had draped himself in religious clothing. If she hated him, then she would find some pleasure or satisfaction in the next moments. But she had a hard time hating. So far in her life, she had hated only one person—her stepfather.

"Your son, without telling you, joined up with that little band of killers you put together to unleash this virus. But he joined up too late to get vaccinated."

Al Hassan blinked several times, his expression blank. Apparently he didn't immediately understand.

"Your son, Saddoun, went with the others to the Coliseum and onto the train to Munich. He was taken captive when the train was stopped. Because he wasn't vaccinated, he contracted the virus and died. I was with him shortly before and he begged me to bring a message to you."

"Saddoun." The man's face sagged, and he aged before her eyes. His shoulders collapsed, his neck seemed to shrink so that his head nodded forward and tears began to flow down his cheeks.

Saddoun had refused to talk to anyone, including her, until he got the rash and started bleeding from… well, from everywhere. That's when he'd said he needed to have her go to his father. He'd made her promise that if he talked, and explained as much as he knew about the plot, she would carry his message.

Now it was time to deliver on her promise. "I was with him until he died. He said to tell you he was sorry that he did not obey you, because he loves you and because Allah commands that children obey their parents. And that I should tell you that he hopes you will be proud that he died in the fight against those who would destroy the true faith."

Al Hassan, silent sobs shaking his body, leaned his elbows on the table and buried his face in his hands. Saddoun had explained that he was his father's only son, that he should have lived to carry on the family name. From al Hassan's response, she knew that the man would never recover from this loss.

"You know, your son died a painful, agonizing death."

"He was my son. A good son."

She stood up, message delivered.

Before she left the room, she turned to the man whose hands covered his weeping face. From her heart came her own message. "Would that Allah spare all of us from fools like you."

Cesare grabbed Nova in a hug that crushed the breath out of her.

"I will miss you, you beautiful and courageous creature," he said, not letting her go.

They stood at a safe distance from the blades of the helicopter waiting to take her and Joe to Capri for two days of recuperation. Then it would be back to the States to face an intensive debriefing in Virginia.

From Claiton Pryce, the DDO at Langley, came words of praise for a successful operation, but the debriefing would be no less intense and exhausting. Smith had said that someone from the CDC would also be waiting to pump them for information on the course and nature of the disease, since they'd watched its effects close up during their days with the sick and dying from the train.

"Why don't you come to Capri, Cesare?" she said, hugging back. Cesare had also been offered rest time, but had declined.

He let her go. "I've been to Capri often. And in truth, I want to get back to Principessa. And to my work. But you will find your stay there a delight. I know the hotel. And you both deserve the best."

Cesare turned to Joe, who was patiently observing this farewell with crossed arms. After having watched Cesare tenderly care for ill passengers for several days, Joe had told Nova he thought Cesare was a good man, and a good agent, even though, he'd added, the man could talk your ear off.

"Do not let her be sad over those who died," Cesare said. "I see too much sadness in her lovely eyes. But both of you have to know that between us, we have saved thousands...no, millions, of lives."

"Don't worry, Cesare," Joe said, turning to look at Nova with those dark, intense eyes. "I'll take care of her."

Chapter 45

Nova sighed. It had been one helluva day. The visit to see al Hassan had left her drained. In fact, it had been a nightmarish twenty-one days that felt like a lifetime since Joe showed up in Costa Rica.

An hour and a half ago, she and Joe checked into a private, elegant little hotel on Capri. She stood naked in front of a full-length mirror on the back of the bathroom door in her room at the Villa Aphrodite. Turning sideways, she checked her thighs and buttocks. She had four yellowing bruises on her legs and some nearly healed scratches on her arm from the fall at Sorokin's, but all in all, her body hadn't suffered any severe damage during this op. This time. That wasn't always the case.

She should just be glad to be alive. For the last few

days, that thought had hit her over and over, and every time she had felt a wave of mixed gratitude, and guilt. She'd been given the precious gift of more sunrises and sunsets, and she intended to savor every one. But others hadn't been so fortunate.

She turned the taps on in the bathtub and started water running for an actual bath—no shower. Her muscles and bones needed a long, warm soak, and she had nearly a whole hour before Joe picked her up for a late dinner.

The tub was filling slowly. With the water running hot, she wrapped her hair in a towel and then studied her face in the mirror above the white marble sink. *I'll wear my hair down and pulled behind one ear.* She felt a sudden, oddly disturbing urge to please Joe, to look and smell good for him.

She strolled back into the bedroom with its light gray- and wine-colored décor and crossed to the French doors of the balcony. Provenza had chosen well. When he had asked, "Where do you want to spend your two days of R and R?" she had thought of her father and simply said, "Capri."

Joe, always easygoing, agreed. She felt lifted by the hotel's location, nestled high overlooking the Tyrrhenian Sea atop a cliff of one of Capri's many limestone peaks. She pushed the doors fully open and walked outside into the warm, humid night. A salty-tasting breeze caressed her face.

The music of sea against rocks rose from below. Lights of homes, hotels and restaurants twinkled along the dark curve of the island. Except for a scattering of tiny white pinpricks in anchored boats close to the island, the sea itself presented a vast, deeply black void. No moon tonight. She loved the perfect blackness of an ocean at night. Utter tranquility, such a blessing after so much violence and grief.

On the way back to the bathroom, she stopped a moment to shut off her laptop and close its lid. She'd written to Star and Penny and answered a ton of e-mail.

The best e-mail had come from Robin Scott, the girl from Costa Rica, Nova recalled as she sunk into the tub of hot water. Costa Rica felt a lifetime away. But Robin had just returned home and written to tell Nova how she had taken her "wise" advice. I learned, and won't ever forget, that if I don't give up and try hard, I can do a bunch more than I think I can, the girl had written.

Nova had decided that she would not give up, either. She had the talent and the temperament for Company work. And above all, she believed that nothing more surely guaranteed that evil men would prosper than if good men—and women—did nothing.

I'm also determined never to give up when something is important, Nova had written to Robin. I'm so happy you've found how empowering that can be.

How ironic that the message she'd conveyed during a chance encounter with this teenager had been the very message she herself had needed to reaffirm.

Nova lifted the tub's plug with her big toe. Time to dress.

As she rose, she noted that she hadn't polished her toenails or fingernails. Should she? She always traveled with three polishes that pretty much covered any color outfit she might select. Maybe just toenails. She didn't think Joe would particularly like fingernail polish on her, but he might find toenail polish intriguing.

She shook her head. Where was this surprising urge to please him coming from? To want Joe to see her as a beautiful woman? At some point in their exploits, he'd already seen her at her very worst...and her very best when she was dressed to seduce. Why, tonight, did she want him to see her not as his partner, but as a living, breathing and passionate woman?

The Villa Aphrodite provided fluffy white terry bathrobes. She slipped into hers and strolled into the bedroom. She went over to the stereo and put in a CD the hotel had provided—Diana Krall's *The Look of Love*.

What should she wear?

This was weird. Really weird. She had planned and schemed over what to wear for more men than she could remember, but tonight something deep inside compelled her to dress up for Joe.

She had six outfits with her. One by one, she took them from her bags and spread them on the king-size bed.

She chose the outfit that Cesare had said, as he was paying for it, was "devastating." The pants and camisole were a rich royal blue, the camisole clinging tightly to her body and revealing her navel if she stretched up even the slightest bit. The see-through cover-up—swirls of two shades of blue and two shades of green shot through with thin, bold strokes of fiery red—was cut so that it fell off one shoulder to reveal the dark-blue strap of the camisole against her skin. Casual, but very, very sexy.

She stood still, seemingly rooted into the luxurious,

thick gray carpet. What the hell *was* it exactly that she wanted to say to Joe?

She looked at the clock built into the bedside stand. She had only fifteen minutes until he arrived.

When he did knock, she never felt more alive.

"Wow!" he said, tilting his head to the side with a cocky grin plastered on his handsome face. "You look fabulous."

As he often did, he wore a silk shirt tucked into slacks. Tonight the shirt was jet black. She hugged him, then stepped back. "And I smell like...?"

"Shalimar."

"Not bad, Cardone."

"You wear it quite often."

He noticed that her French doors stood open. "How's the view from your balcony?"

She followed him out.

He leaned against the railing and looked down. "Quite a drop. Couple of hundred feet. Your view is definitely better." He turned, took her hand gently in his. "How about I have breakfast tomorrow on your balcony instead of mine?"

His hand warmed hers. Totally delicious. Totally alive. She wanted him to kiss her. She wanted him to make love to her. She said, "We'll see."

He pulled her closer. "I'm glad you're not hurt. I'm even more glad you're going to quit working for the Company. I don't like worrying about you."

"I'm not going to quit. I decided this morning."

"You told me you wanted out."

"I thought I did. When I said it, I did want out. But I've changed my mind."

He let go of her hand, frowning, and crossed his arms. "How can you change your mind that fast?"

"It wasn't fast. Well, maybe it was. But it's the right decision."

"It isn't the right decision. This business is crazy. It's dangerous. You're right to want out."

He was getting worked up remarkably quickly. She smiled, trying to lighten things up. "Ah, yes, but it's also exciting work. And it's rewarding."

"Man, I was so damn excited about this evening. About dinner. About this whole mess being over without either of us being dead. And now you blitz me with this?" He turned around and stomped into the bedroom.

She followed him inside. "Look, *you're* not quitting, are you?"

"This is my profession. With you, well, there's plenty else you can do."

"But I'm not a quitter either. I just wrote a young girl telling her that a person should never quit when they're doing something important."

"Important!" He grabbed up her discarded bathrobe from the bed. "How many times have you met some other man in a hotel room wearing one of these?" He threw the robe onto the floor, glaring at her.

"Is that what you're so angry about?"

"Is that why you do it?"

She felt herself stiffen, as if he'd flicked a deep, psychological switch. Only moments ago, she'd been reaching out, aching with gratitude for being alive, wanting to be as close to him as humanly possible. Her tongue for a moment seemed glued to the inside of her mouth. Joe knew that she'd killed her stepfather. And he knew why. What in the name of everything holy was he thinking about her?

"Get out!" she finally managed to say softly. Then stronger. "Get out!"

He opened the door then said, "You are one damned stubborn woman."

"Get out of my room."

He slammed the door.

She took several steps backward, put her hands to her temples. *I can't believe he thinks that. God, I thought he knew me.*

A knock startled her. "Nova, I'm sorry. Let me back in."

She didn't move. He tried the door, but of course it had locked automatically.

"Let me in, please. I want to apologize. Right now. But not through the damn door."

"Go away."

"Look, there are people out here. I feel ridiculous."

She wasn't going to hash over ancient history, but the truth was that for years after her stepfather's abuse, the act of sex had meant absolutely nothing to her. She'd completely deadened herself to it. Then slowly in Germany with Jean Paul, she'd begun to recover her trust in men, enough to be open to the possibility of love. And so many times with Joe she'd had this exciting feeling that, were she to let herself be with him, it wouldn't be just a meaningless act anymore. It would feel good. Maybe even joyous. It would be an act of love.

"Nova!"

Another thought struck her. *He is jealous.*

Jealous meant he cared. And maybe it was true he worried about her when things got serious. She just needed to make him see that working for the Company was just as dangerous for him, just as hard on her.

She took her hands away from her head and listened for another knock. It did not come.

Maybe she should go to his room, knock, and ask him to let her in so she could apologize.

No way. Who had started this whole damn thing?

She turned toward a large decorative mirror and stared at a woman all dressed up to please the man who pleased her…heart.

She heard a sound from the balcony, turned, and there he stood in her balcony doorway.

"I'm not going to let you run away from me this time," he said. He strode across the room, grabbed her hand, pulled her into his arms. Then, tenderly, he kissed her.

Warm. Dizzy. She felt his hand pressing her close and savored the taste of his lips. The kiss she would make last forever. A kiss that made her whole, sweet and whole. So sweet.

She caught her breath, and his tongue parted her lips and slipped inside her mouth. He was hungry for this, too. A warmth spread in the pit of her stomach and blended with a sudden throbbing between her legs.

He said softly, "I want you, Nova Blair. I want you like I've never wanted another woman or ever will."

He kissed her again, and this time she let her tongue explore his lips, urge them aside, and enter his mouth.

His hands moved over the camisole down to the hollow of her back. She pulled out his shirt and let her fingers linger over his smooth skin. Beneath it were muscles like chiseled marble. God, how she loved the smell of his hair and skin—all of him.

"Make love to me, Joe," she whispered.

His hand found her breast. "No bra," he said softly, his breath warm on her neck.

She let one hand glide over the firm abs.

He shivered and then slid his hand up under the camisole. She felt her nipple go hard to his touch.

"Oh, God," she murmured, shivering as well.

"I want you so badly. Don't know how long I can wait."

She took his hand and led him to the bed. He took off and cast aside the see-through top and the camisole, and then his shirt.

He kissed her again, his erection hard against her belly. Her whole body ached to have him inside her, hard like that. Hard and strong and determined. And so sweet.

He took his time, slowly pulling her panties down, kneeling in front of her. He sat her on the edge of the bed and slowly spread her legs. When his mouth touched her, she moaned. She was losing control.

"I'm going to come," she said.

He stopped at once. "Not yet," he said. "Not yet. Not so fast."

He stood, scooted her fully onto the bed and climbed over her. His lips found her lips. His tongue flicked, then savored her nipples. Her belly button. His hand worked a magic unlike anything she'd ever experienced—because she cared. She loved. Soon she heard herself moaning again. "Please," she said.

She was hot, her skin felt slick, and so did Joe's. "Yes, now," he said, before putting on a condom.

Their bodies joined, moved as one.

"Nova!" he urged, his voice husky, a whisper like an incantation.

Fantasy became reality. Oh, yes. And then…an explosion…a wave of heat, flying, loosed from all bonds.

Oh, my God.

He groaned and then collapsed beside her. They lay quiet a moment. He rose on his elbow and kissed her eyelids, her forehead, her lips. Then, crossing his arm over her chest, a heavy, relaxed weight, he drifted away from her to his own place of bliss.

She touched his hair, inhaled the scent of it. This man is worth any risk.

Later, they wakened and showered together—a long hot shower with no words and lots of kisses—then they climbed back into the bed. She lay in his arms in a contentment and peace that surprised—no, astounded—her.

He said, "I am sorry, Nova. Really. I will never do that again, never accuse you. We're not children. Your life is yours. I just want you, if you can, to let me be a part of it."

Was he saying he wanted her forever? For a year? More? Less? How soon would he be drawn away to a younger woman? Could he really accept it if she continued to work for the Company? If she allowed herself to fall in love with Joe, could she bear it when he was off on some dangerous assignment? Or when he was flirting with another woman for the job?

"I'm a big risk-taker," she said. "You are, too. What

will be will be. No one is ever guaranteed anything but now."

And this now was glorious.

* * * * *

Chapter 1

The problem with being a spy was that when it was as breathlessly exciting as Jennifer Garner made it look, something had gone horribly wrong.

Alisha planted a hand on a hip-high stone wall and vaulted it, coming down hard on a round stone on its far side. Her foot—it was bare; she'd kicked off the three-inch leather heels the instant she knew she'd been made—slipped. Her ankle twisted, and she fell so fast she had no time to think through the tuck and roll. A bullet sang over her head, slicing the air with a supersonic whine. Even in the midst of flight, one part of her mind focused on that unique sound, and she shot a wordless thanks toward the stone that had saved her life.

She was back on her feet before the thought was finished, running low to the ground. Her ankle throbbed with protest, not broken but displeased with the weight of speed. Alisha ignored the thrums of pain, focusing instead on the sounds around her. From behind were voices, angry men who wielded the guns whose bullets whined over her head. The wind shrieked as loudly as the bullets for a few seconds, battering her in her crouched run. She put her fingers to the ground when she needed the balance, letting the wind buffet her a few feet one way or the other. It leant her the randomness she needed to break any patterns that the gunmen might pick out in the pre-dawn morning.

One other sound, even more critical than shouting men and bullets, thudded in her ears: the sound of the surf, smashing against cliff faces only sixty yards away. Sixty yards…fifty…forty… She might make it, if flinging herself off a hundred-foot cliff was considered making it.

Damn! Another bullet shrieked over her head and Alisha stumbled forward, forcing herself to make the clumsy action into another roll. Her ankle protested again as she pushed through to her feet, coming up at an angle from her previous trajectory. Her jacket and skirt were dark, warm brown that normally set off her skin tones, but in the pre-dawn grayness, all that was important was that she didn't stand out against the dark like a beacon. A voice lifted in frustration behind her and she huffed a breath of relief. Thirty yards to go, and they'd lost her. More bullets whined, but they were off to the right, following the path she'd been on rather than her new one.

The countryside was not meant to be raced over in darkness. Unkempt knots of earth seemed to leap up, lumps that felt as hard as tree roots against bare toes. Rough-edged stones scraped her feet, though those, at least, offered surprisingly little pain. Calluses built from years of yoga, practiced bare-foot, provided remarkable protection for the soles of her feet. Panicked, early-morning get-aways weren't why she practiced the ancient art, but for the moment, Alisha was grateful for any tiny advantage she had been granted.

The ground fell away into divots that sent her tripping and scrambling forward. Bull in a china shop, she thought, but it didn't matter, so long as she stayed relatively quiet. The wind would hinder her pursuers as much as it knocked her about, throwing the sounds of her passage in directions she'd never taken.

Ten yards. The next thirty feet were the critical ones. To make the jump, she needed all the momentum she could get; she couldn't afford to remain crouched, not with the thunderous waves below ready to grab her and dash her against the cliffs. Alisha straightened up into a full-out run, long legs flashing with speed and urgency. Pain sizzled up the big nerve along the outside of her right ankle, the damage from the twist more profound now that she demanded everything from her injured body.

"There!" She heard triumph in the voice behind her. Alisha didn't dare take the time to look over her shoulder, not with twenty—fifteen—feet to go. Eyes lifted, hands straight with sprinter's concentration, she kicked on a burst of speed, trusting adrenaline to get her through the sharpness in her ankle that meant the sprain was worsening with every step. More shots rang out, the deadly chime of air itself protesting the way it was being torn asunder.

Ten feet. Five feet. She gathered herself, thighs bunched, gaze focused on a far point, dozens of feet past the body-shattering stones at the foot of the cliffs.

Now, she thought, and gave her whole being over to the leap from the cliff's edge.

Alisha flew.

For a few seconds it was freedom, pure and glorious. Nothing in the world but herself and the cool early morning air. The wind screamed and cut away any sounds of pursuit, swallowing the howl of bullets chasing her. It was as honest a moment as Alisha could remember: no one and nothing, not even gravity, held sway over her. A single thought intruded—perfect. It was the thesis of yoga: a state of acceptance so complete that not even the next breath seemed important. Absolute purity for a few glorious seconds, before sheer adrenalized glee set in.

She hit reality in a dive, fingers laced together over her head, arms bent just slightly, enough that her elbows couldn't lock and shatter with the impact. The water was cold, breath-taking; for the first seconds, it took all Alisha's effort to not inhale with the shock of it. But that would be her doom, and the data she carried would never make it back to her handler. She struck out blindly, kicking forward and deeper into the water. It would confound her hunters if she never surfaced, and, down deeper, she might slip between the currents that smashed water against the cliffs.

Her lungs burned as she kicked, panic setting in to the hind part of her brain, the order to *Breathe!* almost irresistible. Alisha kept one hand extended in front of her, still kicking as hard as she could, and fumbled in her skirt's waistband with the other. There were two discreet pouches there. One held what memory told her looked embarrassingly like a wrapped condom. Alisha curled her fingers around that one and brought it to her face, shoving it firmly into her mouth. She kept her mouth closed tightly over it until she'd fit it between her lips and her teeth, like a kid with an orange peel stuck in her mouth. It felt ungainly and awkward, but it would saver her life.

It took an act of pure faith to exhale the last air in her lungs out in a salt-tainted burst of saliva. This time, like every time, there was one frozen moment of sheer animal terror as she dragged air in through the cleared pores of the filter, a moment when she expected the technology to fail and for water to flood her lungs.

This time, as it had every time, the breather worked. Damp, salt-flavored oxygen rasped into her lungs. Alisha swallowed a silent gasp of relief and kicked forward into the cold water, panic fading into confidence of survival.

With the diminishing of fear came memory. Alisha managed a very faint smile around the awkwardness of the breather. It was the breather—or one like it—that had gotten her into the spy business in the first place. The breather, and Marsa Alam, on the Red Sea.

She's noticed a slight man with an American accent wandering the beach almost daily. He had looked dapper, but had been far too old—at least in his forties!—for the nineteen-year-old Alisha to be interested in. They'd nodded politely at one another, and to her relief he hadn't seemed to be interested in conversation beyond exchanged hellos. She had been there for the scuba diving, not making friends with expatriate Americans.

It had been her last day in Marsa Alam when he had approached her, diffidently, carrying two of the breath-ers. "They work like this," he'd said, and showed her how the ungainly little package blossomed into a piece of Bond-like technology. "Try it," he'd offered, and even a decade later, Alisha had to fight off a grin that always threatened to turn into laughter when she remembered that moment. He might as well have added, "The first hit is free."

When she surfaced two hours later, a little dizzy— the breather, he told her, only provided enough oxygen for about sixty percent lung capacity—she'd wanted to know where on earth she could get one of her own.

"Langley," he had said, very mildly, watching Alisha with careful, honest consideration.

And that had been it, Alisha thought ruefully, not for the first time. They'd had her at hello.

BRINGS YOU THE LATEST IN

Vicki Hinze's

WAR GAMES

MINISERIES

Double Dare

December 2005

A plot to release the deadly DR-27 supervirus at a crowded mall? Not U.S. Air Force captain Maggie Holt's idea of Christmas cheer. Forget the mistletoe— Maggie, with the help of scientist Justin Crowe, has to stop a psycho terrorist before she can even think of enjoying Christmas kisses.

Available at your favorite retail outlet.

PRESENTS
The Cardinal Rule
December 2005

THE FIRST BOOK IN
Cate Dermody's
NEW HIGH-STAKES SERIES

THE STRONGBOX CHRONICLES

To agent Alisha McAleer, the mission seemed straightforward: recover a coveted artificial intelligence combat drone for the CIA. Then she found out whom she was up against:

The Sicarri, a deadly clandestine organization...

Her former partner, turned mercenary...

And her own bosses?

Available at your favorite retail outlet.

HOMICIDE DETECTIVE
MERRI WALTERS IS BACK IN

Silent Reckoning

by Debra Webb

December 2005

A serial killer was on the loose,
hunting the city's country singers.
Could deaf detective Merri Walters turn
her hearing loss to advantage and crack
the case before the music died?

Available at your favorite retail outlet.

If you enjoyed what you just read,
then we've got an offer you can't resist!

Take 2 bestselling love stories FREE!

Plus get a FREE surprise gift!

Silhouette® BOMBSHELL™

THE IT GIRLS

Rich, fabulous...and dangerously underestimated.

*They're heiresses with connections,
glamour girls with the inside track.*

*And they're going undercover to fight
high-society crime in high style.*

Catch The It Girls in these six books
by some of your favorite Bombshell authors:

THE GOLDEN GIRL by Erica Orloff, September 2005

FLAWLESS by Michele Hauf, October 2005

LETHALLY BLONDE by Nancy Bartholomew, November 2005

MS. LONGSHOT by Sylvie Kurtz, December 2005

A MODEL SPY by Natalie Dunbar, January 2006

BULLETPROOF PRINCESS by Vicki Hinze, February 2006

Available at your favorite retail outlet.

Silhouette®
BOMBSHELL™
COMING NEXT MONTH

#69 DOUBLE DARE—Vicki Hinze
War Games

For U.S. Air Force Captain Maggie Holt, Christmas had always been about eggnog, mistletoe and holiday cheer...until the biowarfare expert discovered a plot to unleash the deadly DR-27 supervirus at a crowded mall on Christmas Eve. Now Maggie needed a double dose of daring—and the help of the DR-27 antidote's handsome inventor—to defuse certain tragedy.

#70 MS. LONGSHOT—Sylvie Kurtz
The It Girls

After the suspicious deaths of several top show horses, the Gotham Rose spies called on socialite Alexa Cheltingham to go undercover as a grubby groom. Her riches-to-rags transition wasn't easy—mucking stables was a far cry from partying on Park Avenue. She had to protect the mayor's show-jumping daughter, hunt for the horse killer, even dodge a murder rap— all while resisting her chief suspect's undeniable charms....

#71 THE CARDINAL RULE—Cate Dermody
The Strongbox Chronicles

Talk about mixed allegiances! Agent Alisha McAleer's latest assignment involved stealing the prototype of an artificial intelligence combat drone from her CIA handler's own son. And others wanted the drone—including a clandestine organization called the Sciarri and her former partner-turned-mercenary. With even her bosses proving untrustworthy, Alicia was on her own. Again.

#72 SILENT RECKONING—Debra Webb

Going deaf hadn't stopped Merri Walters from rising to the rank of homicide detective. But she had a new set of problems. Her old flame was now her boss, her new partner didn't want to work with a woman and a serial killer was on the loose, targeting country-music starlets. Posing as killer bait seemed suicidal, but Merri marched to her own tune, and wouldn't let anything—or anyone—stand in the way of nabbing her man....

SBCNM1105